Tennessee
TRANSPLANTATION

Tennessee
TRANSPLANTATION

ANITA PHELPS LOCKHART

WESTBOW
PRESS
A DIVISION OF THOMAS NELSON

WestBow Press books may be ordered through booksellers or by contacting:

WestBow Press
A Division of Thomas Nelson
1663 Liberty Drive
Bloomington, IN 47403
www.westbowpress.com
1-(866) 928-1240

Because of the dynamic nature of the Internet, any web addresses or links contained in this book may have changed since publication and may no longer be valid. The views expressed in this work are solely those of the author and do not necessarily reflect the views of the publisher, and the publisher hereby disclaims any responsibility for them.

Certain stock imagery © Thinkstock.
Any people depicted in stock imagery provided by Thinkstock are models, and such images are being used for illustrative purposes only.

ISBN: 978-1-4497-7498-1 (e)
ISBN: 978-1-4497-7497-4 (sc)

Library of Congress Control Number: 2012921060

Printed in the United States of America

WestBow Press rev. date: 12/3/2012

CONTENTS

CHAPTER 1.	Ann's Idea	1
CHAPTER 2.	Peckville, TN	6
CHAPTER 3.	Adelaide	10
CHAPTER 4.	Settling In	16
CHAPTER 5.	The Shopping Excursion	20
CHAPTER 6.	Going Traveling	29
CHAPTER 7.	Bessie	44
CHAPTER 8.	The Monster Machine	55
CHAPTER 9.	The Peanut Butter Shuffle	65
CHAPTER 10.	Going Home	71
CHAPTER 11.	Glen Adams	77
CHAPTER 12.	Mannequin Madness	84
CHAPTER 13.	A Little Buggy	94
CHAPTER 14.	Ann's Motorcycle Ride	101
CHAPTER 15.	Running Errands	107
CHAPTER 16.	Hundred Acres	118
CHAPTER 17.	Addie's Options	136
CHAPTER 18.	Historical Society Meeting	144
CHAPTER 19.	Something's Up	153
CHAPTER 20.	Trouble Abrewin'	165
CHAPTER 21.	A Tour for Teddy	170
CHAPTER 22.	A Hero's Reward	184
CHAPTER 23.	Adventuresome Addie	192
CHAPTER 24.	Smoky Mountain Trip	199
CHAPTER 25.	Open House at Rainer Manor	206
CHAPTER 26.	Eve of Departure	212
CHAPTER 27.	Headed North	217

CHAPTER ONE

Ann's Idea

*T*he idea popped into Ann Flanders' head from out of the blue, as she and husband Frank were riding along on one of their road-runs. That's how they referred to the jaunts they took around the Central NYS countryside where they lived. They were about 75 miles from their home this Autumn afternoon admiring the remnants of fall color which still lingered here and there even though the colors were past their peak. The Flanders had adopted singer Willie Nelson's country hit "On the Road Again" as their personal theme song. That was their favorite thing to do, drive around the countryside. Ann and Frank often marveled at how their horizons had expanded with the purchase seven years before of a small economy car. The gas mileage was fantastic! Upwards to 35 or 40 miles per gallon at times.

Four years ago, they began the first of their annual treks South. These trips started out being three to four days' duration and soon became eight to ten days long. During several of their trips, they discovered Tennessee and it was there they planned to spend the balance of the winter months, beginning in February, with an eye to permanently retiring there someday if it suited them. They loved the Upstate Central New York area where they resided, but the thought of the ice and snow every winter had really lost its charm.

Frank and Ann had just had dinner at a chain family restaurant, each enjoying a full dinner. They were pleased over the price since they had not only used a diner's coupon (buy one, get one of equal value free) but also received a Senior Citizen's discount as well. The restaurant and the long drive there had made it seem like a mini-vacation, turning Ann's thoughts to Tennessee. She reminisced about the times when waitresses had questioned her age when she ordered from the senior menu for those over 55. Although her auburn hair was streaked with gray, it had not faded to the degree one would expect of a 58-year-old woman. Fifty-eight, she mused. Why that's almost 60! She glanced over at Frank. He looked his age, if all you considered was his white hair and white streaked eyebrows. Yet his smooth skin belied his age of nearly 62. Premature white hair was a family trait on his mother's side and his hair was the same color as it was 30 years ago. Only his eyebrows gradually turning white had made him look his years. It's good he's always been active, she thought. He didn't drink, stopped smoking quite a few years back. He had begun smoking later in life than most people, which was a plus. Frank's father, only brother and uncle had all passed away by the age of sixty. This was one of the overriding reasons that Frank planned to retire in February on his 62nd birthday, rather than wait the three years until he was 65. He felt he was already living on borrowed time.

Frank's dream was to retire to Tennessee, build a small place and leave all behind. Ann had retired from civil service two years prior and was receiving a government pension. She had worked sporadically since retirement to complete the required number of social security quarters. She did not expect to be able to collect on it for herself but felt somehow that Frank may benefit. Her plan had been to work full time for the three years but due to the proverbial unforeseen circumstances, had already fallen months behind her agenda. Some of the positions she held had not paid the level of income she required to accomplish her financial goals. The positions obtained that paid the anticipated wage were part time, not the full time employment needed to pay some accumulated bills to enable them to manage on their combined retirement income. A nest egg that she had accumulated towards payment of a second (and only) mortgage had dissolved into investments in several family projects, which used up available funds.

All these thoughts were running through Ann's mind as she tried to come up with ideas to finance the planned two months stay (February to April) in Tennessee. That's when the IDEA hit her. Her active mind frequently fantasized on these drives but she seldom shared these fantasies with her pragmatic husband. Today, however, the idea was so great, she blurted it out.

"Frank, I just thought of an economical way to experience the two months stay in Tennessee to see if it's really where we want to retire. There might be some elderly lady who is on a limited income, in fairly good health, who can't afford the upkeep on her home, could use some companionship and help. It would be a mutually beneficial arrangement. We could do chores, cooking, errands, etc. in exchange for room. We'd have to eat, no matter if we were at home or away, so we could buy the groceries and thus save her money. It'd be perfect!"

The pleased expression on Frank's face told her he agreed with the concept even before he verbalized his reply.

"Yep, that could work," he said.

"She'd have to be independent enough," Ann continued, "so if we wanted to take a trip away for a few days, she would be okay. Of course, if she was an agreeable person, you wouldn't mind taking her along on some of those trips." Ann's mind was off and running with all the possibilities. She had already written to a Chamber of Congress in Tennessee and had received a multitude of literature from both that organization and a real estate broker the Chamber had furnished with her address. She had also contacted a weekly newspaper with an eye to subscribing to it and had received a sample copy of their paper.

The data she had received seemed to indicate the area was a bit more urban than to their liking, so she was now centering her attention on an area a bit more southeast than that county. Coincidentally, they had run into an acquaintance whose daughter lived near this area and the towns he mentioned were familiar sounding to her. It was starting to feel like home and her thoughts were turning more and more to February and the anticipated change of scene.

Ann dreaded leaving her friends and family behind, but Frank was quite possessive and she could seldom enjoy their company. Still it was a comfort to know they were not that far away. One of Ann's good points was her love of people which they seemed to sense and she usually got along well with almost everyone she met. The quickest way to get her dander up was to misunderstand her intentions, but she was working on that aspect of her personality. She would seem an unlikely femme fatale, being overweight for at least 30 years. This had not had a tendency to diminish the interest the opposite sex held in her. They felt comfortable with her and she enjoyed these friendships. At least along with the weight, she had gained friends among her own sex which were scarce when she had been younger. A defense mechanism was her witty (she hoped) repartee in reference to her weight.

"I only weigh one hundred and hefty," was one of her favorite quips. "I'm on a seafood diet. I see food and I eat it." "I'm a light eater. I only eat when it's light out," adding "Thank God for Mr. Edison!" People may not have suspected her true weight as she was 5' 5" tall and carried herself as though she weighed less. In her mind's eye, she felt she DID weigh less, until her scales, AND her husband --- both with equal candor --- would tell her the truth and make her face the unhappy reality. Frank, at 5' 6" was also overweight but still several pounds lighter than Ann. A friend of theirs, years earlier, in describing the couple to others, remarked "BIG woman, little Man," and Frank thoroughly believed this description even after years and extra pounds, had accumulated.

They bounced ideas back and forth, covering the pros and cons of this latest notion of Ann's. Each one tried to think of reasons why it might not work.

"The biggest problem you'd have would be suspicion. There are people out there who are so greedy, they would take advantage of the elderly person. Once you convince them you mean well, everyone can relax and enjoy the mutual benefits of such an arrangement." Ann continued: "Probably the best idea would be to go to the local police, introduce ourselves, and let them check us out. Maybe they would mention our plan to someone and let them contact us. I like that approach better than just running an ad. I really doubt anyone would respond to an ad saying: 'Wanted – an elderly person, preferably female, who lives alone and requires companionship. Will do odd jobs, run errands, in exchange for room. References.' Of course, sometimes someone looking for a companion will run their own ad." Ann saw Frank nod in agreement with her statements.

The sudden appearance of a doe and her fawn approaching the road from a wooded area distracted them and the conversation shifted as their attention turned to these arrivals. The animals stopped in their advance toward the highway, but did not appear frightened. As Frank slowed their vehicle to a crawl, Ann eased the window down and cooed softly to the deer. Frank was used to this and his usual suggestion when they encountered deer was: "Talk to it, Mommy." The animals would usually react by being lulled by the sound of her voice, then turn and slowly retreat to cover. Ann's usual conversation with these gentle creatures consisted of softly admiring them and telling them how beautiful they were, as well as thanking them for allowing Frank and herself to see them. They seemed to spot more deer than others in the same area, often commenting that the deer seemed to be waiting so they could see them before the animals sought cover.

CHAPTER TWO

Peckville, TN

*T*he months passed quickly and it was finally February. Ann had contacted one of the motels named in the literature she had received from the TN Chamber of Commerce. She arranged a special weekly rate, which although a strain on their limited budget, would be much more economical than one would expect. The motel management agreed to discount their usual rate due to it being their off-season and the thought of the guaranteed income, although less than full rate, interested the manager. Because of the Flanders continued search for alternative accommodations, they were asking for a week-by-week agreement on the special rate. Ann convinced the manager that there was no need for daily room service or linen change. This enhanced the mutual agreement. The only thing missing from the smooth flow of their plan was the right person who needed them.

Peckville, TN, was as pleasant a town as they could have hoped for. It boasted a small park with the prerequisite gazebo, a library and most important of all, a local diner which supplied a central place for the area residents to meet and chat. The men would loiter over coffee and donuts while their women shopped. It was reminiscent of the role that the general store played in serving as a gathering place in the 'good old days'. Frank and Ann enjoyed the walk there from their motel room for breakfast and often ate their supper there. Lunch was usually somewhere on one of their road-runs exploring the area. They would either pack a light lunch or stop at a mini-mart along the way for a meat and three (or two) or a sandwich. They found that rather than the usual pre-packaged fare one would expect at a mini-mart/gas station; the food was often freshly prepared and hot off the griddle. Biscuit sandwiches, chicken patty sandwiches and the like were often available. One place they were often drawn back to was an old run-down house about five miles from town. Frank drew sketches of what it would look like if restored. They wanted to check into the ownership of the property on the chance that it could be purchased. An outstanding feature of the house was the pillared front porch. Their interest in researching the availability was squelched because it was so much larger than their original concept of a retirement home, plus the fact that the cost of repairs really didn't fit with their financial constraints.

"We could check the tax rolls and see if perhaps it's up for delinquent taxes," Ann suggested in the course of one of their many conversations regarding the house. "We still haven't been here long enough to know if this is where we really want to settle, though."

"Well, it's just an idea," was Frank's reply. The talk turned to the game plan for the day. They were walking to the diner for breakfast. As they neared the diner, the lone waitress spoke to a Deputy Sheriff as she refreshed his coffee.

"Here comes my New Yorkers, pleasant couple. They want to find a place to spend the rest of the winter. Staying at the Comfort motel, temporarily." She turned to greet the new arrivals.

"Morning folks. Your usual, Missus?" She spoke in the soft Tennessee drawl that the Flanders were becoming used to. They thought their own northern accent must be harsh to the southerners' ears.

Ann's response was, "Yes, Missy, one egg over hard, grits and biscuits." Missy knew one of the reasons she liked this couple was that the lady was willing to try their local menu and enjoyed it on a regular basis. Missy, a fun-loving young lady with medium length blonde hair and a trim figure, was the diner's best asset.

The deputy sized up the out-of-towners. He'd already observed them as they drove about town. One thing in particular he'd noticed, was that the man, although a bit heavy-footed on the accelerator, seemed to be an excellent, courteous driver. On several occasions, the deputy had observed that Frank had averted accidents with other, less skilled, drivers.

"More coffee, Tom?" Missy offered.

"No, guess not, Missy. I promised to drop some bread and milk off to Addie Rainer out south of town 'fore I go on duty. I hate to see her so far out there alone, but she's stubborn and won't give up the old place." He dropped his voice at the latter statement as if to keep the strangers from knowing about this solitary resident who might be easy pickings for the unscrupulous. He felt a bit ashamed of this notion since these did seem like nice, ordinary folk. It didn't pay to take things for granted though, as Ann's obvious interest in what he said did not escape him.

"Deputy," Ann spoke up. "My husband and I have thought about the possibility of exchanging odd jobs and companionship to an older couple or person in exchange for room and board. Do you think this lady might be interested in this type of arrangement?"

Deputy Tom Cates glanced towards Missy before responding. "Well, I doubt she would. She has a large family who tends to her every need..." His voice trailed off as he realized the contradiction of what he just said to his earlier statement about picking up the groceries for Addie.

Missy spoke up encouragingly, "Yes, Tom. These folks have mentioned to me that they'd like such an arrangement, but I didn't even think of anyone at the time. You'd sure have your work cut out for y'all. That place is really run-down."

Frank and Ann exchanged hopeful looks. "South of town, you say?" Frank joined the conversation. "Run-down? That would be that old place on Route 3, with the columns? Could it be?"

"Yep, that's the place. I'll ask her, that can't do any harm." He arose to leave. "I'll let y'all know what she says. I can leave word here with Missy." The fact that they were so open with their plans reassured him. That they would discuss their intent with a member of the area police dissolved his initial fears. He also trusted Missy's instincts and she apparently felt these were trustworthy people. He would, as he usually did, keep an eye out for any problems out at the Rainer place if this arrangement did come about.

It turned out that Adelaide (Addie, to her friends) Rainer had a very depressing week. Rainwater had leaked into the kitchen through a newly developed hole in the roof. The lawn and grounds were a mess. The young lads who used to hire out to do lawn work at a reasonable rate, all seemed to have jobs. Fast food restaurants and gas stations paid more than old ladies could. She'd just about decided it might be time to give up the old place; though she felt sure that would absolutely kill her. Deputy Tom's arrival with her groceries and the proposal from Frank and Ann Flanders was perfectly timed. She agreed to have Frank and Ann come out the following afternoon. Her excitement over the plan did much to dispel Tom's remaining doubts. He personally stopped by the motel to convey word to the Flanders of Addie's invitation.

CHAPTER THREE

Adelaide

*D*eputy Tom Cates led the Flanders' Buick out of town on County Route 3 to the intersection of Rainer Road and Route 3. Not that it was necessary to direct the couple to Adelaide Rainer's home but he wanted to be there at the initial meeting between the couple and the elderly woman.

The Rainer house faced Rt. 3 with a U-drive, set off by crumbling stone pillars, which circled right up to the front door. Tom turned left onto Rainer Road and entered a second drive down that side road which was not visible from the main highway. Because grass had grown over the front drive, the lawn unkempt and the house in desperate need of paint, it did indeed look abandoned to an unknowing passerby. The second drive off the side road was not used too much more, but you could see signs of occupancy on that end of the house.

Frank estimated that it wouldn't take all that much to improve the condition of the lovely old southern home. One supposes you'd call it a mansion, but in its present state of disrepair, it didn't seem to qualify for such a stately nomenclature. Lesser men than Frank would have turned around right there, but hard work didn't scare Frank. He thrived on challenge. He had worked all his life, performing chores as early as four or five years of age. At age 12, he was assigned caretaker duties at a local church. His chores involved unlocking the church doors and starting the fire so it would be comfortable for the parishioners when they arrived for services. Even the year before that, at 11 years old, he worked on a neighbor's farm for wages, driving tractor and other farm-related chores. He actually managed the farm while its owner worked away from home during the day. His maternal grandfather had instilled in Frank a sense of pride in his work and Frank was a perfectionist so every task he undertook was a work of art.

Ann, on the other hand, was a romantic dreamer who believed in Frank's abilities and appreciated his down-to-earth approach to things. She was given to lofty ideas and was an avid reader. Satisfied to while away time with a book or magazine, she needed Frank's more practical attitude to keep her feet on the ground. He was more than competent to cover this aspect of their relationship, so the couple had managed to maintain a comfortable life together. Both were capable people, valued by their respective employers in whatever position they held. Ann loved words and had displayed a talent for writing poetry. She published a chapbook of her verses but it suffered the same ignominy most such 'vanity press' endeavors share.

Adelaide Rainer was a lady in her late 70's. Arthritis had limited her movement but had not crippled her. She cooked her own meals, if she felt like cooking. She didn't get around much since she had never learned to drive. Unlady-like, her mother has insisted and so Adelaide dutifully followed her mother's lead. While Addie's husband had been alive, he drove her wherever she had to go. In the years since his death, she had remained alone in the house, relying on the town taxi for the few excursions she made to the doctor's and once a month to do her main shopping. Living so far out of town, she found this an expensive necessity. Recently, it had been increasingly difficult to entice the taxi driver to leave his stand in town to come the distance, causing him to miss out on the more lucrative short runs for town residents. Charlie Westwood, the town's sole taxi owner, had retired six months ago. The man who bought him out was in it more for the money than to make friends. Tom Cates recognized the need and would periodically check in on Adelaide and pick up essentials for her as necessary. He extended the same courtesy to several other oldsters in the county who had no near kin or neighbors to run errands for them. This small consideration on his part played an important role in these people being able to maintain their independence. Tom realized that there were other things that these senior citizens needed to have done, but he was only one person and his time could stretch just so far. He went out of his way for Adelaide since she had no children and her closest kin was a sister living in a nursing home over in Asheville, NC. Adelaide hadn't seen her sister in 30 years. Her only other living relative, as far as Tom could remember, was a nephew who lived in Atlanta, GA.

For these reasons, Tom hoped this proposed arrangement with the Flanders could work out, but he knew much could go wrong to jeopardize its success.

Adelaide's gray head bobbed up to be seen in the glass window of the back door as she scurried to answer Tom's knock. She was becoming apprehensive about this idea. How much would it cost her? What would she have in common with these snowbird northerners? What could they possibly talk about? She peeked around Tom for her first look at Frank and Ann Flanders. The man looks older'n me, she thought to herself, what help could he possibly be? His wife's real heavy, can't be too ambitious, she decided as she opened the door and ushered them through the kitchen and into the darkened sitting room where she snapped on a light and offered them a seat. Each of the visitors perched uncomfortably on their chair, all beginning to wonder why they were even considering such a venture.

Adelaide glanced from one to another of her guests, as she was beginning to think of them. She was starting to get 'cold feet' about proceeding with this plan. Strangers in her home? She could barely look after her own needs, much less cater to company. What did they expect of her?

Ann was the first to speak. "Frank, doesn't Mrs. Rainer remind you of Dad's cousin, Arlene?" Frank nodded in agreement; he had been thinking the same thing. She did resemble the spinster relative Ann had named. Arlene, now deceased, had been a school teacher and had always spoken in crisp tones, enunciating her words precisely. She held everyone in suspicion as Adelaide now seemed to do.

Ann continued to speak. "I suppose Deputy Cates has told you about us. We want to spend two months here in the area to see if we want to settle here now we're retired. We still own our home in New York State and plan to return to summer there. I'll be honest; we're on a tight budget and can't afford to spend the money to stay in a motel the whole two months. We've started looking into renting but everyone we've talked to so far wants us to sign a year's lease. Frankly, we don't want to be locked into such a long-term rental. Renting a furnished place is too high a cost and renting an unfurnished place would necessitate driving back up north, renting a moving van to bring the furniture needed to sparsely furnish a place. That would cost as much as buying second hand furniture down here and we really don't want to make such an investment. There would also be storage on those items over the summer." Ann paused for breath and looked closely to see if she could determine Adelaide Rainer's reaction to her words.

Frank joined Ann in explaining their intentions. "I see there are chores that need doing around here and I'm handy with my hands and mechanically inclined, so I can keep busy."

Adelaide had noticed his hands were those of someone who had indeed done manual labor most of his life. She liked the manner both had of looking directly at you when they spoke. She had overheard a comment Ann had softly made to Frank as they first entered the room. Indicating the curved front china cabinet, she had breathed, "Look Frank, it's almost identical to mine at home." Adelaide prided herself as being able to size up people as soon as she laid eyes on them. Not that she'd seen many people in recent years, but she still trusted instincts.

"We feel since we have to eat no matter where we live, we would pay for the groceries and do chores to pay for our board. We could run errands for you, take you shopping and to appointments. Not that we'd be at your every beck and call, but I think we could work out something reasonable, Mrs. Rainer." Ann still didn't know how to read Adelaide's demeanor, to know if this plan was acceptable to her.

Adelaide glanced towards Tom. She could tell that he felt what Ann was saying sounded okay to him. It was starting to hit her that this might be a welcome solution to some of her problems.

When Adelaide stood up, Frank did too, motioning to Ann to rise as he felt she was ready to dismiss them and their crazy scheme. With an impatient gesture, Adelaide indicated Frank should sit back down.

"Will y'all join me in a cup of tea, or coffee?" She then added, "Come, Miz Flanders, you might's well get used to where things are."

"Yes!" Ann replied, thinking 'she really does remind me of Cousin Arlene. Right to the point, no monkey business about her. You'll always know where you stand with her.' She moved to join Adelaide as she walked stiffly towards the kitchen. Adelaide's sharp eye took in Ann's stiff movements as well.

"Y'all seem to have a touch of arthritis too, Miz Flanders." Adelaide said this in a kindly manner.

"Yes," said Ann, "Only slows me down on stairs and if I sit for a while, but I manage okay the rest of the time."

Everyone had decided on tea, so under Adelaide's direction, Ann filled the tea kettle and set out cups and saucers. "This is such a pleasant kitchen. May we have our tea here at the table? I know Frank and I would be more comfortable." At Adelaide's nod, Ann stepped to the front room to invite the men to join the women in the kitchen, smiling to herself as she noted their relief at the thought they would not have to juggle tea cups and saucers on their knees.

Shortly after finishing his tea, Tom left the three alone to become better acquainted and went on his way satisfied they had hit it off as he suspected they would.

He took the time to stop briefly at the Peckville Diner to tell Missy the results of the meeting.

Their visit could not have been more cordial. The Flanders obviously had developed an affection towards the family homestead. While Ann and Addie chatted and got to know each other, Frank, not much to be idle, busied himself with oiling and tuning up Addie's old lawn mower. He was anxious to try it out so set about mowing the front lawn. Addie, pleased to see how industrious he was, decided then and there this would be a workable solution to her dilemma.

It was decided that Frank and Ann would move in on Saturday, two days away. They all agreed to have dinner together the following evening to celebrate this new union. Addie hadn't dined out in a very long time and really was looking forward to the companionship of her new friends as well as the assistance they offered towards the maintenance of her home.

CHAPTER FOUR

Settling In

*A*delaide and Ann made their way slowly to the second story of the house where Adelaide gave Ann the grand tour. The rooms were generous sized but barren in appearance with shades drawn. Accumulated dust caused Ann to sneeze, but there was no clutter to have to be cleaned up. This was a cause to rejoice for Ann since she was unable to throw anything away. She and Frank referred to themselves as depression babies who used what they had and didn't buy new unless one was absolutely forced to.

There were four empty bedrooms on the second level with a central hall that circled the top of the stairs. The open hallway ran from one end of the house to the other. Long French style windows let in the rays of the sun and cast a cheery light over all. A small alcove was set midway down the hall towards the rear of the house. Two built-in seats abutted the recessed shelves, filled with books, which were at the center of the alcove. Adelaide touched one side of the bookshelves and the whole alcove pivoted, granting access to an attic room containing relics of a more peaceful age. As Adelaide turned on a light, Ann saw several pitchers and washbasin sets, which she knew would be coveted by antique dealers. Leaning against a far wall was a cloth tri-fold screen, commonly referred to nowadays as a room divider. She smiled at the sight of a 'thunder jug', an old-fashioned necessity which perched under one's bed for any nightly nature calls. Ann estimated that there was more than enough furniture here to furnish the four empty rooms upstairs, if Adelaide allowed her a free hand in restoring these rooms.

"I haven't been upstairs in a very long time," Adelaide spoke, causing Ann to give a start. She had been quite engrossed in her re-decorating plans. The entrance to the attic room intrigued her and she wondered about the reason for the hidden door.

"Adelaide, was this house part of the Underground Railroad System?" Ann referred to the name given to the route used in pre-civil war days to smuggle slaves out of the South to the North. Ann thought it was ironic that some people then couldn't wait to leave the South and now there were people in the North who couldn't wait to come South. The difference was that the northerners wanted to escape the bondage of ice and snow, not a sometimes cruel master who sought to own them, body and soul.

"Well, so the story goes. This house wasn't always in my husband's family, so we really don't know its exact history. As I said, I haven't been up here in so long, I'd forgot what I had up here. We bought the place furnished from Mr. Rainer's uncle. I've been afraid to come up here alone; afraid I'd fall and not be found in time. I don't relish nursing any broken bones if I did survive a fall. It'd definitely be a nursing home for me if I did break anything." Her independent speech convinced Ann that she and Frank had found just the right person who needed them as much as they needed the place to stay.

When they cautiously retreated to the first floor of Adelaide's home and inspected the downstairs rooms, Ann noticed the height of the ceiling in the kitchen at the very back of the house was much lower than the ones in the front. This would disguise the existence of the attic room, she felt. Really clever of the builder, she decided.

There were five rooms downstairs. The formal living room was just to the left of the front entrance. The room extended about twenty feet. To the right of the entrance, actually a part of the main room, was a library area with a long bookcase along the front wall of the room. Two rooms opened off that end of the long room. Actually, three, since one was a full bath that probably occupied what once had been a pantry. The other two rooms were bedrooms. One might have been a lesser sitting room and the other may have been part of the living room originally, which possibly had taken up the whole front of the house. The placement of a bay window in the front bedroom reaffirmed Ann's decision that the room had been part of the living room. A second bay window was situated to the right of the main entrance. The dividing wall in the bedroom was a tad too close to the bay, she felt, to have been part of the initial construction floor plan. On the far-left wall of the living room was a huge fieldstone fireplace. At the rear of the formal dining room was the door that led to the kitchen. A door at the back wall of the bath also provided access to that necessary room from the kitchen.

The kitchen contained a combination wood/kerosene stove providing for warmth as well as cooking. It was one of those big old stoves with a water reservoir so you had a ready supply of hot water when the stove was in operation. In a small basement, once a vegetable cellar, was an old furnace. It had been fueled by wood or coal but Frank would soon convert it to burn oil and have it clunking along. If you overlooked the noise, it was an efficient, economical means of central heat. Adelaide marveled at how versatile Frank was; he seemed capable of any task, performing plumbing, heating, electrical, painting, carpentry and mechanical jobs equally well.

Thus began the first of busy, happy days with three tired adults falling into bed each night and sleeping quite soundly. Adelaide especially, was sleeping better than she had in ages. She felt quite secure knowing she was not alone.

By mutual agreement, they had decided on a test period of one week. If any of the parties felt the deal was not working out, they would part company at the end of the week.

Actually, three weeks went by with everyone busy, when they realized the end of their test period had passed by without any one of them giving a thought to it. Frank scraped and painted. Addie donned old clothes and tended her long-neglected rock garden while Ann dusted and cleaned on the inside of the Rainer Manor. Frank located remnants of an old picket fence and with a small investment in materials, soon had it erected. His pride in accomplishment, coupled with Addie's pleasure in seeing her home being rejuvenated, added to his satisfaction. Ann happily recorded a weight loss of 15 pounds in the three weeks since they joined forces with Addie.

CHAPTER FIVE

The Shopping Excursion

*A*ddie and Ann had hauled out clothing stored in an upstairs closet and spread it out on Addie's bed where she sorted through the items. She had decided that since the agenda frequently included dinners out that she should dress up more. She had several lovely outfits of the classic designs that never go out of style, but she had decided it was definitely time to get a new coat. The one she had been wearing was too threadbare to be seen out in, she declared. She may be on a constrained budget but she wasn't destitute yet, so no need to look like it. Besides, with Frank and Ann purchasing all the groceries, she had a little extra money.

When Addie mentioned to Ann that she'd like to go shopping sometime, Ann's response was: "Grab your purse, Addie, we're off!" After explaining their errand to Frank, they were. This gave Addie cause to think about how a shopping trip for her in the past, meant days of planning before she ever got around to going. It was different, but Addie was learning to become as spontaneous as the Flanders.

Obviously, Adelaide hadn't been shopping for clothing in a long time. Ann's heart went out to her when she saw Addie's face grow pale as she checked the price tags. She seemed drawn to a black coat of Chesterfield style, the type of timeless design Ann felt she would select. The $99 price tag made her shy away from a final decision and forlornly told the saleslady she wanted to think about it. On the drive back home, Ann tried to cheer her with suggestions on how she could get the coat without paying the whole amount at once.

"You could charge it to a store account," Ann started to say.

"Humph! Never charged anything before and I'm too old to start that nonsense now." Her set face did much to convince Ann that approach was out of the question.

"Well, you could get it on lay-a-way or wait until it goes on sale, or I could…"

Ann broke off, as Adelaide snapped, "No, you couldn't! I don't borrow money either." Her stern face softened into a tired look. "But I appreciate your offer, Ann. I would put it on lay-a-way but I wanted it now. You see?"

Ann's smile told Addie she did understand.

When they arrived home, Adelaide excused herself, as she wanted to lie down and rest. Ann took a cool drink of soda out to where Frank was working and recounted their unsuccessful shopping experience. After a few moments of conversation, she decided on a new tack. Adelaide was so tired, she never awoke as Ann started her car and drove off towards Afton, twenty miles southeast on Route 3. She quickly spotted the specialty shop she was seeking. There on a hangar – in Addie's size – was a classic Navy Chesterfield coat. Ann paid the price on the tag, took up her purchase and retraced her steps to her car. She drove around until she located her next planned destination. Returning to the car a few moments later, she was back at the Rainer house before Addie arose from her nap. Ann's smile convinced Frank she had been successful in her excursion.

"Found a Sally Ann store, did you?" He asked.

"Yessir," Ann said happily, "and found just the right one, too!"

Several days later, Adelaide asked Ann if she would take her to the supermarket to pick up a few items. Ann suggested they drive to Afton instead of Peckville. She had an ad insert from a shopper paper she had picked up when driving around.

"Not only can we save a little money, but we get a nice ride out of it as well." Ann was sure both reasons would appeal to Addie. She was right.

"When do we start? I haven't been to Afton in 'bout twenty years." Adelaide eagerly accepted Ann's suggestion. Addie had told Frank and Ann that her late husband had been dead fifteen years so Ann reckoned it had been five years before that time when the couple had ventured very far from home. She also remembered Addie saying it was thirty years since she had seen her sister. It frequently was a topic of conversation between the Flanders that the trips they took so casually would be a big deal for some people, requiring much more advance planning than Frank and Ann found necessary.

Exactly what Addie had thought herself. Ann knew it probably cost most people a lot more money to take the same trips she and Frank enjoyed. They still were also aware that there were people who take the same trips for less, by really cutting corners. This would involve camping out and purchasing ingredients for sandwiches at a grocery store instead of eating in restaurants. This was not the Flanders' idea of a vacation, however.

The two ladies said their good-byes to Frank. It was more to his liking to stay there and scrape paint instead of 'wasting' time shopping.

The drive to Afton was pleasant, their conversation lightly punctuated frequently by a gasp or "Oh, My!" from Addie as she noticed the many changes (new homes, business development, improved roads) that had occurred along the route in the years since she had last traveled that way. Near town, the road joined an interstate highway and the four-lane bridge over a deep ravine set Addie nearly speechless.

"I had no idea that they had made all this progress," she ventured. "I feel as though I've suddenly stepped out of the dark ages and into the 21st Century! The bridge has really shortened the trip over. Seems like no time and we're here!"

"I'm glad I mentioned coming over here, then," Ann said. "I hoped it would be a pleasant change for you." As she pulled the car into a parking place, she told Addie she had a quick errand to run. Opening the glove compartment, she handed a small packet to Addie.

"Here, leaf through these coupons and see if there are any you can use. I try to use the manufacturer's coupons whenever I can. Sometimes the stores double even triple them. If you have a store coupon from a newspaper or shopper ad for the same item, it's quite a savings."

Addie busily sorted through the stack of coupons and did not watch which direction Ann went as she strode away from the car. Entering a dry cleaning shop, she presented a yellow slip from her purse. The attendant retrieved a plastic encased garment from a nearby rack.

"Here you are, Miz Flanders," the girl read her name from the slip. "That will be six dollars." As Ann paid, she spotted a white envelope attached to the plastic along with a pink copy of the slip Ann had presented.

The attendant noticed Ann looking at the envelope and spoke. "The cleaner found that pinned inside the lining. We didn't open it. I'm sure the contents are intact."

"Oh, I have no doubt of your honesty, thank you." Ann gathered the garment and left the shop. 'What else could I have done?' she wondered to herself. She walked to the car and opened the trunk, slipping the dry-cleaning into it. Addie was still sorting through coupons as Ann slid behind the steering wheel. She started the car and drove to the grocery store where she and Addie planned to shop.

"I'd forgotten how much lower prices are in a supermarket," Addie said as she moved her cart through the aisles. "When you have to rely on others to pick things up for you at their convenience, you just have to pay the going price. I began to think everything had gone up sky-high, but I see there are still bargains to be had."

"I didn't realize there was anything we really needed," said Ann. "Have I missed anything on your lists?"

"Oh, not at all," was Addie's quick response. "I guess I was just anxious to get out and poke up and down, see what's new. I also have a special recipe I want to try. You and Frank have been buying all the groceries and I want this to be my treat. Remind me to get some 'cahns'." They entered the next aisle that contained cereals.

"'most four dollars for a box of cereal! Imagine that!" cried Addie.

"Look over here, though, Addie. You can get the house brand for about half that. Frank and I like it as well and if they carry the generic brand, it's even lower. Best part is, these other ones are frequently made by the same brand name manufacturer. Just slight differences, like smaller or broken pieces. Such as salad olives. You cut them up anyway, so why not pay less and get the ones that are already in pieces?"

"Makes sense to me," replied Addie. "I like the idea of using the coupons, too. I thought you only got five or ten cents or even pennies off. I was surprised to see some for 25 and 50 cents off."

"You ain't seen nuthing yet," quipped Ann.

After the two ladies cashed out their groceries, Ann paused at a bulletin board near the store exit. Arranged on the board were little pads of printed matter. Selectively tearing off two or three slips, she continued out the door.

"What's that?" queried Addie, not wanting to miss out on anything.

"Rebate coupons. You send these in with box tops, labels or bar codes from the product with your receipt for the purchase and they send money back to you," explained Ann as she passed the slips to Addie.

"Why some of these are for the same items we used the store and manufacturer's coupons on! Seems 'most like stealing." Addie shockingly responded.

"It's all part of their advertising budget. They feel if they can get you to try their product one time, you'll like it and continue to buy it."

"Ann, it's really nice to get out and about in the world again. I have to admit, this world you and Frank have shown me is totally new. I feel like I've been in a cocoon."

They reached the car where Ann loaded their bags of groceries into the trunk. Before closing the lid, she retrieved the garment she had picked up at the dry cleaners. She went around to the passenger side and laid it in Addie's lap.

"How's this suit you?" Ann asked.

"Whatever have you got here?" Adelaide lifted the plastic wrap enough to disclose the garment, then continued speaking. "Oh, Oh, what a lovely coat!" The dry cleaner bag contained just that. The navy blue Chesterfield coat identical, except for color, to the one Adelaide admired in the shop back in Peckville.

"Where'd you get this? However..." Addie's voice trailed off; she was at a loss for words.

"It's yours if you want, it Addie. Maybe you won't want it after I tell you how much I paid for it," Ann teased.

"I can't afford this, Ann, and I won't accept such an expensive gift so y'all just have to take it back." Her hand tenderly stroked the coat but she was firm about not accepting it.

Ann decided she shouldn't keep Addie in the dark any longer; it was time to be truthful.

"Addie, back home we shop quite a bit at what my daughter-in-law, Lisa, calls 'Sally Ann' stores. Actually they are Salvation Army or Goodwill thrift stores. I've bought items with their original price tag still attached. Well, while you napped after we got back from shopping the other day, I zapped over here to Afton and found a 'Sally Ann'. Imagine how thrilled I was to find this. Just what I was looking for. Sorry it's not black. Someone had mixed it in with the men's coats and they had just discovered it and moved it into the Ladies' section. One of the sales ladies said she'd worked there three years and it had been there as long as she had." Ann glanced at Addie to see her reaction to hearing the source of the purchase.

"It's just like new, Ann. How much was it?"

"Five dollars. It was more, but I hit it on a green tag day; fifty-percent reduction on all items with a green tag. Actually, the dry cleaning cost more than the coat!"

"How thoughtful of you to do this for me. It's lovely!" Noting the white envelope attached to the plastic, Addie asked, "What's this?"

"Oh, I forgot about that. The cleaners found it pinned to the lining. Probably extra buttons or maybe somebody's mad money. Open it Addie, and see what you have."

Addie eagerly opened the envelope after first holding it up to see if the sunlight would show them any clue as to the contents. Inside, wrapped in a plain sheet of typing paper, were two bills. One was a fifty dollar bill, the other a hundred. Both ladies gasped simultaneously.

"Oh, Addie, now you can go to Peckville to get the black coat you really wanted."

"Shouldn't we try to locate the donor of the coat?" She looked up at Ann.

"Well, I really don't think they would have any record after three years or more. If the person who it belonged to had donated it, they certainly would have come looking to get it back during that period of time."

Addie conceded Ann was probably right.

"I feel it's your money, Ann, you bought the coat." She was adamant, but Ann would have none of her arguments.

"Now you can get your black coat." Ann repeated her earlier suggestion.

"Why I don't need that black coat. I have a perfectly lovely navy blue one here. Blue is a better color for me anyhow. I'd rather invest it in a new refrigerator."

"Good decision, Addie. Now if you're ready to call it a day, let's head back home."

"Yes, I'm ready to go. We've had a busy day. I've learned a lot from you today, Ann. I never realized there were so many ways a body could save money."

"I've got a few more cards up my sleeve, Addie. If that new refrigerator has a large enough freezer section, I saw a day-old bread store here in town. You could stock up a supply. I've successfully frozen milk, even. You might consider picking up a small microwave oven. You could cook up a main meal and make your own TV dinners. There's nothing like good home cooking. I do that at Thanksgiving and Christmas. It stretches the leftovers out without us getting sick of same old, same old."

"Well, Ann. You're just full of money-saving tips. Wherever did y'all get these ideas?"

"Back home, my family never bragged about how much they spend on anything the way some do, but about how little the cost. Most of my friends did too. One office I worked in, about four of us gals used to spend our Friday lunch hour chasing down rummage sales. When we got back to the office, we'd show off our bargains and do the Peanuts gang greeting dance. Well, our version of it anyway." Ann laughed at these memories.

"That must have been a sight to see." Addie smiled to think about that scene. If the other ladies were plump as Ann, it must have been a sight, for sure. Addie realized she'd laughed more these past few weeks than in the years since Mr. Rainer had passed away. Laughter was coming easier to her with some of the worries and pressures eased wondering how she was going to make ends meet.

The return trip was as pleasant as when they drove over to Afton. Each lady feeling comfortable with the other as if they had known each other for a much longer period of time.

CHAPTER SIX

Going Traveling

*B*efore supper that evening, Frank and Ann strolled around the outside of the house, inspecting what had been done and what was left to do. The place seemed somewhat improved with the scraping done all around even though the new paint had not been applied on the front side as yet.

"I think it would be a good time to take Addie on a trip to see her sister," Frank suggested. "Once I get the front of the house painted, I have the hardest work done. After that, I think we should start exploring around during the week, maybe take a few days off here and there and be around here weekends. Three- or four-day weekends sometimes, two-day weekends other times. We could get into some kind of routine. Be sure Addie has everything she needs and once in a while just pack her up and take her with us."

Ann waited patiently until Frank paused for breath. "That's a great idea! If she gets to see her sister, she'll have her trip in and won't feel left out when we bomb out on ours."

"My idea exactly," said Frank. "and you know me, I'd hate hanging around while you guys visited. So this way, everyone's happy and I get something worthwhile accomplished without you gals underfoot."

"I'll worry about you, here alone." Ann fussed. "I'll be afraid you'll fall off the ladder or some such thing."

"You know I won't be careless. Besides, I'd bounce if I fell."

"Well, if you promise, but I'll still worry. Is there someone you could get to help you? It'd be worth the money to hire someone wouldn't it?"

"Not a bad idea. There's a kid keeps riding his bike past here. Stops and watches me. I don't think he's headed anywhere, just checking up on my progress. Maybe I can hire him to supervise me." Frank knew Ann recognized his tongue-in-cheek speech wasn't all that serious, but it eased her mind to know he wouldn't be totally alone.

Frank continued with his thoughts, "I can't wait to see the look on Addie's face when you tell her you'll take her to Asheville. Hey, there's my sidewalk superintendent right on time!"

Ann glanced in the direction Frank was looking. A young boy, probably 11 or 12 had eased his bike to a stop. His face reddened when he realized they were looking at him and he started to ride away.

"Son!" Frank called. "Wait a minute; I'd like to ask you a favor."

The boy paused a second, then turned around and started towards Frank and Ann. They noticed he seemed to have difficulty in pedaling the bicycle. They introduced themselves and he reciprocated.

"My name's Teddy. Teddy Bisbo. I live down there a ways. I see you been fixin' up Miz Rainer's place when I ride by on my school bus. I hope y'all don't mind me coming over to watch. I don't never come on her property." He looked hesitantly from one adult to the other.

"What I wanted to ask you, Teddy, was if you wanted to earn a little money to help me out. You wouldn't have to paint or climb a ladder, but just be my legs and hand me things."

"Gol-lee, sure, all right!" Teddy exclaimed. Sounded like an easy job to him. He was already drawn to this project. He found himself fascinated by the miraculous results this man seemed to perform by his steady work. It almost looked easy to see all that he accomplished in a short period of time. "When do I start?"

"Well…" Frank began slowly. "I want you to clear it with your folks. If it's okay with them, you can start tomorrow after school."

"There's just my Ma. I'll ride right home now and ask. I know she'll say yes. And oh, there's a teacher's meetin' day after tomorrow, Friday. I don't have to go to school that day." Teddy said excitedly.

"Wait, I'll write a note to your mother with the details." Ann was always business-like. She hated to leave anything to chance.

They discussed wages and the agreed-upon amount was duly stated in the note to Mrs. Bisbo. Just before Teddy left, Frank spoke to him about the problem he had pedaling his bicycle.

"Looks like the pedal's bent. I could fix that for you," Frank offered.

"That'd be great, Mr. Flanders. I don't have any tools to fix it."

The man and boy worked together and after a bit, the bike was oiled and re-assembled. Teddy eagerly tested it. Pleased with its performance, he gave a wave and headed home.

"Ann, from the description Teddy gave, he lives a mile and a half from here. I was thinking Teddy might not mind checking in on Addie days we aren't around."

"You're reading my mind as usual, Frank. I was thinking exactly the same thing. Anyway, I feel much better about leaving you on your own. Let's go tell Addie to pack her nighty 'cause if she feels up to it, we're going bye-bye."

It didn't take much convincing to talk Addie into preparing for the journey. She alternated between tears and laughter. She expressed her delight in the idea by hugging them both.

"I thought I'd probably never see my sister alive again. I just hope nothing happens to her now I'm almost there. Oh, what if something does happen before then? Will she know me? It's been thirty years. Oh, I can't wait, I can't wait!"

"Addie, it's only a four hour drive. In four hours, you'll span 30 years," Ann spoke softly. "Do you want me to help you pack?"

"I can manage. It'll help time pass. You know, Ann, you've mentioned how you two take trips on the spur of the minute. Well, I think I can see why you do. Waiting for the big day to arrive can be agonizing. I'm so glad I didn't know till just now about this trip." She busied herself setting the table for their supper.

Supper that evening was a light one and a quiet one. Everyone had much on their mind. Adelaide was too excited to eat. Ann was almost as excited as Addie. Frank was mentally scheduling all his work, yet a bit envious of the ladies' plans. It had been quite a few years since Ann had taken a trip without him. Prior to retirement, she had occasionally traveled in the course of business in one of her positions. She had taken three long vacations alone over the forty years they had been married. For the past fifteen years, the only time they were apart was while each was at their respective nine-to-five employment.

Sleep did not come easily to anyone in the Rainer house that night. Ann remembered experiencing the same excitement over the years as a child on Christmas Eve, or the nights before a birthday. As she grew older, this same sense of anticipation pervaded the nights before beginning a new job and on the eve of her retirement. Actually, Ann thoroughly enjoyed life. Each day was new and exciting to her, like a clean sheet of paper. She kept a journal of her daily activities, seldom missing a day. Usually such happened on a day that was more exciting than usual. She knew that to most people, her life would probably be boring, but since she was the one who lived it, that was fine with her. Oh there were probably a few minor changes she would make, but overall, she liked the hand life had dealt her.

Eventually even Adelaide drifted off in a fitful sleep. She dreamed of being a young girl again sharing happy times with her sister. She was requiring less sleep as she grew older so it was not surprising that she awoke early the next morning, even before the hour set for her alarm to go off. Ann did not set an alarm as she felt a natural awakening was best. Years of early rising to 'punch a time clock' had lost its charm and this was one of the biggest pleasures she found in retirement. Truthfully, Ann was a night person. Any attempt to go to bed earlier than 11 pm would cause her to toss and turn, resulting in her being more tired in the morning than if she stayed up later. Frank, on the other hand, could drop off to sleep in an instant and arise early in the morning, raring to go. (Ann would say: "I'm raring to go, too. Go back to bed!")

The smell of fresh coffee brewing, bacon and eggs cooking woke both Frank and Ann at 5:30 am. Quick as a flash, Frank was dressed and Ann threw on her robe. Just as they left their room, Addie was calling "Breakfast's ready" from the kitchen.

"We're not waiting on protocol, Addie. Smells real good." As they approached the kitchen, another aroma greeted them.

"Addie, are those fresh biscuits I smell? What a treat!" Ann exclaimed.

"Yes, Ann, it is. I want to take some to Bessie and so I made plenty. We'll leave some for Frank to have while we're gone." Addie relished the praise they gave her for her cooking skills. Any cook will admit they enjoy cooking for others as much or more than for themselves. Addie was no exception to this.

Ann, as usual, was through eating before Frank. She excused herself so she could get washed up, brush her teeth and hair and dress. She noticed Addie had already dressed for the trip and had her overnight case by the door. It would be torture to Addie to delay their departure needlessly.

As soon as she was dressed, Ann returned to the kitchen where Addie was washing the breakfast dishes. Ann dried them and put them away. When Addie was done, she wrapped up the fresh biscuits, packing some for her sister and reserving several for Frank. It pleased her that they openly enjoyed her cooking. In just a few short weeks, they had become as family to her and filled a void in her life as her hospitality filled their need.

Finally, it was time to bid goodbye to Frank. As he always did, Frank hugged Ann and kissed her goodbye. He cautioned her to 'watch out for the other guy.' Then to Addie's astonishment, he gave her an embrace and told her to give one to Bessie. Addie turned quickly so he wouldn't see her eyes well up with tears.

Frank snatched up both Addie and Ann's cases and placed them securely in the trunk of the car. As he shut the trunk lid, Addie handed a key ring with several keys to him.

"What's this, Addie?" He asked.

"The key to the house, the back barn and Mr. Rainer's car. I don't know if it will even run anymore. I feel bad that you'll be without a car while we're off gallivanting. Maybe you can get it running."

Frank recognized the key as a Ford key, but couldn't determine the year. His love for automobiles was evident to Addie by the care he took of his own. If there's anyone I'd trust Bert's car to, it's Frank, Addie thought. It was obvious Frank appreciated her thoughtfulness; he felt honored by her gesture.

"I figured I'd have to rent Teddy's bike if I needed to go anywhere. Thank you, Addie, I'll check this out."

With a wave of his hand, he turned towards the house, then pivoted to watch the ladies drive away. Ann gave a short toot on the horn as they turned left on Rainer Road, left again at the stop sign at Route 3, to head towards Afton where they would take the interstate to North Carolina and Asheville.

Addie was silent for the first few miles. Ann respected her need to withdraw into her thoughts and memories. The desire to see her sister after such a long separation was overwhelming, but so were the anxieties over the condition of Bessie's health. She had not had word in several years. Addie faithfully sent greeting cards at Christmas and Bessie's birthday, but no response was forthcoming.

There was a germ of fear growing in her mind as to whether her sister was still alive.

Finally, Addie broke her silence. "I feel selfish at taking you away from Frank, Ann."

"Addie, it was his suggestion that we do this now. When he gets caught up with the big tasks he's scheduled, he'll be ready for a break. He thought, and I agreed, that you should see your sister before any more time passes. Frank will keep busy." Then to change the subject slightly, she added, "I do like that Bisbo boy. He seemed eager and able to help in just the short time he was there yesterday."

"Well, that makes me feel better that this was Frank's idea. I agree with you: I like Teddy Bisbo, too. I've seen him ride his bicycle by many times. He never stopped. Probably was scared of 'the old witch in the haunted house.' Do you know, Ann dear, you and Frank have done more for me than make improvements on my old house. Ya'll have done so much for this old soul of mine, too. Do you realize you've dragged me into the 20th century?"

"Kicking and screaming all the way?" Ann laughed. "I always said that's how I got my daughter into womanhood. I'm only kidding, Addie," she continued, seeing Addie looked like she was about to protest.

They made small talk about the scenery, the route, and the changes, some of which had been noticed and discussed on their initial Afton trip. Ann recounted some of the trips she and Frank had undertaken. Addie seemed grateful to have Ann chatter on about these things which took her mind off the fears she had been developing about Bessie.

"Look, Addie! See the crosses on the hillside over there? It is always a comfort to me when I see those." She indicated a grouping of three crosses; two yellow ones flanking a larger white cross. This scene is repeated across the countryside. Ann and Frank had come across them many times in their travels throughout the Southern states. They encountered them as far north as Illinois, but only once had they noticed any in their native New York State.

"I don't remember noticing them afore. It's good that someone is not ashamed of their faith." Addie reflected on the scene. Ann proceeded to tell Addie about the many times they had viewed the crosses in their travels.

The sight of the crosses did much to lift their spirits. Ann was stirred by Addie's remark about the display of faith. Ann's own faith in God was very strong. She didn't force her views on others. She knew she was probably too reticent about sharing it with people she didn't know well. Some people found it offensive to have someone share the Gospel. Ann did not consider herself religious, believing that religion was man-made. She was a believer. She tried hard to be an example of Christ's love. People sensed it when they were around her, but sometimes they just didn't always understand what it was they were experiencing. A young co-worker had once told her she was too good to be true, that she was unreal. Ann would be the first to tell you she was far from perfect. She had a little framed saying on display which read: 'Be patient with me, God isn't finished with me yet!" (Frank had a saying about her as well: 'You're too heavenly minded to be any earthly good.' So they were at an impasse in that department.)

The miles to Afton passed quickly. Addie apologized to Ann for not being able to guide her better along the route.

"None a these roads look at all familiar to me and it's been such a long time that I have no idea which way to go. But you don't seem to have any problem at all."

"I'm used to being the navigator. I looked over the map at home and wrote down the routes we'd use. Actually I'm good at numbers so I remember the route numbers. You can be a help by looking for Route 78 signs. Once we get on that, it's clean sailing right on down. You can be acting navigator this trip and I'll be acting chauffeur. I'll try to live up to Frank's example."

"I have no doubt at all in your abilities, Ann. I have complete confidence in you. Look! There's your route over there!" Addie was pleased to have spotted the sign. A huge van was parked so it was difficult to see the sign unless you were on your toes. A few blocks down, the traffic to Rt. 78 detoured straight through downtown causing a delay, but after a half an hour of negotiating the busy streets, they were finally back on the more direct route. Ann gave a sigh of relief when the Interstate access ramp loomed into view. Addie echoed her sigh. Several miles down the road, Ann pointed to a sign which read: 'REST AREA TWO MILES. MODERN FACILITIES.'

"I gotta rest my area, so I'll pull in up there," said Ann.

"Good, I'll avail myself of their modern facilities as well." Addie was tickled to note Ann's smile at her witticism. She was starting to relax as the miles rolled by. She enjoyed Ann's companionship and it was evident Ann felt the same.

In fact, Ann often thought of how Addie seemed like family. Ann admired Addie's quiet acceptance of her lot in life. Addie would comment on how much more convenient life was since Frank and Ann had become a part of it. She never harped on the negative side of LBTF, as she was beginning to call her Life Before The Flanders. Addie had picked up Ann's habit of using acronyms to abbreviate frequent sayings. Even Frank had his favorites. ASAP (As Soon As Possible), TGIF (Thank God It's Friday) among others.

It felt good to the ladies to get out of the car and stretch their limbs. They took advantage of the 'facilities', and decided to have a CB (coffee break) before they headed back out on the road. Ann had brought a small thermos of coffee so they sat at a picnic table for their break. Addie was visibly relaxing now though she did verbalize some of her fears.

"Ann, I may be taking you on a wild goose chase. Suppose she has passed away and no one told me?"

Ann consoled her: "I suppose that is always a possibility, but I'm sure her son would have contacted you if that were the case. You know the old saying, 'no news is good news'."

"Of course, he would have let me know. Thank you, Ann, for pointing that out to me." The ladies arose and went to the car. As they continued their drive on the interstate, Ann asked Addie if she had a pencil and paper. Addie did and wondered aloud why these were needed. Ann enlightened her.

"When I was little and on a trip with my parents, my two brothers and my sister, Mom and Dad would introduce us to a game to while away time and keep us from fighting among ourselves. One, which is still my favorite, is spotting the different states' license plates. The object is to see how many states are represented, but since I'm so obsessed with numbers, I count how many times I see each state's plate. I warn you though, it can become aggravating if you see a plate that looks unlike any you've written down but you never get close enough to actually determine the state. You also can't count the state you're presently driving in." Addie agreed it was a pleasant diversion to help pass time. She made it more of a challenge by creating two columns on the note page, crediting Ann or herself with the first spotting of a state's plate, as it occurred.

"Can you just imagine trying to do this on a narrow two-lane road?" asked Ann. "Thank God, Frank never was interested in joining me in this pastime." So probably more for safety reasons, than compassion, Addie won her first game of this when the count was later tallied.

The combination of the game, keeping an eye on the scenery, counting the sightings of the crosses and their quiet conversation kept Addie's thoughts occupied so time passed more quickly than it otherwise might have. Addie's face registered her amazement that they had reached the 'WELCOME' sign at the North Carolina border.

It seemed not too long after that they had reached the Asheville exit.

Ann intently studied the signs indicating the various services one would expect to find at an interchange along an interstate highway. She had given this a lot of thought, going over all the possible conclusions to this trip. She decided it was time to share her game plan (though not her motives) with Addie.

"Here's the plan, Addie. Because of the Afton detour, we've been five hours. I'd hate to get to the nursing home just at their mealtime. We'd be hungry and not at our best. I get a headache sometimes when I'm hungry, so I propose we have a light lunch--- some soup--- perhaps a sandwich, too. Then we'll go find a nice motel or bed and breakfast place, get settled in, wash up, a nap if we like and go to the nursing home during afternoon visiting hours. I know you're anxious to see Bessie so I'll let you decide what you want to do."

Addie thought the plan over. It was apparent to her that Ann had thought this through and she recognized that Ann was concerned about Addie's welfare. A light lunch made good sense as she was almost too excited to eat, but some soup would taste good and a cup of tea as well.

"Yes, that seems like a good idea, Ann. Did you think it necessary to locate our quarters for tonight so soon?" asked Addie.

"Frank and I have had one or two uncomfortable nights over our travels by waiting too late to pick out a motel for the evening. The sooner you select one, the better off you are. Since we aren't trying to make it to another city tonight and we know we'll be here a few days, I think it's best. Since it's after checkout time, we'll pay the same rate as if we were checking in at 4 a.m. tomorrow morning. Soooo, for the same price, we have the convenience of our own 'digs', even though temporary."

"What good common sense you have, Ann. I am the beneficiary of your experience, not to mention your kindness as well…" Addie broke off as Ann signaled a turn into a truck stop. "Are you needing gasoline already?"

"No," replied Ann. "This is a truck stop chain Frank and I are familiar with. So far we've never been disappointed with their meals. They maintain clean rest rooms, too. Wait till you see this place, Addie. It's like a mini-mall inside. Almost everything you need while you're traveling, you can find at a truck stop."

"Another new experience. Something different every day. I never realized how much fun a body could have just from the simple things. I keep wondering how you and Frank can afford to eat out as often as you speak, but I see you manage money very well." She spoke admiringly.

"We always say, people wouldn't believe it even if they could follow us around," laughed Ann.

Ann deftly maneuvered around the traffic and located a parking space. Luckily, it was near enough to the entrance so the ladies did not have to dodge cars to get to the door. As Ann had predicted, it was a whole new world inside for Addie. As Addie had frequently remarked, Frank and Ann had exposed her to the 20th Century. Not that she was unlearned, it was just that the sheltered life she had led since her husband's death had not exposed her to much of the progress the world now takes for granted. Addie had never purchased a television set. Never having had one, she felt no need for a TV. She had no contact with her neighbors and had no desire to keep up with the Jones anyway. She was brought up in an era where people got along with what they had, 'making do,' as they said. Still she found this a great learning experience and eagerly embraced all the new sensations of sight and sound.

"Just another day in the Adventures of Addie and Ann!" Ann quipped, causing Addie to laugh.

After browsing through the shop portion of the truck stop, they proceeded to the restaurant area where they seated themselves in a booth equipped with a telephone and a miniature TV. A waitress soon appeared at their side with glasses of ice water and menus. She took their beverage order, told them of the daily specials while indicating to Addie the section of the menu listing their Senior Citizens' meals. Since Addie had joined Frank and Ann on more than one occasion of dining out, she had knowledge of current prices. Her pleasure upon seeing the discounted Senior meals was evident. They each ordered hot tea and on hearing that the soup of the day was chicken rice, promptly settled on a bowl apiece. Ann knew from experience that a cup would be sufficient for her taste but she wanted Addie to have enough to suit her. If Ann ordered merely a cup, she felt that chances were that Addie would follow her lead.

Their order was served quickly, accompanied by a small plate of dinner rolls. The two enjoyed their nourishing lunch. As they were sitting over a refill of their tea, Ann excused herself and went to the Ladies' restroom. During her brief absence, their waitress stopped at their table.

"Is there anything else I can get you ladies?" she inquired. "Do y'all think your daughter will want any dessert?"

"She said not," Addie replied. She felt no need to correct the waitress on their relationship. Addie and Bert had never had any children nor felt a loss that they hadn't. It was nice, however, to feel like part of a family. When Ann returned to their table, Addie told her of the waitress' comment.

Addie remembered something Ann had said earlier and asked, "What did you mean, Ann, when you said we'd either find a motel or a bed and breakfast? What exactly is a bed and breakfast? It's really self-explanatory but where do you find one?"

"It's just as it sounds, the name for a private home, usually an older one, where you can get a room to stay overnight. Much like the old tourist homes. Besides a room, you are provided breakfast also. It's a quaint idea and you are treated more on an individual basis than at a motel. They both have their benefits."

'I recall staying in tourist homes several times and once at a motor court. The forerunner of these modern motels. Bert and I stayed at a motor court in Nashville on our honeymoon."

Their light lunch check came to only $4 plus tax. Addie insisted on paying the tab while Ann left the tip. Addie noted that she calculated the amount and left more than 15%. Ann explained that the waitresses were now taxed on 8% of the restaurant's business as tip income, regardless if they received that amount in tips.

"Some people don't realize that and either tip lightly or not at all. If I leave a little extra, it helps make up some of the difference." When Ann finished her explanation Addie thought how like the Ann she had come to know to be considerate.

The ladies returned to their car where Ann studied a pamphlet she had picked up at the cashier's counter in the truck stop. It was a map of Asheville. Locating a certain place on the map, they headed out to find their intended destination. It turned out to be a small motel run by a middle-aged couple. They obtained a double room for two nights. It was outfitted with two double beds, the usual furnishings and included a television set and a telephone. While Adelaide freshened up in the bathroom, Ann placed a telephone call to Frank to tell him the name of the motel and telephone number in case he wanted to contact them over the next several days. He was pleased to hear they had arrived safely and reported that his work was moving along smoothly. He and Teddy had just stopped to grab a bite to eat.

"I'm just about to call the nursing home now to ask about Bessie Turner." Ann wanted to be able to allay Addie's fears.

"See you in a few days. Tell Teddy we said 'Hi'. I love you."

"Me, too," was Frank's response as they both hung up.

Ann next dialed the number for the nursing home. After a brief conversation, she returned the receiver to its cradle with a perplexed look on her face. Addie emerged from the bathroom unaware that Ann had been on the phone. Ann shared the call she had made to Frank but said nothing of her second call.

CHAPTER SEVEN

Bessie

*A*ddie decided she'd follow Ann's suggestion to lie down briefly, "Just to catch a few winks."

Ann took up the phone book and wrote down a few numbers in her ever ready note pad. Slipping out the door with purse in hand, she located the nearest pay phone and made a few calls.

She returned to their motel room to freshen up. By the time she was finished, Addie was up and sitting at a table near the window of their room. She was doing some figure calculations and said to Ann, "When we get back home, take me to my bank. I'll take out the money for the paint to finish up. I'll hire someone to do all that front. It's too much to expect Frank to do it all."

"He'll probably not agree to it, but I'll let you two settle it. Are we all set to go?" Now that's a foolish question, Ann thought to herself, seeing Addie was already donning her coat.

They left the motel and headed towards the eastern part of town. Ann had done her research well and quickly found the street she was looking for. As she made her way along Pleasant Boulevard, Addie cried out.

"Ann, you went by the home! Pleasant Rest is back there on the right!"

"Addie," Ann spoke gently. "While you were resting I called there. Bessie's no longer there."

"Not there? When did she … leave? Where is she now? Is she? Oh, my…Is she dead?" Addie's consternation showed in her face and echoed in her words.

"No, dear, she's not dead. But Pleasant Rest wasn't very helpful, I'm afraid. It seems sometime three years ago, she had a spell where she had to be hospitalized. By the time she was ready to be released from the hospital, the home had accepted a new resident who replaced her." Seeing Addie's questioning expression, she continued, "Oh, it's quite customary. If the room isn't paid for, they're not obligated to hold it. And the government medical plan doesn't allow duplicate payments for both the home and the hospital. It's either one or the other. Frank's mother was in a local nursing home. They charged her $700 a month for two months while she was hospitalized and when she could return to the home, they said they weren't equipped to care for her. I believe they planned this all along and I feel it was very dishonest to charge her to keep the space open. Worst of all, they charged her the same price as if she were there being cared for and eating their food. It should have been a reduced rate since they weren't rendering any services to her other than holding the space!" Ann said indignantly.

"Oh, my, I hope I never have to be in a home. Did the Pleasant Rest people tell you where she is now?"

"No Addie. They said they don't maintain records for change of address for former residents."

"Where are you headed then, Ann?" Addie decided Ann appeared as if she knew where she was going.

"I believe she's at the County Home for the Aged. So we'll just check it out."

"The poor house?" Addie was shocked. "Why didn't someone let me know? My own sister!"

"They don't call them Poor Houses anymore, Addie. There is a lack of residences to handle everyone who requires nursing home care. It's regrettable that some people who are in nursing homes don't always require that in-depth nursing care but would do as well or better in the communal-type residence where everyone has their own apartment. They have central services or people who check in on you; but those are not easily found either. So the county-run homes take the patients in until there is room in a nursing home for them. Many times there's a problem with overcrowding." She stopped speaking when she saw Addie give a shudder, deciding she'd already told Addie more than she cared to know about such places.

"It can't be too much farther, from the directions I got," said Ann. Soon they sighted the rambling grounds of the County Home for the Aged. Ann turned into the drive leading up to a huge official-looking building. She parked in the visitor's parking lot and said to Addie: "Why don't I go in and check to see if this is the right place? Save you walking all around until we're sure. Okay?" She spoke kindly. She could image how anxious Addie was. All these delays, just when Addie felt she was finally there, must be unsettling to her, to say the least.

"Yes Ann, I 'spose that's best." As she spoke Addie looked towards the veranda of the Home, where residents milled around whiling away time. Some were in wheel chairs; several accompanied by white uniformed attendants. There seemed to be no visitors in sight.

Before she left the car and Addie, Ann suggested that they pray for a successful conclusion to their search. Addie quickly bowed her head at Ann's suggestion.

"Heavenly Father," Ann began. "We come before You in love and admiration and gratitude for all of the blessings You have given us. Father, we especially ask for You to bless our venture to find Bessie. We pray that this long separation between Addie and Bessie be over.

We know it is in Your power to grant us what we ask. We worship You, we adore You. In Jesus' name. Amen."

"Amen," added Addie. "Amen!"

Thus fortified, Ann strode purposefully up the front walk and into the main building to a reception counter and asked if they had a resident named Bessie Turner. The reception clerk punched the name into a computer and confirmed Mrs. Turner did reside there and gave Ann the building and ward numbers. She pointed to a chart under a plastic sheet on the counter, which gave an overall view of the Home's campus. Ann found this helpful and thanked the clerk for her assistance. All the way to the car she rejoiced and thanked God for guiding them safely and quickly to their destination.

"Is it too much to hope," Ann whispered, "that Bessie will know Addie?"

Addie was disappointed when Ann returned to the car, slid behind the wheel, placed the key in the ignition and started the vehicle. Addie took it as a sign it was an unsuccessful quest. Her spirits brightened; however, as they turned right from the parking lot, not left, as they would have to return to the main street.

"She is here, Ann, is she?" Addie asked excitedly.

"Yes, she's in Ward 18, Building 6. Prepare yourself, Addie. These places can sometimes be grim and depressing."

The Building 6 parking lot was a bit closer to the building than the main parking lot had been to the office. There were several parking spaces reserved for Staff and some marked for Visitors Only. Ann parked in one of the visitor spots and escorted Addie into Building 6. She read the directional signs posted in the corridor lobby where all the corridors converged at the Central Hall. There was an information desk but it was not manned at the moment. There was no need for information, since Ann felt she had all she needed with the data furnished her at the main reception area. She found a sign indicating Wards 17 to 20 were down corridor A to the right of the central hall. Leading Addie down the corridor, they quickly located Ward 18. There were eight beds in this ward. (Ann calculated to herself that if all the wards had eight residents and each of the ten buildings had twenty-four wards, there were over 1000 people cared for at this facility.)

Addie looked around her, confused. The old women almost all looked alike to her. Several were sleeping in their beds; two or three were sitting up in either lounge chairs or wheelchairs. Three beds were empty with no sign of their occupant around. One of the empty beds looked vacant as it was stripped of any bedding and no personal effects placed on the nightstand present for each resident. Another bed was made up with a cheery quilt thrown across it. The nightstand held pictures, cards and a plant resulting in a more homey appearance than the others reflected. The last empty bed was also stripped of the bedding. On the nightstand was a box containing someone's personal belongings.

"Ann, look!" gasped Addie as she indicated a sign sticking out of the box. It was a printed signed such as was hanging on the occupied beds. Ann could see the last three letters of the sign. It read "- - - N E R" She hurried to the box and pulled out the sign. It read 'TURNER' and Addie burst into tears. It seemed so frustrating to come so far, after such a long time and see her sister's things boxed up as if to pack away. An attendant came in the room and when she saw Addie sobbing, asked:

"Did y'all know Miz Warner?"

Ann explained, "Mrs. Turner. Mrs. Rainer is Mrs. Turner's sister."

"Oh, but you see, Miz WARNER passed away. I'm moving Miz Turner's things over to the bed near the window. I thought it'd be cheerier. She loves to see the flowers. She's down in the TeeVee lounge watching her soap. Don't tell her about the move. It's a surprise. She didn't mention y'all were coming so I guess that will be an even better surprise. She deserves it. She's so pleasant to be around. Dry your eyes, Ma'am. I sure am sorry for the mix up." The aide continued, "If you can keep her busy there for a while longer, I'll be all done here."

Ann put her arm around Addie's shoulders both to comfort her and to brace her up.

"My legs are all rubbery, Ann."

"Mine, too, Addie. But come on, the search is nigh over!"

The two ladies walked down the hall in the direction the attendant had indicated they would find the TV lounge. On entering, they found two silver-haired ladies engrossed in the TV program. As they hesitated before entering the room, the station break came on signaling the end of the half-hour show. One lady arose to leave, saying to the other.

"Mary, I don't think I'll watch the next one today. I'm feeling edgy. Maybe I'll walk about a bit." Seeing Ann looking at her, she smiled and asked, "Are you here to see Mary?" Mary looked up expectantly but not recognizing Ann, she turned back to her TV program.

Ann was in the lead with Addie partially hidden behind her. Ann responded to the older woman's question. "We're looking for Bessie Turner."

"Well, you've found her. What can I do for you?"

Ann realized that Bessie didn't see Addie. She said, "I understand you have a sister, Adelaide Rainer. If you like, I can arrange for you to see her." As soon as Ann spoke, she was sorry to tease Bessie as she immediately started to weep.

"Oh, I miss Addie so much! I haven't seen her in so long!"

Addie delayed no longer. Stepping around Ann, she reached out to Bessie to hug her. It was heartwarming to see the happy faces on the sisters. Both began talking at once.

"You are a hard person to find!"

"However did you find me?"

"No one told me you were here."

"Who brought you? How did you say you found me?"

"Ann, my friend Ann brought me and found you. I was so worried about you."

"I've so much to tell you."

"And I you. Where's Ann? I want you to meet Ann."

Ann had stepped out into the hall. She felt the sisters needed some private time for this long-overdue meeting. Ann needed a tissue. Tears were streaming down her face. She had known all day the risk she was taking to bring Addie this distance with no assurance they would find Bessie. Yet she knew it was a gamble they had to take. She silently praised God that their trip had a happy ending.

Bessie and Addie appeared in the doorway looking for Ann. Ann found herself wondering why Bessie was in the nursing home at all. She was mobile and alert. It seemed unnecessary for her to be here. Ann decided she should find out who Bessie's doctor was and learn more about this matter.

The three of them, with Bessie leading the way, went to another lounge down the hall. A TV was on there but the room was vacant so Bessie turned it off. Addie introduced Ann formally to Bessie and briefly explained their relationship and all that Frank and Ann had done for her in the few weeks they had been staying with her.

Ann found she was taking a liking to Bessie. She was a very sweet lady, stooped with a dowager's hump which gave her the appearance of being shorter than her true height. Ann surmised that Bessie had osteoporosis, and probably in a great deal of pain at all times. Yet throughout she seemed to maintain a calm and positive attitude.

After a while, Ann excused herself and left the sisters to visit. She wandered to the nurses' station for Wards 17 through 20 where she asked the charge nurse who Bessie's doctor was. The nurse said Bessie did not have a private physician, but was attended to by the Home's doctor. The nurse answered all of Ann's questions confirming that her suspicions were right about Bessie's osteoporosis and that it was complicated with a bone density problem. It all boiled down to the fact that Bessie couldn't live alone because of the ever-present danger of falling and breaking one or more of her thin bones. She also had a case of adult-onset diabetes which was diet-controlled. Apparently she had surgery over seven years ago and was accepted into Pleasant Rest as a convalescing patient. Paperwork was overlooked and Bessie was absorbed into the system. Other than Addie, the only living relative was her son, an executive living in Atlanta. Once a month, he placed a call to Bessie and would dutifully visit on her birthday in June and at Christmas. Bessie was never invited to his home, presumably because she was too weak to travel. Ann thanked the nurse for the information and went back to where the sisters were.

Addie asked Ann if it would be possible to take Bessie to dinner with them.

"I'm sure we can get the 'okay' from the powers-that-be. Let me go check it out," offered Ann.

"I don't think I have anything proper to wear," worried Bessie.

"Don't give it a thought," Addie said. "I can loan you something of mine." Ann thought that was a great idea and suggested that Bessie come as she was, just throwing on a coat. She could shower at their motel where Ann and Addie could fuss over her and get her all dolled up.

As Ann headed down the hall towards the nurses' station, there was a flurry of activity in the area of Bessie's ward. Ann had been in enough hospital situations (not to mention watching TV hospital dramas, a lesson in themselves) to recognize a serious episode. All available medical personnel had been summoned to the bedside of one of Bessie's elderly roommates. One nurse's aide remained at the station. Ann approached her and asked about their plan to take Bessie out to dinner. The aide retrieved Bessie's coat from her locker, bringing the visitors' coats from the ward as well.

"Does she have a purse?" asked Ann. With this reminder, the young lady went to a locked room and returned with a leather handbag, obviously very expensive. Her son's gift, Ann decided. Probably never takes her anywhere so she can use it, she fumed.

"There's no money in the purse," the aide told Ann. "If you want her to withdraw some, you'll have to do it at the main office."

"No need," Ann replied. "Thank you for your help. We'll be on our way. Oh, is there a curfew?"

"If they are not remaining overnight, we like them to be here by eight. It's less disruptive to the others."

"That sounds reasonable," said Ann. "Is she taking any medication we'll need to have with us?" At Ann's question, the aide checked Bessie's chart.

"Not until her morning meds." She was no more specific than that, which left Ann wondering what type of medication that was.

Ann slipped a ten dollar bill into Bessie's purse before she took the coats down to the ladies. She didn't want Bessie to feel destitute but she knew there was no reason for her to have to spend money during their planned outing. Rather than spend time at the main office, this seemed the most convenient manner in which to handle it. Ann believed it would be less upsetting to the ladies to leave right then without being in the middle of the Ward crisis. This is what they did.

Bessie enjoyed the drive to the motel. Both ladies seemed in such good spirits, Ann realized how much this visit meant to them. Once more it caused her to think about how the everyday things that most people take for granted can be the answer to prayer for others.

When they arrived at the motel, Ann suggested perhaps the ladies would like to rest a bit before they dressed for the evening meal. The room was inviting looking. The bed pillows were plumper than one usually found in motels. The lamps had soft globes which cast a warm glow over the room. At the far end of the double room was the vanity lavatory while to the left was the bathroom. To the right of the sink area was an open closet. Accordion-type vinyl doors lay flat against the wall. These could be pulled across to shield that end of the room from sight. It was particularly handy if someone was opening and closing the outside door while a second person was washing up at the lavatory. Instead of drapes at the window, they were outfitted with vertical blinds. The walls and furnishings were of a soft pink and beige combination with glossy prints on the wall, which carried the same color scheme. Two lounge chairs were on either side of a table. A relaxing atmosphere in all.

Both Addie and Bessie decided Ann's idea was right up their alley. Ann claimed one of the lounge chairs, while the sisters reclined on the beds. Although Ann planned to read, not nap, it wasn't very long before her eyes closed and her magazine slipped to her lap. Bessie was asleep even before that. The security of being with her sister, added to the relaxing surroundings, worked like a sedative. Addie was so excited she was sure she would not rest. Before long though, she too dozed off. They rested for about 45 minutes when Bessie awoke with a start which roused the others.

"I'm sorry to waken you," Bessie apologized, and went on to explain what woke her up. "It was so quiet. Too peaceful. You get used to the commotion in the back-ground and the lack of these sounds, woke me."

Ann understood what Bessie meant. She had heard similar comments when city kin came to the country to visit. They subconsciously missed the din of the city which they had become accustomed to. The quiet of the country kept them awake.

"I can't believe I slept so soundly," commented Bessie. Addie agreed that she, too, had rested well.

As the sisters were selecting an outfit for Bessie from the several Addie had brought with her, Ann leafed through the telephone directory to see what restaurant might appeal to them, frequently asking for suggestions from Addie and Bessie.

"What do you feel like eating? Plain or fancy? Casual or dressy?"

Bessie spoke up, "Do you know, I sort of like the idea of eating where you and Addie had your lunch. I've never been at a truck diner before. Addie said the prices were reasonable."

"Stop," interjected Addie. "Truck stop is what they call it. They serve huge servings to the truckers or senior citizen meals if you're not up to so much food."

They agreed to eat there this night and the next day they would reconnoiter the area to pick out another place to eat.

Bessie thoroughly enjoyed her introduction to one of Asheville's truck stops. She was astounded, as Addie had been, to see all the items for sale there. Addie escorted her about the shop as if she were a seasoned veteran traveler.

After they left there, Ann drove them around the city and the ladies exclaimed over all the sights and sounds of the city and its lights.

They finally returned to the motel. Ann called the Home to tell them that Bessie would remain with them overnight. The mood of the motel room turned into that of a teenage girls' pajama party as the sisters talked long into the night before they could get settled down and drift off to sleep.

CHAPTER EIGHT

The Monster Machine

*F*rank's Friday, as it started out, was not quite as eventful. With Teddy's help, the work he had laid out for the day was moving along nicely. They had accomplished so much, that after their lunch break and Ann's phone call, Frank suggested they check out Addie's car.

As they walked to the back barn as Addie called it, Frank made mental notes of the work needed to update the maintenance of the outbuildings. Up to now, he had concentrated his efforts on the house. This was his main objective and once this was completed, he and Ann would settle more into a routine of alternating work and pleasure. It was in Frank's makeup not to shirk work and he respected the fact that buildings would last indefinitely with the proper upkeep. Without attention, they could quickly crumble. He considered such a fate an insult to the carpenters who so carefully constructed the buildings.

As Frank pointed out certain things about the buildings to Teddy, he was pleased to see the attention Teddy gave to what he was saying. Teddy's interest was evidenced by the questions he asked Frank. Teddy was eager to learn all he could. He soaked up the information Frank was sharing with him. He had paid close heed to whatever task Frank was doing from their first encounter when Frank had repaired Teddy's bicycle pedal. Teddy decided this man was like a walking encyclopedia of facts. Frank remembered following his grandfather around in the same manner when he was even younger than Teddy.

The two reached the door of the back barn behind which sat a Ford of unknown year and model. To Frank, a mechanic and car bug, it was a moment to be relished. To Teddy, who had never had much intimate knowledge of ANY car, it was so exciting he was about ready to burst. Frank prolonged the moment with a little humor.

"Behind door number one, if you select it, is..." parodying a popular TV game show host. Finally, he put the key in the padlock on the double barn door, turned it and with Teddy pulling on one door, Frank on the other, it opened to reveal --- a tarp-covered automobile. From the outline of the car beneath the covering, Frank estimated it was between a 1949-1951, two-door model from the apparent size. He appreciated Teddy's well-mannered behavior. Some boys his age would have let their curiosity get the best of them and would try to rip the tarp off. Frank preferred to inspect the lay of the tarp to be sure it wasn't caught on anything or stuck to the car in any way. If there were any road tar or tree pitch anywhere on the auto when the tarp was placed on it, the tarp would adhere to the car like glue.

Frank carefully went over the whole car, gently lifting the cover and found that there were no areas where the cover was stuck. With a nod to Teddy, who took up one side of the tarp, they eased it off the vehicle.

The car was a green 1950 Ford custom, two-door coach. Frank was thinking that a car, if stored for the same period of time up north would not be found in such good condition. The salt and sand applied to the northern highways in the wintertime, would have caused massive rust damage. None of this was evident on Addie's car. It was a fine machine, Frank thought admiringly. It had been properly elevated with blocks so that the tires did not make contact with the barn floor. Frank worried about the internal mechanism, wondering how that fared over the period of storage.

Frank and Teddy were so absorbed in their find, they did not see or hear the approach of an automobile. It wasn't until a figure appeared at the barn door, they realized they had company. The visitor was Tom Cates. Tom saw they were engrossed so greeted Frank by name.

"Hello Frank, Teddy. You've got quite a find there."

"Oh, hello Tom," Frank returned his greeting. "Addie said if I could get it running, I could drive it. It's in good shape but it's been stored so long, I doubt she'll even turn over." Frank was puzzled when Tom shook his head 'no'.

"I wouldn't worry none about it starting, Frank. Addie's had me start it up for her every few months for the past several years. Before he retired, Ray Shafer at the Ford Dealer, used to check it out every six months for her. Y'all be amazed how sweet it sounds."

"I guess that explains why the tarp slid off so easily. I thought it hadn't been off in 15 years." Frank moved easily about the engine compartment, checking the oil level, fan belt, spark plug wires as well as other wires, to be sure they made the proper contact. He connected the battery cables to the battery terminals and turned the fan by hand. The engine was freed up as he expected based on Tom's comments. Tom recognized Frank was an experienced mechanic, leaving nothing to chance. He noted Frank, when checking the oil, had rubbed some between his thumb and finger, feeling its weight.

"Why did you feel the oil?" questioned Teddy, who had also noticed Frank's added action when checking the oil level.

"I was testing the viscosity of the oil. The feel of it tells me if it's got any lubrication left to it. Sometimes people drain regular oil and put in a thinner weight oil to store a car. Actually all you need to do is drain the old oil and replace it with new oil. You shouldn't run it to turn over the motor, but just hit the starter periodically to be sure nothing's froze up inside."

"Why's that, Frank?" asked Tom. "I thought you actually had to start an engine and let it run awhile to be sure everything's well lubricated."

"The combustion causes acid to form in the oil." Frank answered. "That's just what you don't want to happen." Satisfied that everything under the hood was in good order, he slipped in behind the wheel. As Tom and Teddy looked on expectantly, Frank placed the key in the ignition switch. With a grandiose flourish, to amuse his audience, he proceeded with his elected task.

"Gentlemen, start your engines!" Frank quipped. All three broke into grins as the old Ford began to purr. Teddy and Tom applauded appreciatively. Frank let the car run briefly before he shut it off. Everyone worked together to take the car down off the blocks. With Frank operating a jack, Teddy and Tom pulled the blocks out from under the front wheels. Then the jack was transferred to the rear of the auto and the operation repeated. When all four wheels were on the ground, Frank invited them on a test drive the length of the driveway. Tom was 'tickled pink' that his arrival on the scene was so timely as to be part of the test drive. At the end of the long drive, Frank brought the Ford to a halt and asked Tom if he wanted to operate the vehicle on its return run up the drive.

Tom was eager to try out the old car. He felt paternal towards it since he had been tending it for Addie the past few years.

"It sure runs like a charm, Tom," Frank told the deputy. "Your attention has paid off. I'd hate to think the shape she'd be in if the motor hadn't been turned over in 15 years." Tom glowed at the praise of the older man he had come to respect.

"Frank, what do you think a car like this is worth?" queried Tom.

"Oh, I guess about two to four thousand." Frank replied. "My Hemming's had one original about $1,750; restored, 2 to 3 times that with some as high as $7 – 8000. This one is in such good condition, one-owner, low miles, it can easily bring $2000. I used to have one like this but it was a four-door. What a sweet car that was!"

Teddy really enjoyed the conversation between the two men and felt lucky to be in this place, at this time. He had not guessed that this day would turn out to be so interesting. He finally worked up the courage to join in the conversation and ask the question that was foremost on his mind.

"Mr. Flanders, how much do you 'spose one of these cars cost brand new?" Teddy asked respectfully.

"Oh, probably less than two thousand," was Frank's reply.

Teddy's eyes widened when he heard that. "You mean it's worth more now than when it was brand new! Imagine that!"

"Inflation alone would account for some of that," said Tom. "Plus the fact that anything over 25 years old is considered a classic. This car is over 40 years old." Tom explained patiently, as he eased the car back into the barn. "Frank," he continued, "if you're in the area next May, what do you say the three of us take in the Antique Auto Show over in Afton? I'd sure enjoy looking at those cars with an expert such as yourself at my side."

"I doubt we'll be around that late in the Spring, Tom, but if we are, I don't see any reason not to go."

"Teddy, you and I can plan on it even so. Okay?"

"That'd be great, Deputy Cates. Thanks!" Teddy enthusiastically accepted Tom's invitation. "Mr. Flanders, what's a Hemmings?" Teddy was determined to ask the second question that had been bothering him ever since Frank had mentioned it.

"That's a hobby car magazine, sorta like a catalog. They're full of ads for old cars and parts for sale or wanted," was Frank's explanation, then he went on to say, "Now you know what a Hemmings is, have you ever heard of a Henway, Teddy?"

Tom and Teddy both looked quizzical as Teddy answered, "No sir, I haven't. What's a Henway?"

"About two pounds," Frank laughed. Tom caught on first. Teddy wasn't far behind him in picking up on Frank's joke. Frank's humor was clean if perhaps a bit dry sometimes.

"Well, men, I have to get back to painting or I won't ever get finished," said Frank.

"I have my overalls in the car," offered Tom. "I'd be glad to give you a hand."

Frank readily accepted his offer so the three of them pitched in, getting even more work done than Frank could have hoped for. They took a break in mid-afternoon for soft drinks and snacked on the goodies Addie and Ann had left. Frank brought out the automotive book he had mentioned earlier. Tom leafed through it briefly, then passed it to Teddy to look at. He left it open to the Ford section and Teddy looked up the year 1950, reading through the models until he came to the type car Addie owned. He soon found that Frank's estimate was close. He began looking up other cars he had heard the two older men discuss. He was very careful as he turned pages, a fact that was not overlooked by Frank.

The talk changed from cars to motorcycles. Tom asked Frank if he had any experience with them. Frank acknowledged he had some.

"I have a Harley Sportster but haven't been able to get it running smooth," Tom mentioned. "Do you think you might give it a look over?" The two men went on to discuss year and model of Tom's bike. Teddy was all ears, as usual, taking in all this mechanical talk, new to him.

Break over, the three went to work. Time passed quickly and when it came time to quit for the day, Teddy promised to be back bright and early the next day. Frank offered to pay him for his time so far, which pleased Teddy. Originally he had planned to use his earnings towards a newer second-hand bike, but since Frank had fixed the pedal and oiled it up, the old one operated so smoothly, he decided to keep it.

This money he would give to his mother. He couldn't wait to see her expression when he handed it to her.

It was a justifiably proud mother that gratefully accepted the money offered her that evening. Unknown to Teddy, she put a portion of it aside to start a savings account for him, silently vowing she would add to it until the total sum Teddy had presented to her was accumulated. For the moment, a higher financial priority beckoned.

When Teddy had pedaled off towards home, Tom invited Frank to join him at the Diner in Peckville for supper.

"They have a pretty good fish fry," Tom added as an enticement, "But then you've probably eaten there Fridays."

Frank had, and agreed with Tom, it was very good. He accepted Tom's offer to take him to town. It would save him cooking his own supper and provide some needed diversion.

The fish fry was tasty. It reminded Frank of their usual Friday night fare at home in NY State. They enjoyed what they considered, and almost everyone else agreed, was one of the best fish dinners one could eat. They went to the same restaurant every Friday evening and felt like they were family. They often referred to it as the best kept secret in Central New York. It sure wasn't their fault it was a secret, since they told everyone whenever the subject of dining out arose.

It was a pleasant evening. After their meal, the two men drove to Tom's home where Tom displayed his Harley for Frank to check over. Again Tom was impressed with Frank's mechanical knowledge.

In the corner of the garage, Frank spotted an older model industrial floor machine.

"I haven't seen one of those in years, Tom. Where on earth did you come across it?"

"My dad had a cleaning service. He swore by that machine. You know it?" Tom asked incredulously.

"I worked at that factory for almost twenty years. Does it still run?"

Tom doubted it did, but secretly thought if anyone could make it work again, Frank was that person.

Their attention turned again to the motorcycle. Tom started it up and Frank listened to it run for a few moments then bent down and adjusted something in the motor area. The engine began running a bit more evenly than when it was first started. Frank asked Tom if he could take it down the road for a test run. Tom readily agreed, sure that Frank would not have asked if he had never driven a motorcycle before.

Frank had a slight bit of difficulty in climbing on the machine, which worried Tom a bit. Frank saw his expression and commented that his old limbs had a touch of arthritis and were sometimes stiff. Once astride the Harley, he had a comfortable manner about him, as of someone used to the saddle. He gunned the motor a few times, eased the bike out of the drive and onto the road. Going slow as he was initially, the bike wobbled a little and now Tom was really getting nervous. Frank gingerly tested the brakes, then stepped up his speed slightly, tapping the brakes again. Satisfied that he knew what the machine's response would be, he turned the handle-grip accelerator so that his speed quickly came up to the posted speed limit. He drove down the road and around the bend until he was out of Tom's sight.

Tom was reassured by the caution Frank was exercising in testing the brakes. The ease in which he sat on the Harley also was comforting, still Tom worried about the 'old man.' He had come to like Frank and certainly didn't want him to get injured. He also liked his motorcycle and did not want to see that damaged either! Suddenly from the opposite direction, Tom heard a fearsome roar! Distracted from looking towards the direction where Frank had disappeared, he turned to see what on earth was coming down the street from the other way.

A streak roared past him and he was just going to run for his car to give chase to this intruder when it dawned on him that it was his own Harley with the 'Old man' driving at speeds the motorcycle had never seen under Tom's hand! Soon, at a much slower rate of speed, the Harley and Frank returned. Frank was grinning sheepishly at Tom.

"Sorry, Tom, I shouldn't have done that, but you know these Harleys, they take their own head and you can't stop them!"

It took a few moments for Tom to gather his composure and shut his gaping mouth. He kept looking at the motorcycle in disbelief that this monster belonged to him.

"Frank, I have never seen anything the likes of that! I still can't believe it's my old bike! You didn't let on to me that you're a racer. I 'most had cardiac arrest. You almost had just plain arrest. I was about to chase after you and give you a ticket. You sure had me fooled, coming from that direction!"

Reluctant to have the evening end, the two men chatted over coffee in Tom's kitchen. They talked more about cars and motorcycles and Frank told him about some of the many models he had owned. It was more in conversation about their different characteristics rather than bragging, since it was not in Frank's makeup to talk about his possessions as some people are prone to do.

"My son has the last Harley we owned. It got too big for me to enjoy wrestling with. Between me and Momma and the bike, it was beginning to feel too much like work. So we got a lighter weight bike. The old Hog's still in the family." Frank modestly did not admit that he now had two motorcycles awaiting his return to the North.

Since the hour was late, Tom asked Frank if he would like to take the bike home and keep it there for transportation until Ann and Addie returned from their trip. Frank eagerly accepted Tom's generous offer since he was obviously sincere about it.

"Now don't make me have to track you down for terrorizing the county," Tom grinned. "Not that I'd ever be able to catch you. I don't know if I'll dare ride that monster again."

Frank assured Tom that he had gotten his kicks out of that demonstration and apologized again. "I usually don't do that on anyone's machine but my own. Just got carried away. I think I missed my bike more than I realized these past months." The two men shook hands and Tom told Frank he'd try to stop by again to give him a hand.

"That's a threat, Frank. Not a promise."

"You're welcome anytime, Tom. Wish I could put you on the payroll."

"Not to worry, Frank. See you soon."

"Night, Tom. See you. Thanks again for the loan of your wheels. It'll sure be handy." Tom watched Frank ride off. Seeing the ease with which he handled the machine, he began to realize the extent Frank had conned him earlier with the hint of inexperience reflected by the wobbling and hesitancy displayed as he first rode away from the drive. Who would believe that under that silver hair and calm demeanor was a speed demon such as Tom had witnessed this evening. He shook his head as he turned to enter the house and snap off the outside light.

A content Frank wheeled off towards the Rainer home. The night was warm and stars blinked down on him. He was very appreciative of Tom's offer to use the motorcycle until the ladies' return. It was a generous gesture on Tom's part. No one would understand this any better than another bike owner.

Once at home, the motorcycle was carefully garaged and again Frank checked the oil as he had before he had begun riding it that evening. Pleased that there was no change in the level, he retired to the house. Making sure that things were A-OK in the kitchen, he shut off the lights and was off to bed. It didn't take him long to fall asleep. He'd put in a busy day.

CHAPTER NINE

The Peanut Butter Shuffle

*S*aturday and Sunday at Asheville went all too quickly for the three ladies. When Ann called to tell the people at the Nursing Home that Bessie would be remaining overnight with them, she made arrangements to return to the home to pick up Bessie's medications she would require in the morning.

Saturday began with a light breakfast followed by a trip to a beauty salon where they all received a shampoo and set. Bessie was treated to a manicure and pedicure, after which she declared she felt totally pampered. Lunch at a restaurant at the mall followed. Ann requested a window seat so they could enjoy watching the shoppers pass by. She explained that people-watching was one of her hobbies.

After their lunch, the ladies browsed through several shops. Both Bessie and Addie expressed consternation at the prices. When they paused to rest on a bench, Addie related the story of her coat to Bessie. Bessie liked the idea of shopping at 'Sally Ann's' and wondered if Asheville didn't have one. Off they went in search of a phone booth where Ann quickly perused the phone directory to get the address of the Goodwill Mission Thrift Store. Once armed with that information, the ladies gleefully exited the mall and were off to their destination. Ann was happy to retreat to the comfort of her car.

Bessie had a ball looking around the store. She selected a lovely dress from among three she tried on, marveling at the price ($5.99). Addie picked out a gray pin-stripe suit at $7.99.

When it came time to cash out their purchases, Addie commented to the cashier. "I'm afraid there's been a mistake, Miss. I have too much change."

"No, Ma'am, that's right," smiled the young lady. "These are green tags which are half price today. $7 plus tax for both."

"For both?" echoed the sisters simultaneously. They practically skipped from the store. Addie recalled the remark Ann had made about the times she and her friends from work had successful shopping excursions.

"Ann, I believe Bessie and I have learned your peanut butter dance," Addie laughed.

"Peanut butter dance?" asked Ann.

"Yes, the one you and your friends did when you got a big deal."

"Oh, you mean our Peanut Gang dance," explained Ann. "Yes, you two have that down pat!"

Just about that time, Bessie was admiring her purchase when she discovered the dress still had its original price tag affixed under the sleeve.

"Why, this is brand new!" she exclaimed. "It was originally $35!"

"JACKPOT!" Ann cried out.

"BINGO!" Addie chimed in.

On the ride back to the motel, Bessie asked if one of her roommates could accompany them to dinner that evening.

"I'm having so much fun, I feel selfish not sharing it with Mary. Do you all mind?" she inquired.

Both Addie and Ann thought it was a fine idea. A call was placed to the home and arrangements made to pick up Mary and go to an early supper. When the agreed-upon hour came, Mary was ready and waiting for her dinner dates. The foursome ventured out to dine at the restaurant they had selected. It was a steak and seafood house, elegantly appointed with glass chandeliers, etched mirrors, the whole nine yards. The ladies were obviously enjoying themselves and the restaurant staff were not yet very busy due to the early hour, so they devoted more attention to the ladies' table than one could normally expect. This added even more to their pleasure. Bessie told Mary all about their shopping trip. Mary was torn between envy and being glad Bessie had such a nice day.

"I can't thank you enough for including me in your plans for this evening," Mary began when Addie interrupted.

"Think nothing of it. You're like family to Bessie, so when she suggested it, it seemed like the natural thing to do. We should have thought of it ourselves, sooner."

Ann readily agreed with Addie. Mary's eyes welled up. She had never married and had no family, frequently feeling left out when other residents at the home had visitors. This evening meant more to Mary than she could express. Addie recognized the gamut of emotions Mary was feeling. She quietly engaged Mary in conversation, sharing the recent changes being wrought in her life. She decided that kindness was like a little snowball on a mountaintop. As it rolls down the hillside, it gathers more snow to itself until it doubles in size. She told the others of her metaphor. Mary commented that meanness could also resemble the runaway snowball, creating an avalanche of its own.

"That's true," Addie agreed.

The ladies had dawdled over dessert and coffee but the restaurant was beginning to fill up and the table was needed. Since it was still early, Ann suggested they drive around town before they returned Mary to the nursing home. They drove down the main street business section and through the residential areas. Ann located the city park and stopped the car at a pond there. Fishing some crackers from her ever-ready survival kit, she shared them with the others. Each took a few and crumbled them up, tossing the crumbs to the geese and ducks populating the pond.

"This is the most fun I've had in ages," said Bessie, "and it isn't costing us a penny."

"I'm learning from Ann and Frank," Addie put in, "that money don't buy happiness. It's a gift people give one another. Usually their time, sharing a laugh. Well, listen to me! I'm becoming a philosopher in my old age."

"I couldn't have put it better, Addie," was Ann's comment. "I'm proud of you."

"We have had a nice day," Bessie reminisced. "I'm so glad y'all could join us, Mary."

"Oh, I wouldn't have missed it," Mary replied. "But I really think I best be getting back." Reluctantly, the ladies got back into Ann's car for the drive to the home.

On the ride there, Mary couldn't help teasing Bessie about the touch of Tennessee that was beginning to creep into her speech. "I will need someone to translate for me after you're done with your visit."

Bessie laughed, "I was hoping nobody noticed. I am starting to mimic you, Addie."

"I caught it, if no one else did," Addie sniffed, pretending to be hurt over their teasing. "Ann, how come you haven't picked up our way of speaking?"

"Because I'm working real hard not to. I'm afraid folks will think I'm mimicking them. Truth is, I have always had a problem of echoing whatever I hear. I'm like a sponge in that respect, and do so unintentionally. I've made people really mad at me 'cause they thought I was mocking. A friend and I visited her family once in Michigan while her two sisters, who were living in the South, were also visiting. We were only there two days and went home with such drawls. We got hysterical on the return trip on the train because we couldn't remember how people in New York spoke. Not to mention the time I offended friends from Brooklyn because I picked up their accents. I'm afraid I will slip if I relax. But it's work trying to keep my New York pronunciations especially since I'm not hearing it. Frank is starting to sound like he was born here. He spent some time in the northern part of New York State and the small town where he lived spoke similar to people in the South. He's easily slipping back into that way of speech." Ann paused for breath, then went on to say "I once visited a good friend in Germany. We were sightseeing and were overheard by a couple, obviously American, who realized my friend seemed to know her way around so they approached us with some questions. I felt by their lack of accent (to me) that they were from Upstate New York as well. I asked them if they were from the Rochester area since they sounded the same as some cousins of mine from there. They were! In fact, they lived about two blocks from my cousins. How's that for pinpointing a location?" she boasted.

Ann's concentration was now devoted to looking for landmarks as they were nearing the street the Home was on. Once there, Mary received a hug from each of the others before they left her and drove off to their motel for another restful evening.

Sunday was passed pleasantly. Ann walked to a coffee shop and bought coffee and pastries and the Sunday paper. They spread the sections out and totally relaxed. At ten o'clock, they dressed and drove to services at a non-denominational chapel Ann had noticed on their Saturday drive around town. It turned out to be an excellent choice as they received a very warm welcome. The services were unstructured with members of the congregation witnessing to the ways the Lord was working in their lives. Ann was very touched when Addie spoke out and told of the changes in her life, crediting the Flanders for their part. The music was uplifting, especially the last piece. It was sung a cappella, though not in the formal sense, just their voices blending together in worship and praise. Bessie described it well as sounding as she imagined the voices of angels would sound. Addie and Ann agreed. Ann was reminded of the little Chapel she had attended back home.

CHAPTER TEN

Going Home

*A*ddie and Ann both slept fitfully that night. Addie was anxious to be home in her own bed while Ann had not been apart from Frank for this length of time in years. It was a comfort to her to know he would be missing her as much, if not more. They had that kind of relationship, built from years of being together, sharing experiences and working towards the same goals.

The next morning, Ann used her credit card to pay their motel bill. She explained to Addie that there would be no finance charge as long as she paid the bill as soon as she received the statement. Ann did not believe in carrying large sums of money around, preferring the convenience of a credit card instead. They had agreed to split the cost of the trip. Ann had to overcome Addie's objections since Addie was insistent that she wanted to foot the entire cost. Ann stood her ground and it was decided that when the credit card statement arrived in the mail from Ann's bank, Addie would then pay her half.

They figured the amount from the bill Ann received at checkout. Addie expressed amazement that it was so reasonable. The motel offered a ten-percent discount to members of the American Association of Retired Persons (AARP), which Ann belonged to; that caused the charge to be lower than normal.

Ann remembered to tell the owner that they had an extra person staying two nights. He waived the usual charge for the extra person. He had noticed Bessie's presence and appreciated Ann's honesty in informing him of the additional member of their party.

"Hope you ladies plan on staying with us next time you're in town."

"You can be assured of that," Ann promised. "We'll be back often to visit Mrs. Turner."

After they bid the proprietor goodbye and were walking to their car, Addie commented "If you are knowledgeable enough, I can see where you can take advantage of various discounts," she paused, then added, "And you're a knowledgeable young lady!"

"Young?" laughed Ann. "Not a good adjective to describe a retired person, Addie." You could tell it pleased her to be so addressed.

They had breakfast at their now-favorite truck stop. Their usual waitress took their orders then spoke apologetically to Ann.

"I'm sorry, Ma'am, but I have to see proof of age. I've been criticized for giving senior citizen discounts when I shouldn't have."

"No problem," replied Ann. "I understand. In fact, I find it flattering. Here's my driver's license," she added as she retrieved it from the depths of her large purse. The birth year verified her age as 58. This eatery set the minimum age for senior citizens at 55, while other places established their minimum age at 60. Ann and Addie both had to laugh at the look of disbelief on their waitress' face.

"Thank you, Ma'am," the girl said politely.

Addie said "I don't have a driver's license so ya'll just have to take my word for it."

"Up home, they have you get a non-driver's I.D. card from the Sheriff's Department if you don't drive. Most places won't cash checks for you unless you have either a driver's license or the non-driver's I.D."

Addie thought it was pretty funny to have to have a license <u>not</u> to drive.

Ann continued by telling how once when she paid cash at a store for purchases rather than write a check or use a credit card, the clerk at the register, insisted she produce ID when Ann tendered the money. When she questioned the clerk's reasoning, the girl was quite indignant and insisted it was store policy.

"Now, I guess I've heard everything," declared Addie.

Their breakfast was served and they dug in. After their meal, they went to cash out and Ann was surprised to see they failed to charge her for her coffee. The cashier indicated a sign behind her that read: BEVERAGE FREE, IF RED STAR APPEARS ON YOUR RECEIPT.

"You lead a charmed life, Ann. Hope some of it rubs off on me."

Once outside, Ann broke into her peanut butter shuffle.

"Doesn't take much to make me happy," Ann smiled. "Save me 50 cents and I'm jest as happy as ah lark!"

Addie realized that what Ann said was true. It reminded her of the old adage, 'a penny saved is a penny earned.' She repeated it aloud. She had not missed Ann's slight hint of drawl, but decided not to mention it.

Ann commented, "Outside of stores, you frequently will find pennies lying on the sidewalk or in parking lots where kids drop them because they mean so little to them. It still takes only 100 of them to make a dollar. I can't believe they just throw money away."

Addie reflected on a sign she noticed over a small dish that contained pennies at the cash register in the truck stop. 'HAVE A PENNY, GIVE A PENNY, NEED A PENNY, TAKE A PENNY.' That made more sense to her than just throwing them away.

"I've seen more than 100 soda or beer cans and bottles lying alongside the road on our trip," spouted Ann. "That's over $5 just lying there."

"That'd sure go a long way at our Sally Ann Shops, wouldn't it?" asked Addie.

"You bet," was Ann's reply, grinning to herself, as she realized Addie was picking up a thing or two about this economizing kick. She would be the first to admit Addie was frugal before she and Frank came along, but now Addie was learning she could still be economical, yet get a few luxuries for herself without a huge investment of her limited income.

The return trip went smoothly. This time Ann took an exit past Afton. It was a few miles longer but would eliminate the detour through the city that had delayed them on Friday.

When they reached the now familiar Route 3 that led to Addie's home, they both heaved a sigh simultaneously. Addie then dozed in her seat for about twenty minutes and they were finally on the last mile strip towards Addie's. Addie roused herself and was again looking at the scenery. She commented that traffic seemed rather heavy for the road.

"No," replied Ann. "It's been steady, just seems to have backed up for some reason. Maybe they're doing some road work up ahead."

It appeared to them that the slow-down was right near Rainer Road. They could see the few cars ahead speed up past the Route 3/Rainer Road intersection, yet could see no sign of any road equipment or an accident at all. Just then Addie let out a yelp.

"Ann! Am I seeing things? Look!" Blurted Addie, pointing in the direction of her property. Ann looked where Addie indicated.

"Oh my! Oh my!" Addie kept repeating.

"Oh my!" echoed Ann. The Rainer house was transformed into what appeared to be a brand-new home. A new coat of white paint enveloped the house, columns and all. There, in the unused circular drive at the front of the house, was Bert's green Ford Tudor. It was this sight that had caused the build-up of traffic as vehicles ahead of them had slowed to take in the unusual sight.

"I almost expect to see Bert behind the steering wheel of the car," gasped Addie.

"Don't go into cardiac arrest on me, Addie."

"Nor you, Ann," was Addie's response. "You almost look like you've seen a ghost as well."

"We did have a green Ford like that, years ago, but ours was a four-door. I'm amazed to see the painting all done. Frank used these three days well."

Ann beeped the horn as they turned down Rainer Road to the drive behind the house. She was tempted to pull in the circular drive in back of the Ford, but that would have marred the picture, she felt. It looked like a portrait from the past as it now stood.

Frank heard the car horn and recognized it as their car. He greeted them at the car with a grin and hugs.

"It looks great, Frank!" Ann praised.

"How did you ever accomplish so much in such a short time?" asked Addie.

"Teddy worked all three days and Tom Cates donated his day off." explained Frank. "Getting the car to run was easy. Hardly nothing to it except a wash job." He was obviously pleased to see his handiwork so greatly appreciated.

Ann got her camera from the car and was taking photos of the whole house and the Ford. She was glad Frank had the foresight to take some 'before' pictures of the house. She would get duplicates developed to share with Addie. She had taken pictures of the sisters during their visit and knew these too, would be precious to Addie.

They enjoyed a welcome cup of tea and regaled Frank with tales from their travels, while he shared the report of his activities while they were gone. He wisely decided to wait until later to tell of the stunt he had played on Tom with the motorcycle.

Ann whispered "Thank You, Jesus, for Your journey mercies on our trip." Addie breathed a silent "Amen!"

The green Ford was not returned to the back barn until after Teddy's school bus dropped him off. Teddy blushed with pride in his part of the restoration of the Rainer place when his fellow students on the bus buzzed over what a big change in the property.

He was glad he had paid attention when Frank had talked about the old car, as he was able to explain what make and model it was. His peers marveled at his knowledge, one older boy exclaiming, "Gee, I didn't know you knew so much about cars, Teddy."

Before he headed home, Teddy called to Frank to tell him about the other kids' reactions.

"Guess it's okay to put the Ford away now, huh, Teddy? I figured you deserved a glimpse of it first. You played an important part in all this. I couldn't have done it as fast without your help," Frank said generously.

CHAPTER ELEVEN

Glen Adams

*T*uesday, Frank, Ann and Addie took it easy. No big projects were planned for the day and they all rested except for a brief excursion into Peckville for a few groceries.

Wednesday morning found Frank at work scrutinizing the outbuildings to see if there was any dry rot or structural damage to contend with.

Addie and Ann began sorting through boxes of books in the hidden attic. Ann pointed out the value of some of the older farm directories. Addie had one for every year from 1900 to 1929. These listed the occupants of every home, indicating the occupation of the head of the household.

"If you don't want to keep these, Addie, I suggest you donate them to the library or town clerk. They are a great help to people who are into genealogy and researching their family roots. It zeros in on a year and then they can get a copy of the census for that year. The census usually lists ages and dates of birth for the residents.

"You know, Addie," continued Ann, "you should think about using some of these antiques to decorate your rooms. Maybe open up the house for visitors once or twice a week and charge a small admission or just let them make a donation. It's something to think about, anyway. If you decide to do that and kept these directories on your own library shelves, it would entice visitors. The types of people who are interested in paying to tour these old houses are mostly quiet, gentle people. The kind you would welcome into your home."

Addie and Ann began a list of items Addie had stored. When it was completed, they made their own tour of the house with both making suggestions as to where to display these items to the best advantage.

"Enjoy your things, Addie," said Ann, "or sell them and enjoy the financial security this added income would afford you."

They decided it was time to break to make lunch. As they entered the kitchen, a vehicle was heard driving in the far drive. It was a gray pickup truck. A pleasant looking, white haired gentleman emerged from the driver's compartment and engaged Frank in conversation. Shortly after his arrival, he and Frank came into the house. Frank introduced the newcomer to the ladies.

"Addie, Ann, I want you to meet Glen Adams. Mr. Adams, this is my wife, Ann Flanders and Adelaide Rainer who owns the property. Addie, Mr. Adams here, well, I'll let him tell you himself."

"Glad to meet y'all, Miz Rainer, Miz Flanders. My son owns a farm down Rt. 3 towards Afton. He recently lost a barn to lightning. He's looking to rent or lease one to store hay. He asked me to stop by and ask if y'all was interested in maybe renting out any of your buildings."

"I'll have to think about it, Mr. Adams, and let you know. I want to talk it over with Frank and Ann. I have no idea the going rent if I was to consider it," adding, "Where's my manners? Do sit down and join us for tea or coffee, if you prefer."

Mr. Adams accepted Addie's invitation and the four sat down. After some conversation, Ann quietly arose and put together some sandwiches. She set small plates and silverware on the table. She took a container of cottage cheese and a dish of potato salad left over from Tuesday's supper from the refrigerator. After mild protests that he didn't want to intrude, Mr. Adams consented to stay for lunch. He found himself enjoying their quiet company and the easy camaraderie among his hosts. The men discussed the condition of the outbuildings. Frank remarked that because the roof of each was intact, the buildings remained structurally strong, with straight rooflines. This was an indication that the frames of the building held up well despite their age.

After lunch was over, they dawdled over beverage warm-ups. It did not go unnoticed by the Flanders that Glen, as he asked to be called, and Addie were hitting it off.

Ann placed a call to the Peckville Realty to see what the market rental price was for farm buildings. She knew Addie would probably not charge the full going rate but it was a factor to consider and would give her an idea of what to ask if she decided to rent to the Adams'.

Glen finally got up to leave, vowing to return soon to see what Addie had decided to do about the offer. After his departure, Addie asked Frank what he thought about the idea.

"If you charged a reasonable price and they threw in the labor to keep the buildings maintained, I think you'd do well to accept it. But that's your decision, Addie. I can't make it for you," was Frank's answer.

"Ann?" Addie turned to see what Ann had to say.

"I agree wholeheartedly with Frank," Ann responded. "Mr. Adams seems really nice and if his son takes after him, you should have no problem. The buildings aren't being used, they're empty, and this way you'd be putting them to work for you and helping them solve their storage problem at the same time."

"I don't have fire insurance on the barns," Addie said, "just the house. I should increase the coverage to include them."

"We'll check it out. Usually, outbuildings are covered by a percentage of the overall house coverage. You don't have to have separate insurance for them. But as I said, we'll call your agent to be sure."

"Mr. Adams is a widower," Frank commented. Both Addie and Ann laughed because no one had asked and Frank's statement was out of the blue. He took their ribbing good naturedly but said, "I knew you were both dying to ask!"

"Well," laughed Ann. "There should be a special discount for widowers!"

Addie blushed like a teenager at the teasing, but secretly enjoyed the affectionate manner in which it was delivered.

"Sorry, Addie," murmured Ann as she gave Addie a quick hug, "We shouldn't be teasing you so. Ready to go back at it?" She said, referring to the task of sorting out the items stored in the attic.

"I s'pose so," replied Addie. "I don't relish the job but it needs doing."

The women went back upstairs to continue their work. They worked awhile in relative silence, once in a while commenting on some aspect of what they were doing.

Ann broke the silence to ask about something that had been rolling around in her mind. "Addie, is there a museum around Peckville? Some of those clothes are in good shape and it's a shame they're not someplace where people can see and enjoy them. I was also wondering if there was a historical society in the area," Ann finally paused.

"A museum? No, I don't think so. There used to be a History Society years ago. I've been out of the social circle for so long, I don't even know if it's still active or not. Most likely Tom Cates would know about those things." Addie put a lot of stock in Tom, he had solved problems for her in the past, and she felt he had all the answers.

The ladies finally decided to call it a day. When they realized what time it was, it was definitely going to be a late supper that night. Frank suggested that they go into town and have supper at the Diner that evening. No one had to think twice before accepting his invitation and began taking turns at cleaning up in the bathroom and getting changed from their work clothes for their trip to town.

"It's times like these that I miss the second bath we have at home," sighed Ann. "But it really isn't a problem since we're not in any special hurry."

The leisurely drive to Peckville was punctuated by the sighting of several deer that had ventured down to the valley to graze for their supper. They counted at least six including one buck, two doe, two fawns and a yearling. Addie had been the first to spot them and the others praised her keen eyesight.

When they arrived at the diner, they were pleased to see Tom Cates' Sheriff car parked in front. Entering, they all greeted Tom and Missy.

Returning their greeting, Missy exclaimed, "Well, Miz Rainer, Miz Flanders, haven't seen you ladies in here for quite a spell. I understand from Tom here, that y'all have been travelling! How's your sister, Miz Rainer?"

"Oh Bessie's fine, Missy. We enjoyed our trip. Ann's the one to go with. She's a good driver and a wonderful navigator. How've y'all been?"

"Good, Miz Rainer," was Missy's reply.

"Great, Addie," said Tom. "Frank tell y'all bout his ride on my black monster?" Then seeing the puzzled look on Addie and Ann's faces, he quickly changed the subject, "Meatloaf's great tonight, folks!"

"Sounds good to me," Frank quickly agreed. "Ann, how about you and Addie? What are you having?"

Everyone decided to go with the meatloaf dinner, knowing that the meals served at the diner were not only delicious but ample.

Addie remembered she had a question for Tom. "Tom, is there still a history society here in Peckville?"

"Yes Ma'am. Peckville Historical Society. They meet at the library once a month except in the summer. Miz Perkins at the library can give you all the info you need about it."

"Good, we'll go over to see her one of these days,'" Addie responded. She explained to Tom why she was interested in the society, telling about the books and old clothes she and Ann had been sorting. "Ann suggested that these items be on display somewhere and it seems like a good idea to me."

"Display? I've got an idea," Missy chimed in. "Remember that old ladies' store used to be on Main Street? The window mannequins are stored up over the general store. Ned's Momma and his aunt ran the ladies' shop. I bet he'd sell them reasonable."

"Yes! They'd be perfect, Missy!" Ann made no attempt to hide her enthusiasm. "If Addie wants to pursue this, would you like to help us? Maybe talk to Ned and see what he wants for them?"

Addie picked up the thread of the conversation. "If we can get the dress dummies, y'all could join us in dressing them up, Missy. Ann, should we arrange them all, set up the farm directory library and invite the historical society to have their next meeting out at the house?"

"That's an excellent idea, Addie!"

Their excitement was contagious. Frank and Tom each tried coming up with suggestions to fit the scheme of local history.

"Frank," Tom asked, "have you seen that buggy up in the rafters in Addie's back barn? It's suspended overhead behind Addie's car."

"Yeah, I saw it up there. I could get it down and set it out front with a mannequin sitting in it."

"I'll help you get it down, Frank," offered Tom.

Addie turned the conversation to the visit by Mr. Adams. After telling of the offer, she asked Tom if he knew the family, certain that he would.

"I know them well. I went to school with Bobbie Adams. He's younger than Billy what runs the farm. They're fine folk. I think y'all should seriously consider renting the barn to them, Addie. 'Course it's up to y'all."

By the time they finished their meal, it was decided that Missy would approach Ned Foster. He was a morning regular at the diner and she could easily sound him out about the mannequins. It pleased Missy to be included in on this conspiracy, as innocuous as it was. She promised to call Addie after she had talked with Ned Foster.

The evening drew to a close as Tom bid them a farewell. This caused Frank to check his watch. Realizing how late it was getting, he spoke up. "Hey, if we don't get going, we'll still be here at breakfast time!"

Addie quickly agreed with him as Ann arose and gathered her sweater and purse in silent consent. They had put in another busy day and it was time to head home.

CHAPTER TWELVE

Mannequin Madness

At ten o'clock, Addie's phone rang. Ann, alone in the kitchen, answered it.

"Ann, it's Missy. I spoke to Ned. He said he has three adult mannequins and one child. All women. He'll let them go for $50 apiece. I thought that way too steep for such old things. He came down to $150 for the lot. Do you reckon they're worth it?"

"Let me check around to see what they cost new. It would be nice to have the older ones if they're usable, but if newer ones are less, then maybe we should go that route."

"I didn't let on why I wanted them," Missy volunteered.

"Good! No sense in jumping the gun on our plan, Missy."

After she hung up the phone, Ann first checked Addie's telephone book to see if any Afton numbers were listed. Not finding the one she desired, she dialed information and asked for the phone number of the biggest department store she remembered seeing in Afton. When she obtained the number, she dialed it and asked for their purchasing department. A pleasant sounding lady answered the ring.

"Purchasing, Miz Parsons. May I help you?"

"I hope so, Ms. Parsons. This is Ann Flanders calling from over near Peckville. I want to set up a display using store dummies and I don't know where to start to locate some. I wonder if you could tell me your source and the approximate cost. I realize it's an imposition, but I would really appreciate any help you can give me."

"Well, this is a new one to me. Don't know anyone ever asked me such a question before. What's this display for?"

"It's for an Historical Society meeting, though I expect it will become a permanent display at the old Rainer Place out on Route 3," explained Ann.

"Oh, I see. Well, we buy the dummies at a supplier over in Knoxville. They cost us $150 new. That's with our business discount."

"Ouch!" said Ann. "I guess I didn't realize they were so expensive." Her disappointment hung heavy in the air.

"We have some old ones gathering dust in the storage area. Since it's for the Historical Society, I'd be authorized to donate obsolete equipment to a worthy cause. We could give you six. I believe there's three ladies, one man, a little boy and girl. That way, I can convert unused stuff to a tax write-off and gain needed space in the storeroom."

"Oh! Perfect! Thank you SO much! When can I get them? Before you change your mind," Ann laughed, while wondering silently where she would get a truck to haul them.

Ms. Parsons told Ann the hours the store was open and said she should come to the office and ask for her, Meg Parsons.

As soon as she got off the phone from speaking with Meg Parsons, Ann couldn't resist calling Missy at the Diner to share the news with her.

"Peckville Diner, Missy speaking."

"Missy, guess what? I called over to Afton Mall and talked with a lady named Meg Parsons at the department store. She made me an offer I couldn't refuse," Ann fairly gushed the news out.

"Oh, Oh, that's great! How much? How many?" Missy questioned Ann.

"She GAVE them to me. Rather they're donating them to the Peckville Historical Society, for use at the Rainer House display. We're going about this backwards. Haven't even contacted the historical society yet. Addie and I plan to go in to the library this afternoon."

"I believe their next meeting is a week from Thursday. If we are to have that display up in time to entice them to hold that meeting out there, we'll have to get cracking!"

"Do you think they could possibly change their meeting place at this late date?" Ann asked.

"I reckon they could. It's a small town. By phoning around they could easily accommodate a change. 'Sides, everyone's just abuzzing about how nice the Rainer Place is looking. I bet they're just adying to get out there and see it for themselves."

"Things are just falling right into place," Ann commented as she and Missy rang off.

Addie came in from the outside, her cheeks rosy from the gardening activity she had been engrossed in. Ann quickly brought her up-to-date on the recent telephone conversation she was engaged in regarding the mannequins. Addie's joy at hearing about Meg Parsons' donation was identical to Missy's.

"How are you going to pick them up, Ann?"

"You'll laugh, but I thought about just going over to get them with the car. Wouldn't that be fun? But it would take more than one trip. Or maybe I could stick two or three in the trunk and just stuff the rest in the back seat. I'm scared I'd damage them by packing them in carelessly though."

Addie's cheeks seemed even rosier as she shyly ventured a suggestion. "Well, perhaps we could impose on Mister Adams to pick them up in his truck. He seems real obliging, maybe he's even a member of the historical society."

"Good idea, Addie! I couldn't think of who we knew with a truck, but I bet he'd be happy to do this for us. I'll give him gas money. Shall you call him or do you want me to?"

"Oh my, no! You call him. I'd be too embarrassed to!"

The call was placed and a pleasantly surprised Glen Adams readily agreed to donate his time and truck to their project. In fact, he suggested since he wasn't doing anything that afternoon, he could run the ladies over to Afton on their errand. His truck was a club cab type, which held five passengers, so there would be room for Frank as well.

"Oh yes, I'll need Frank. Are you sure you don't mind doing this? I insist on paying for the gas," she continued over his objections. They agreed to be ready when Glen came by at one o'clock.

Ann walked out to where Frank was putsying in the back yard and told him of the things that transpired that morning. He indicated he would be able to accompany them on the trip to Afton, which was a relief to Ann. She realized that she had not checked his schedule before she set up the arrangements with Glen. Frank finished up the chores he was involved in and went in to clean up for lunch, and the afternoon's jaunt.

"I really don't need to go today, Ann," remarked Addie when Ann and Frank entered the kitchen.

"Oh no, you don't back out on me now, Lady!" Ann insisted. "Don't you know you're part of the bait for this trip? I know Mr. Adams is looking forward to your company." She laughed to see the stunned look she was getting from Addie, whose cheeks were extremely red now. Much more so than when she had finished her outdoor work earlier.

The ladies prepared lunch while Frank cleaned up. He seldom got dirty when performing any work, a feat that many an on-looker marveled at over the years. Ann appreciated his cleanly manner and was aware that there were a lot of women who'd give anything to have a man such as Frank.

After their lunch, Ann washed up the dishes so they wouldn't be sitting in the sink when they returned. She felt it was so much easier to do them up quickly before the food had a chance to stick to them. Her thrifty nature insisted that it took almost as much water to rinse them off as it did to wash them. Even though the water was not metered at the Rainer place, Ann remembered her childhood training in water use. One just did not use it wastefully. It didn't happen often at home, but the times when the pump did run dry, and the extra work it created for her father to prime the pump to obtain a flow were not forgotten.

Addie changed from her gardening outfit into a dress and was ready by the time Ann finished the dishes. Ann decided to wear the slacks that she had on so it only took her a few moments to freshen up. The three of them were ready when Glen Adams pulled into the back drive at exactly one o'clock.

After loading some old blankets into the truck to wrap the mannequins in, Frank and Ann climbed into the jump seats behind the passenger seat of Glen's pickup. Addie sat in the front seat with Glen, still protesting that it wasn't necessary for her to take up space. The aroma of Old Spice after-shave lotion lingered in the cab of the pickup. It was clear to the Flanders that Glen was looking forward to the afternoon as a social outing rather than a burdensome errand to accomplish for a neighbor.

"I was glad you called me today, Miz Flanders," began Glen. "I was bored with TV, and needed some diversion. Now, Miz Rainer, tell me all about these dummies we're getting from Afton."

Addie was flustered but gamely told Glen about their plans to have the historical society meet at her home and how they wanted to set up the display of the old clothing to enhance the antiques and the farm directory library.

"That sounds just dandy," Glen responded enthusiastically to their idea. "I always planned to join that club but just never got around to doing it. Maybe I could help you set up the display?"

The four chattered on during the drive to Afton as if they were long-time friends. Glen had some suggestions to make about the planned meeting and gladly shared some of his memories of the area with them. Ann was at the ready with her notebook and took down some of Glen's information to add to a draft pamphlet, she was planning to prepare on the area's history. She intended to discuss this with the librarian-historian to determine if such a need existed. She knew acceptance of such an item would be more widespread if it was endorsed by the historical society than if written by an outsider. However, she could ghostwrite it, if necessary or just furnish the data she had obtained to the society and someone there could write it.

All too soon it seemed, they arrived at the department store. Ann located the purchasing department and introduced herself to Meg Parsons, a woman in her early forties. Meg was of average build, evidently single since she wore no wedding or engagement rings. She was eager to hear more of the planned display that Ann told her about as they walked to the storage area.

"Perhaps you'd like to come out and see it when we set it up. We'd certainly love to have you visit. You are playing an important part in making it become a possibility with your offer of the mannequins. If you couldn't make the meeting, come at any time you are able. Just let us know so that we will be there when you do come out."

"Thank you, Ann. May I call you 'Ann'? Please call me Meg. I notice y'all are not from around here. How did you become interested in Peckville history?"

Ann briefly explained how she and Frank wound up staying at Addie's, then added. "I'll go tell them to bring the truck around back here. You'll meet Addie. She came with us. Luckily, Mr. Adams' truck has enough room for us all."

A short time later, Ann directed the truck up to the loading dock that Meg had instructed they should use. Meg was waiting with a cart on which the mannequins were stacked. Frank and Glen wrapped them in the blankets they had brought with them and laid them gently in the bed of the pickup truck. Glen mischievously placed one of the lady mannequins on the seat next to Addie, motioning for Addie to move over to make room for it.

"There's no room for this one back there. She'll have to ride up here. Hope y'all don't mind." Addie was speechless, but slid over to the center of the front seat next to where the driver would sit. In the back, Frank and Ann were cracking up at this new arrangement, but were careful that Addie wouldn't notice their amusement.

With the truck all loaded, they bid goodbye to Meg. Ann promised to keep her posted on the activities of the historical society and Meg assured them she would come to Peckville to see the display, when notified it was in place.

They were headed back to the interstate highway, when Glen noticed a red light flashing in his rear view mirror.

"Frank, must be an accident, somewhere. There's a police officer coming with his lights aflashing. Better yield the road to him." Glen pulled the truck onto the shoulder of the road. "Dang, if he's not after me!" he added incredulously as the patrol car pulled in behind him.

Once the two vehicles were stopped, the officer alit from his car and approached the pickup with his hand on his gun.

"Something wrong, Officer?" asked Glen innocently as he rolled the driver's window down. The police officer scanned the interior of the truck glancing at each occupant in turn. Finally his eyes rested on the third passenger in the front seat. His face flushed.

"Would that lady please put some clothing on? We have an ordinance against riding around naked in a motor vehicle. I'm giving you a warning this time, but next time, if there is a next time, I'll have to give her a ticket."

The four flesh and blood occupants of the pickup truck began to roar with laughter. Actually, Addie sputtered more than laughed.

"Officer, I reckon you'd better look in the back of the truck," said Glen. "I've a whole passel of them naked people back there. They're dummies, real ones."

"Sorry, sir," the officer began. "We had a complaint called in to the department that there was a truck-full of bare-naked people. Had to check it out. I would suggest you drape something over her or we'll just get more complaints."

"We will cover it, sorry to cause so much trouble, Officer," apologized Ann. She threw her sweater to Addie, who quickly wrapped it around the troublesome object.

As they drove away, Glen expressed his regret to Addie that his prank had caused any embarrassment to her. "You shore were good-natured about all this, Addie. Tell you what, I owe y'all supper for my foolishment. After we get these unloaded, let's head back up to the Cracker Barrel. They put on a good spread."

"You've done so much for us already, Mr. Adams," replied Addie. "If it weren't for these dummies, you wouldn't have got pulled over in the first place."

"No, no, I insist! I haven't had such fun in a long time. 'sides I enjoy your company, Addie. You and Ann's too, Frank. I'd be proud if y'all be my guests."

"Looks like another offer we can't refuse," spoke Frank. He lightly nudged Ann's foot, which she rightfully interpreted as an instruction to follow his lead on this matter. Knowing Addie as well as they had come to, they were both aware that she would not accept this initial invitation of Glen's without their accompanying the older couple. "But tell you what, Glen. I will drive on this second outing, give you a well-deserved break." Glen readily accepted Frank's offer.

There were about three miles from Addie's when they heard a siren.

"Oh, no! Now what?" Glen said as he looked into his mirror. "More mounties." Again he pulled the truck over to the shoulder of the road. The patrol car pulled in behind him. Deputy Tom Cates approached the truck.

"Yes, what is it?" Glen asked. "I wasn't speeding." He broke off when he saw that Tom was laughing.

Tom peered around Addie at the dummy.

"I couldn't resist stopping you, Glen. I heard on my police radio 'bout what happened over in Afton. I figured it'd have to be y'all. Missy told me at lunch that you'd got the donation from that store in Afton and when I heard that report, I knew that somehow it'd have something to do with my friends."

"Yep, it's us. The over-the-hill gang," Ann commented dryly.

The rest of the day went much more smoothly. The truck was unloaded with its cargo safely stored in the back barn until they decided exactly what ones would be placed where, and what garments were required to dress them in the proper period they wished to portray. After this was accomplished, Glen drove home. They would pick him up in the car at the appointed time to drive to dinner. Frank decided to nap before it was time to get ready to go. While Ann began making a list of the clothing she felt would be appropriate to clothe the mannequins, Addie went in to rest a while before she dressed for the evening meal.

The drive to the restaurant was enjoyable, as was dinner that evening. It was apparent that Addie was beginning to relax in Glen's company and was now laughing over the prank he had pulled earlier.

"When I saw all the room there was in that truck bed when you unloaded those dummies, I knew I'd been had. Don't you ever pull a stunt like that on me again, Glen Adams!" was her final comment on the subject.

"No Addie, I won't. But you shore were a good sport about it all. Next week, let's run up to Shoney's for supper and maybe a movie. How's that suit you, Addie?"

This time, it was Ann that nudged Frank's foot. They were not invited on that planned outing, nor did they mind. They were happy that Glen and Addie were getting along so well. They liked both of the older people and thought it great they had made friends with one another.

CHAPTER THIRTEEN

A Little Buggy

*T*eddy Bisbo disembarked from the school bus at 3:30 p.m., the same time as every other day. He continued to bask in the admiration of his fellow passengers which was generated by the part he played in the refurbishing of the Rainer home. Teddy was a bit disappointed when that job was finished. He trusted in Frank's promise that if anything else came along requiring an extra hand, he would consider Teddy first. He didn't want to be a pest to Frank but hoped something would come up soon.

It was with immense pleasure that Teddy saw Frank awaiting his arrival from school.

"Hey Teddy! Got a minute?" Frank called.

"Yessir, Mr. Flanders. Be right there!" and he was.

"Teddy, remember the old buggy in the back barn?"

Teddy eagerly nodded 'yes', curious to learn what new project Frank had lined up. As they walked towards the back barn, Frank explained what he wanted to do. When they reached the barn, Frank unlocked the padlocked doors and flung them open. He then proceeded to drive Addie's car out and park it a ways from the doors. He and Teddy then inspected the buggy and discussed what must be done to retrieve it from its storage place in the rafters. Frank had brought ropes with him and these were looped over rafters then knotted in place to secure the buggy. With Teddy holding the ropes as Frank instructed him, Frank climbed up a stepladder and eased boards from the strategic positions they had occupied for many years. Once this was accomplished, he returned the step ladder to its usual place at the rear of the barn stall. Placing himself in a spot near Teddy, he took two of the four ropes from Teddy, leaving him with the other two.

"Okay Teddy. On the count of three. One, two, three!" Gently the two released the tension on the ropes, giving slack to them equally as they slowly eased the buggy to the barn floor. Frank surveyed the antique vehicle and tested the wheels to determine if they would still operate. As was his usual manner, he oiled them while testing, turning them carefully. Once satisfied the buggy wheels would turn smoothly, Frank grasped the buggy poles and pulled it out of the barn and off to the side. Then he drove the Ford back into its storage place. Indicating a galvanized bucket, he asked Teddy to draw a pail of water so he could wash off the dust that had accumulated over the years. While he worked, he and Teddy discussed possible arrangements of mannequins in the buggy.

"How many did you say there were?" asked Teddy.

"We brought six. I'm not sure how many Addie and Ann will give up. I'd sure like to have a stuffed horse to pull our buggy." Frank told Teddy about Glen being pulled over by the law officer and of Tom's reenactment.

Teddy enjoyed being let in on the joke that backfired on Mr. Adams. Then, reluctantly, he decided he should head for home.

"Don't want Momma to worry 'bout me. I was gonna catch the late bus tonight so she won't be looking for me till bout now." He refused the money Frank offered him for his help. "Naw, I couldn't take that, I didn't hardly do nothing. Just consider it as me helping a neighbor." He smiled as he spoke

"Well, thanks, Teddy. I 'preciate your help. I'd be glad to give you a hand any time you need it."

Ann appeared at their side with two glasses of soda. "Here you are, guys. Thought you might need to wet your whistle." Teddy and Frank gratefully accepted the cool drinks.

After the sodas were down, Frank offered to drive Teddy home so his mother would not be anxious. After considering his offer, Teddy turned it down.

"The walk would be nothing on such a fine day. 'Sides I got my bike hid in the weeds a ways down the road."

"How about a rain check then?" suggested Ann. "Frank will give you a ride home on a nasty day."

Teddy laughingly accepted that good offer.

"I believe I will ask Miz Rainer if I can leave my bike here when I catch the bus, 'steada leaving it in the weeds. I'd feel better if I could lean it against her barn."

"Yes, ask her! I'm sure she'll tell you it's okay. I never gave it a thought or we'd made arrangements before this." Frank was truly sorry he didn't think of it himself. He resolved to be more aware of Teddy's needs.

Ann verbalized a question that hit both Frank and her simultaneously. "Teddy, how do you manage carrying the books and riding your bike at the same time?"

"I got one-handed steering down to a science." Teddy responded. "It's sure a whole lot easier since Mr. Flanders fixed my bike. I'd best go ask Miz Rainer bout leaving my bike here." He hurried over to the back door and rapped on it.

Addie appeared at the window and opened the door when she saw Teddy. Teddy asked her the favor he sought.

"Oh my, yes, Teddy! Of course you can leave your bicycle here whilst you're at school. Probably best to leave it between the back barn and big barn. Or right here near the back door." Addie was all smiles. She liked Teddy and frequently commented to Frank and Ann that his mother had done a good job raising him as evidenced by his manners.

That settled, Teddy headed off towards home. The three adults watched as he retrieved his bike from its hiding place quite a ways down the road.

Frank shook his head, "I cain't believe I never thought 'bout how he got back and forth to the bus stop. Now I think of it, when I saw him riding around here fore we got to know him, he didn't have enough time to walk home and ride back from the time he got off the bus. Course I didn't know just how fer down the road he lived. What?" This last was directed at his wife who was grinning at him. Even Addie was looking at him in an amused manner. Frank did not feel he had said anything funny.

"Are you going to tell him, or shall I?" Ann asked Addie.

"Let me!" replied Addie. "Frank, you're starting to sound like you've lived here all your life." The ladies had not missed the definite signs of a soft drawl slipping into Frank's speech, even though he had not noticed it himself.

"Oh, is that all?" said a relieved Frank. "I wondered why you two were cracking up." He pronounced his words quite precisely that time as if to prove them wrong.

"Don't fight it Frank. It's contagious. You were bound to ketch it sooner or later. I've caught Ann in a drawl or two so you can stop laughing at Frank, Ann." Now it was Frank's turn to laugh at Ann. She didn't mind being the focus of their banter. Frank and she had fully expected Ann would be the first to succumb to the influence of the Tennessee manner of speaking. Ann considered herself a verbal sponge, having soaked up all manner of speech in the past as she had explained to the other ladies while visiting Asheville.

"Addie, if you're going to be ready for your date with Glen, you'd better get a move on," reminded Ann, changing the subject.

Addie turned all red and sputtered "Date? We're just going to supper and a movie." But she smiled and headed backed to the house partly to escape the prospect of their continued teasing.

"What would YOU like to do this evening?" Frank queried Ann.

"Why don't you give Tom Cates a call and see if we could use his motorcycle to go for a ride?"

She could tell by his reaction, she had said the right thing. He scooped her up in a big bear hug. No easy feat, except for Frank's great strength. Almost immediately Ann started to yip.

"Oh, Oh, watch out, you'll break my ribs!" What a couple we make, she thought. Frank's so strong and I bruise so easily.

"I'd like to run to Peckville to Dollar General and pick up something. Maybe we'll see Tom in town." They went in to tell Addie they were leaving and so Ann could get her purse. As Frank cleaned up at the kitchen sink, Ann suggested to him that they hold off on their trip to town until Addie was ready to go. Glen would be picking her up soon and Ann felt it would be awkward if Addie wasn't ready when he arrived and had to answer the door in her robe. Frank agreed. As Ann explained, Glen and Addie were getting along so well, no sense in doing anything that would make Addie feel uncomfortable. Not that Glen would let a little thing like that bother him, but Addie was a proper lady and it would upset her.

Sure enough, Glen, in his eager way, was early and Frank went out to greet him and steer him and the conversation to the buggy, giving Addie the few extra minutes she needed to finish her preparations for the evening. After the men chatted outside a while, they headed to the house where Ann offered Glen a cup of coffee.

"Well, thank you, Ann. Don't want to put you out none, though."

"I have it in the thermos," Ann said. "It's plenty hot.. Hope that's okay?"

"Maybe just a half a cup. Don't want to keep Addie awaiting." Then as she poured his coffee into a mug, "That's fine, fine. Thank you."

Ann turned to Frank, asking if he wanted some.

"Yeah, half a cup, too." He sat across from Glen and the two men continued their talk about the buggy. The talk turned to the Rainer property. Glen expected to bring his son around in a day or so to finalize the lease agreement with Addie.

"That's good," said Frank. "Ann and I will feel better about leaving Addie on her own later knowing there will be people around now and again. Tom Cates has been real helpful to her and looks out for her needs."

"Well, you can be assured, I will be looking out for Miz Addie. I can run her to town for her groceries and any appointments she has." He was so firm about it, the Flanders had no doubt but what Glen indeed would be looking out for Miz Addie.

Addie entered the kitchen and Glen immediately jumped up, but she motioned him to sit again.

"Enjoy your coffee, Glen." A tinge of pink on her cheeks may have been a slight touch of rouge, thought Ann, but she wondered if Addie may have overheard Glen's remark about looking after her. It simply could have been a flush of excitement over the thought of the supper 'date'. It was becoming to Addie, no matter what the cause. A glance at Glen told her that he appreciated how nice Addie looked. If Addie was a sassy teenager, she would say the 'date' was 'no big deal', but it obviously was.

Glen finished his coffee and looked at Addie. "You ready?" At her nod of agreement, he continued, "Well, we're off then. Bye Frank, Ann. Be seeing y'all."

As he escorted her outdoors, Addie saw he had not come in his truck, but a blue, four-door sedan.

"I borrowed my son's car. Figured it was more befitting to take a lady out to dine in an automobile."

Addie protested it had been unnecessary, but her pleasure at his thoughtfulness was evident.

Frank and Ann had followed them outside to see them off. After they drove away, waving as they left, Ann heaved a big sigh and turning to Frank, said, "Why do I feel like I've just sent my daughter out on her first date?"

Frank laughed and reassured her. "Glen's a fine person. She'll be in good hands."

"Oh, I know that and they enjoy each other's company. She never once told me she wished we were going too. That's a good sign."

While Ann stood in the drive, Frank went inside and came back out with her purse.

"All set? I checked out everything inside. No burners on, and I promised Addie we'd lock up if we went anywhere."

"No, just give me a second." Ann always needed one more second. Frank was accustomed to it and waited patiently for her while she ran back inside. Meanwhile he started the car and brought it up to the back door. She emerged shortly thereafter and they were on their way.

CHAPTER FOURTEEN

Ann's Motorcycle Ride

*T*he drive to town seemed to take no time at all. New growth was evident all around and the grass was getting greener. Rhododendrons were beginning to blossom as the temperatures had been on the rise. The advent of Spring was on the land.

Once in town, Frank drove directly to the small department store. They had discovered that the prices there were competitive and most household items were carried in their inventory. Once inside, Ann inquired what they were shopping for.

"I want to get a book bag for Teddy. One of those backpack type so his hands are free to steer the bike. The last few times he's given me a hand, he wouldn't take any money so I decided I'd get him the book bag."

"What a great idea! You're a nice person!" He really is, she mused. Always thinking of others. She joined in the search for the item, instinctively heading in the right direction. Frank thought she did it totally by intuition, but Ann would confess that when she first enters a store she is not familiar with, she looks around for any department signs or, in the absence of any such indicators, looks for other clues. A technique that most shoppers use subconsciously but when done quickly might give a person not accustomed to shopping, the appearance that magic is somehow involved.

The backpacks were located and selection process begun. There were the usual wild-colored ones, the fad ones with pictures of the popular cartoon characters. As Frank looked from one to the other, Ann pointed out some plain ones in solid colors.

"If you get one like this, it will always be up-to-date even if a new fad comes in."

"Right," Frank readily agreed. "Teddy's too old for the kiddy ones, anyway." His eyebrows shot up as he inspected the price tag, adding, "That's about half the cost of those wild ones."

"Yes, and the plain ones will probably hold up just as well."

They agreed on a navy backpack and cashed out at the front register. After placing their purchase in their car trunk, they left the car parked where it was and walked down the block to the diner. A patrol car was parked outside. Since it hadn't been there when they drove into town, Tom couldn't have been inside very long.

Tom and Missy called greetings to the pair as they entered.

"Hello, you two," was Ann's response.

"Hi Missy, Tom," Frank returned their greetings, adding "Tom, you're just the man we're looking for."

"Oh? Nothing wrong, I hope?"

"No, No. We're wondering if we could con you into the loan of your Harley for an hour or so. It's been sitting out there and probably needs to have the motor turned over."

"Well, as you say, Frank, that's an offer I can't refuse. Go ahead and use it. Y'all didn't need to ask, you know."

"I wouldn't use it without your say-so," Frank was quick to reply.

"No, guess you wouldn't, but you have my blanket permission to use it anytime."

"Y'all had supper yet?" asked Missy.

"No, but we'll be back later after our ride." As he spoke, Frank arose and motioned to Ann that they were ready to leave. She followed him out the door, knowing nothing would come between Frank and his motorcycle ride. Ann enjoyed riding but was not such a fanatic as Frank. He insisted it was no fun to ride without her. She would say it was because she held the back end down, and Frank would agree.

The trip back to the house went a bit faster than the one to town. Once there, Ann rummaged around in boxes in their closet until she unearthed helmets and leather jackets. She laid these out on the bed just as Frank came in to see what was holding her up.

"Hey, I didn't know you brought those!" He exclaimed.

"I knew they'd come in handy sooner or later. The whole idea of heading south was so you could get in some clutch time. I'm just surprised you weren't tempted before now with Tom's machine just sitting out in the barn."

"Well, I wanted to concentrate on getting the place spruced up before we started to run and play."

They donned the helmets and leathers with Ann also putting on her black leather gloves. She had changed into a black turtleneck sweater and black double-knit slacks with low cut black leather boots.

"All set, Motorcycle Momma? Let's hit the road!"

While Ann had been changing her outfit, Frank had brought Tom's Harley from its storage and quickly wiped it down, checked the oil and chain. Now he climbed on and started it up. After revving the engine briefly, he motioned for her to jump on. She stepped lightly on the passenger peg and swung her other leg up and over, settling into the saddle with the ease of someone accustomed to a motorcycle, as she certainly was after almost forty years of experience. She had driven motorcycles at one time but now preferred to buddy ride and let Frank do the operating.

With little hesitation, they were on their way. Frank headed in the general direction of Afton then took a side road, which led through piney woods alongside a stream that spilled over flat rocks and mossy stones. The crisp, clean smell of the pines hung in the air. A pile of cut logs was stacked next to a dirt lane, awaiting trucks to haul them to the lumberyard. The heavier aroma of the cut pine added a new flavor to the atmosphere around them. They did not feel the need to talk and conversation was not easy to carry on over the noise of the motorcycle. Over the years, Ann had developed her own codes to facilitate her backseat driving or to call Frank's attention to any sight along the way. A squeeze of her knees to indicate caution, a tap on his shoulder or helmet if she wanted to point out anything to him, a slap on the helmet if he was acting up or showing off or even just going too fast to suit her. It wasn't often she found it necessary to use these tactics as she had tremendous confidence in his abilities. He, in turn, admired her courage and appreciated the trust she placed in him.

Even though it had been months since Ann had ridden, she quickly settled into the saddle and rode the curves, leaning with Frank, fitting her body to his as the cycle hugged the road. From their first ride together, she had heeded his instructions and fought the desire to lean away from the curve that is an instinctive reaction of a novice. You have to learn to resist the urge to do that and lean over into the curves. It seems to defy the laws of gravity.

Circling back towards Peckville, they came into town and wheeled up to the Diner. Once the bike was stopped, Ann placed her hands on Frank's shoulders and tapped his arm. At this signal, he stood up and Ann rose with him. Standing up for a moment, she finally swung her leg up and over the chrome back-rest, and set it on the ground. She stepped away from the bike, moving very stiffly. Frank swung off and walked the bike backwards into its parking place. They placed their helmets on the saddle and hung their jackets over the back-rest. Ann rolled her gloves up and placed them inside her helmet. Walking a bit easier now, they entered the Diner for their evening meal.

Missy was all smiles as she greeted them and asked if they enjoyed their ride. Both answered with enthusiastic affirmatives, aware that their entrance had attracted the attention of the other customers.

Frank's pure white hair had not gone unnoticed by several diners, also white-haired.

"It was great," Frank grinned. "Sure felt good to feel the wind whizzing past your ears! Tom's bike's running tip-top, too!"

"Yes," Ann echoed. "It was really terrific of Tom to allow us the use of his machine. We rode through the Pine Woods off Rt. 3 towards Afton. The aroma of those woods was just wonderful!" she gushed.

They seated themselves in a booth and gradually settled down, ordering coffee and the mini-meatloaf special. Their portions were generous and both knew they would not be able to do justice to the full size meal.

"There's no easy way to carry a go box on those things, is there?" asked Missy.

"And that's the truth!" Ann agreed.

By the time they finished their meal, Frank and Ann were the only customers left. Missy had finished her cleanup chores so poured herself a cup of coffee and joined them in the booth, after refreshing their cups.

They had chatted back and forth when Missy mentioned she had heard of their trip from Afton with Glen and the mannequins.

"I wish I'd been there with a camera to see that. Poor Miz Addie. Speaking of dummies, what did you find out at the library? Wasn't it today you and Addie was going there?"

"Library! Good gosh! We never went there! Yes, it was today. In all the excitement of Addie's date, we forgot to go. Well, hopefully we'll get there tomorrow."

"You're sure cutting it close, if they say yes. Y'all need help getting the display ready on time for the meeting." Missy said timidly. "I could give you a hand day after tomorrow, if you like."

"You're on, Missy! We welcome your offer." Ann readily responded.

"Are you ready to head home, Ann?" Frank cut in.

"Yes, guess we better. Addie's probably worried sick. I should have left her a note to explain why the car was there and we weren't." fussed Ann.

They hurriedly paid their bill and left. They arrived at the Rainer place to find it dark. Frank went off to bed as soon as they arrived home and he had put the bike away. Ann stayed up for a while watching TV. She could not retire so soon after eating but it was never a problem for Frank. He had an excellent physical constitution and seldom suffered from insomnia or other minor discomforts. Just prior to his retirement, he had been subject to headaches, but once the stress of the rat race was gone, the headaches disappeared as well.

Ann watched the late news and headed to bed, leaving a small light on over the kitchen sink as well as the outside light. I WILL NOT sit up like a doting mother!" she insisted to herself.

She did not fall asleep until after she heard a car pull in the drive and recognized the sound as being Glen's son's.

CHAPTER FIFTEEN

Running Errands

*T*he aroma of coffee brewing awoke Addie. She couldn't believe that she had slept so late. She never set an alarm clock to waken her for she always awoke naturally every day at the same time. Since Frank and Ann had been staying with her, the routine had evolved that Addie made breakfast and the smell of coffee usually greeted the day for them. That the shoe was on the other foot made Addie feel a bit uncomfortable. She had slept quite well. She now decided she might just as well enjoy a few extra moments of rest since obviously Ann, or maybe even Frank, had things under control in the breakfast department. It was pleasant just to lie there and rethink the previous evening's activities.

Glen Adams was good company and a courteous escort. They had a leisurely dinner and lingered so long over coffee and dessert that they forgot to watch the time so missed the deadline for the movie's start. Addie really didn't mind and neither did Glen. It seemed unimportant next to their conversation. After a few tentative awkward moments, their talk came easily and they found it fun getting to know one another better. The Adams, like the Rainers, had enjoyed a long lasting marriage. Glen admired Addie for her independent manner. While the Rainers had not been blessed with children, Glen and his wife had raised four. Glen spoke of his two sons and two daughters with pride. They had presented him with seven grandchildren, of whom he was equally proud.

"Do you have any pictures of your grandbabies?" Addie inquired.

"You bet! Don't think you're getting off that easy!" laughed Glen as he proceeded to pull a miniature album from an inside pocket of his suit jacket. "Now, I don't always carry this with me but I wanted to show them off to you."

"You have a lovely family there, Glen," Addie said when she was done looking through the plastic-encased pictures. "There's one boy that seems to favor you quite a bit."

"You must mean Sonny Joe. Really, his name is Glen III. I think he does look like me when I was a tad."

"I don't have any pictures to show you. Bert and I never had any children. My sister, Bessie, has a son. Except for a spell when Bessie was sickly, I didn't hardly ever see him when he was a young'un, nor now either."

The talk eventually turned to the Flanders and Addie was matter-of-fact when she told of the arrangement they had.

"I feel so much better since they've come. I wasn't sickly, but just afraid to do anything. I was always scared I'd fall. Just knowing somebody's there to help if I do have a problem, has given me all sorts of confidence. I surprise myself at all the things I find myself doing nowadays."

"That's good, Addie. They seem like fine folk to me."

"They are, I'm fortunate to have them with me. I'll be sorry to see them leave to go back north."

"I reckon so, but I'll be around, Addie. You can count on my help," Glen reassured her.

"That's a comfort, Glen, but I hate to be burdensome."

"Friends aren't a burden, Addie."

They had talked about everything under the sun, and were amazed to see how fast the time had flown. They had even sat awhile in the car visiting when they returned to Addie's house.

Addie roused herself from her thoughts and arose to get ready for the day. When she entered the kitchen, Ann was setting the breakfast table while Frank was at the stove.

"Was you gonna let me sleep the day away?" Addie chided.

"Oh it doesn't hurt us to get breakfast for a change. You've spoiled us rotten, Addie," was Ann's explanation.

"How was the movie, Addie?" Frank asked innocently.

Seeing Addie's flustered reaction to his question, Ann broke in. "Guess there was a change in plans, Frank."

Addie stammered, "Well…, Well…, service was slow and we didn't make the show."

"As long as you enjoyed yourself, that's all that matters," Ann said. Addie was relieved that the questions ceased and they settled down to eat. Frank served up pancakes but confessed Ann had mixed them up, he just manned the griddle.

They discussed the plans for the day with Ann suggesting they get to the library in the morning.

"Why, that's right! We were supposed to go there yesterday. I plumb forgot all about that!" Addie moaned.

"Don't feel bad, Addie, so did I. I don't think one day delay will cause any problems."

After breakfast, Addie insisted on doing the dishes as penance for oversleeping.

"Now, Addie, there's no rule says Addie makes breakfast; if Addie oversleeps, Addie does dishes," teased Ann.

"Maybe there should be such a rule," Addie quipped. "Can't change my routine now." Addie took her time doing up the dishes unlike her usual manner. She was remembering her pleasant evening out, knowing there would be other such outings, since it was obvious Glen had enjoyed himself as much as she.

Ann intuitively knew what Addie was thinking about and ceased her chatter, finding chores to do in other parts of the house. She dusted the living room, then began to collect laundry items from the bath and the bedroom she and Frank shared. Addie used the hamper in the hall for her laundry. There were no facilities at the Rainer house to wash clothes. Addie's wringer type washing machine had broken down over the years and she had felt no need to replace it. Any laundry she didn't do by hand, she sent out to the cleaners. She and Ann hand-washed their lingerie, but the linens and heavier items they took to the laundry-mat at Peckville. Ann's plan was to take the laundry with them on their trip to town for the visit to the library.

Addie's reverie continued until the last dish was done. Ann considered asking her if she had a delayed case of puppy love, but wisely decided not to.

Frank came in from his outdoor work and tracked Ann down. They had a brief discussion regarding the store dummies. Ann asked Frank to come upstairs where she indicated a stack of clothing and rummaged through a box in the closet until she located the desired articles.

When they returned to the first floor, Ann carried the items they had brought downstairs and Frank picked up the laundry bag. They carried them outside where Ann opened the car trunk for Frank to place the laundry inside, then she handed him the stack of things she was carrying.

Addie declared she was ready to go to Peckville whenever Ann was. The ladies left soon after. On the way to town, Ann was careful not to interrupt Addie's thoughts except to occasionally point out an item of interest. A flock of geese one time and flowering rhododendrons another time.

Number one stop was the laundromat to pop their laundry in the washers. Ann commented to Addie as they got back into the car, that it was not very common to dare leave one's wash in a public laundry and expect to find it still there on your return. She felt assured about doing it in Peckville. Addie agreed that it probably was unusual.

The next stop was at the library. The librarian, Lil Perkins, greeted them warmly. Addie, after initial introductions, asked Ann to explain their mission.

"Mrs. Rainer owns the Gothic home on Route 3 towards Afton. Perhaps you're familiar with it?" Ann asked.

"Yes, I've seen it. It's recently been refurbished?"

"That's the one. Addie here has quite a library of old farm directories for the county as well as some period clothing. She feels that these are items that would be of great interest to the Historical Society. Right now, she's entertaining several possibilities to develop methods for additional income. Before she proceeds along these lines, she wanted to determine what interest, if any, the society might have."

Addie then spoke up, "That's right. To that end, I would like to invite the Historical Society to meet at my home for their next meeting. I don't know if that's possible so close to your meeting date."

Miss Perkins' eyes brightened throughout Ann's dissertation. At Addie's invitation, she was visibly excited.

"What great timing!" she said enthusiastically. "We're running out of ideas to spark interest in our members. This is just what we need to regenerate our club. Let me call around and let them know where we'll meet. I'll call three or four and they'll each call three or four."

"Wonderful! Mention that we'll be open to any suggestions so Addie can consider them."

Addie nodded in agreement with Ann's statement.

"So we can expect y'all to meet out there next week?" asked Addie.

"Thursday evening at seven. We have a week before our meeting; that's plenty of time. I'll place a notice in the weekly. I was going to insert a reminder anyway and I'll put out a sheet on the library door. I'll make it on the computer when I get a chance."

"Could you Xerox a copy? I'm sure Missy will put one up at the diner," suggested Ann.

"Good idea, I'll make several extra and put one in the Post Office as well." The librarian's enthusiasm had not waned.

"I've had some computer experience," Ann offered. "If you want, I could help you make up the poster. What type computer? Apple? IBM? Dell?"

"It's an Apple. That would be just wonderful, if you don't mind."

Turning to Addie, Ann said, "This won't take long." The remark caused the librarian to look closely at Ann.

"Computer's over here." She led the way to the Apple. It had a 3.5" disk drive which Ann preferred to work with. Lil Perkins gave her the flyer from the previous meeting. Ann seated herself at the computer keyboard and turned the equipment on. She then proceeded to bring up the index for the historical society disk the librarian had handed her from a box of disks. She located the file for the last meeting's notice and copied it, renaming it to the current date. She then entered the file and updated the data that had changed from the previous notice, i.e., date and location of meeting. These items were quickly changed by highlighting the obsolete data and typing the new. The rest of the flyer, including the border trim, remained unchanged. Once the changes were made, Ann saved the file and executed the print command. Seconds later, the library's laser printer had spit out the new announcement. The librarian was at the circulation counter with a library patron, so Ann took the new flyer over to the Xerox copier and ran off six copies. All of this was accomplished in less than ten minutes.

"I don't believe I saw what I just did," exclaimed Addie. "I thought the electric typewriter was a wonderful invention, but this beats all!"

The librarian turned around and asked, "Are you ready to print it yet?"

Addie laughed as Ann handed over the original and copies of the flyer. "My gal's way ahead of you, Miz Perkins!"

"Well, I guess you're right, Miz Rainer." Lil said, then turning to Ann, she commented, "You sure do have experience on that machine. Would you be interested in some part-time work here? It don't pay a heap of money, I'm afraid."

"I might," replied Ann, "If I can work it into my busy schedule."

"We'll talk about it next week, if it's okay?"

"All right by me." Ann picked up two copies of the notice and motioning to Addie, said, "Let's hit the road, gal. We'll drop one off at the diner and one at the little gas station out on Rt. 3 and we'll see you next week."

"If you don't mind, Miz Rainer, I'd like to come out a tad early." Lil requested.

"That's fine. If you want to stop in one evening afore Thursday, feel free to do so. I'm usually there. And I wanted to ask you what type refreshments I should serve."

"Oh, we have a refreshment committee who takes care of that. All you need do is furnish the meeting place."

"Done!" answered Ann for Addie and they left to retrace their steps to the laundromat, where Ann planned to transfer their wash to the dryers.

Addie and Ann gasped simultaneously when they got there and went to the washers that had contained their laundry. They opened up washers on either side but there was no sign of their items anywhere.

On a slim chance, Ann walked over to the dryers. There, side by side, were both loads, whites and colors, completely dry. There were no other people in the place, no clue as to who the kind person was who had unloaded the washers and not only put the wet wash in the dryers, but paid the 50 cents for both dryers so the clothes would be dry when the ladies returned. Attached to one of the dryers was a yellow Post-it note that read: "PASS IT ON! HAVE A NICE DAY!"

"Now, that's my kind of people," murmured Ann.

"Mine, too," agreed Addie, then "Ann, how 'bout here? Let's put one of those notices up here on that board."

"Great idea, Addie! Let's!" Ann retrieved one from the car and tacked it up. She removed an old out-dated flyer and used the tack which had held that one.

Stowing the clean laundry in the car, they drove to the Post Office. For 25 cents, Ann used the public copy machine and made another copy. She knew she could have done it at the library for 15 cents or probably even free, but that would have taken extra time. She considered making two copies and leaving one at the Post Office but since the librarian had said she would do so, Ann didn't want to act like she was overstepping her bounds.

The ladies next stopped at the diner where Missy gladly placed the flyer on their bulletin board.

"Missy, did you still want to come out and help us dress dummies?" Ann asked.

"Well, sure Ann, I'll help you dress dummies anytime. What's a dress dummy though and why are you calling yourself names?" quipped Missy.

Coming right back at her, Ann responded, "A dress is something ladies wear, dummy."

Addie looked from one to the other. "You both are beginning to sound addled. I'm sure glad business is slow here today. I think we're all working too hard."

All three burst out laughing at their own foolishness.

"It does seem good to slow down a minute. Missy, I'd like a cup of hot tea. Addie, what would you like?"

"I believe I'll have tea as well, Missy."

Missy prepared their beverages and served them.

"I'll be through here at two. I had the early shift today. I can come by later if you like."

"We appreciate your help, Missy. Plan to take supper with us," invited Addie.

The entrance of several customers had Missy busy so Addie and Ann finished their tea, paid their check and called goodbye to Missy.

"Goodbye, see y'all later," she promised.

Once in the car, Ann asked Addie if there was anything they needed to get before they headed home, suggesting, "How 'bout getting some baked goods for an easy dessert for tonight?"

"That's a good idea, Ann. Better get some milk as well."

A quick stop was made at the bakery for Danish and a cheesecake. As they were selecting their purchases, Addie noticed they had added a cooler since the last time she had been in the bakery. She retrieved a half-gallon of 2 percent milk and added it to the items being rung up. Ann had money out but Addie objected. By now, Ann knew it would be futile to offer any resistance.

Once in the car, Addie told Ann, "I know that it cost more there than at the market for milk, but it is a convenience. I figured our time was worth the change."

"Now you're beginning to sound like Frank," was Ann's comment.

"Well, I know you're all for saving a penny here and a penny there, but you've common sense too."

"I try, Addie. I try."

Before returning home, they shot over to the gas station down Rt. 3 and inquired about placing the meeting notice there. The owner graciously accepted it and posted it in the front window. He seemed honored to be selected to display it.

They got home just about time to make lunch. Addie warmed a can of soup while Ann made tuna sandwiches. There was hot coffee in the thermos from breakfast. When all was ready, Addie called out the door for Frank to 'come and get it!'

At lunch, the women took turns telling Frank about their visit to town with Ann doing most of the talking as usual. They told of their benefactor at the laundromat.

"And Frank, you should have seen Ann dazzle that librarian when she got to work that computer. You showed her things I don't think she knew 'bout her own equipment." Addie exaggerated while Frank nodded in agreement.

"She always amazes me when I see her fingers fly at one of those," he told Addie.

"Well, she impressed Miz Perkins so, she offered her a job."

Frank glanced at Ann.

"Don't worry, only part-time," she reassured him. "I haven't given her a yes or no answer yet. I mentioned my busy schedule. I wouldn't take it if it was too time-consuming. It's probably to do monthly or quarterly reports."

When the ladies cleared the table of the lunch dishes, Frank asked them to come outside a minute. They dutifully followed him out. Walking around to the front of the house, they soon learned what he'd been up to while they were in town.

In the front drive, where last week the old Ford had stood, there was now the buggy, all cleaned up with a new coat of black paint. At the reins of an invisible horse, sat the male mannequin, dressed in old Levi's™, with a Mackinaw jacket and a trooper hat, with ear flappers down, sitting on his head. Standing up in the back of the buggy, leaning towards the seat, were the boy and girl mannequins, also dressed in clothing of a similar time frame. It looked like a scene from a Currier and Ives print.

Frank began to sing out, "If I only had a horse," to the tune of the song 'If I only had a brain', the scarecrow sang in the movie 'Wizard of Oz'."

"Maybe, but you wouldn't trade your brain for it," Ann commented dryly.

Addie declared, "I feel like I've stepped way back in time, now."

"We keep jerking you back and forth between centuries, don't we, Addie. I bet you wish we'd make up our minds."

"I sometimes do feel like I've climbed onto a magic carpet," admitted Addie.

"Welcome aboard!" invited Ann. "Watch out for the air turbulence!"

CHAPTER SIXTEEN

Hundred Acres

*A*ddie went to her room to rest awhile. Ann had suggested she might like a brief nap before Missy came since they would be busy for the rest of the day. No mention was made of the late hour Addie had turned in the night before, but Ann was not surprised when Addie readily accepted her suggestion.

Before Addie went in to rest, the ladies talked about what they should serve for the evening meal. They didn't want anything that took too long to prepare, but since it was Missy's first visit, they wanted to have something she might really enjoy.

"We really have to rack our brains, since they serve quite a variety of food at the diner. Now what would be a treat for her?" Ann pondered.

"I can't think of what would do. I haven't cooked fancy in such a long time."

Frank overheard their conversation and ventured a suggestion on the subject. "How about your shrimp stew, Ann?"

"Shrimp stew? What's that consist of?" asked Addie.

"Everything but the kitchen sink. Bacon, shrimp, clams, potatoes, corn, cream cheese, milk, oh, and onions. It's really easy to throw together and everyone I've served it to seems to like it."

"It's like a chowder, then," stated Addie, "but cheesy tasting?"

"Sorta, it's very filling but surprisingly, you won't notice the cheese flavor. I can run into town while you're resting and get the ingredients."

"Will you be going, Frank?" Addie inquired hesitantly.

Usually Frank would have gone as well, but he could tell by Addie's tone that she would feel more secure knowing he was there while she rested. With a knowing look from Ann, he reassured Addie.

"No, I'll be here. I'm in the midst of something and I hate to leave a job undone."

Addie accepted this explanation as it was very like Frank. Confident that all was under control, she went to take her nap.

Ann quickly made a list to be sure she didn't overlook anything while at the store. She added oyster crackers to the list. She felt as though she should include something else on the menu but was at a loss as to what would be complimentary.

With her list complete, she kissed Frank goodbye and made the run into town. Parking her car in the grocery store lot, she headed towards the market, just as Tom Cates in his Sheriff's cruiser pulled in the lot. He rolled down the window of the patrol car and called to Ann.

"Hello, Ann."

"Hi, Tom, what's up?"

"I'm here to escort the manager to the bank. Been meaning to stop out to see y'all. How was your ride last night?"

"Just wonderful, Tom. We enjoyed it so much. Thank you again for your generosity in allowing us the use of your Harley."

"It was nothin', Ann. I owed Frank the pleasure since he took the bother of tuning it up for me. My schedule's been so hectic, I haven't been able to find any time to ride it myself."

"Missy's coming out this afternoon to help us with the display. She's staying for supper. It's real casual, but we'd all be pleased if you joined us."

"You mean Missy's actually taking an afternoon off? She usually works a double shift more often than not. Rosie's kid's been sick so her hours ain't been regular. I'd like to take you up on your offer, what time's supper?"

"Probably about six. Come earlier if you like. We can always find something to keep you out of mischief."

The arrival of the store manager on the scene closed their conversation.

"Sorry to keep you waiting, Tom," he apologized.

"No problem, sir. I was a tad early, anyway. See you, Ann."

"Yeah. Later, Tom." Ann said as she turned to enter the store.

With the prospect of another visitor for the evening meal, Ann decided to triple, rather than double her recipe. She was glad she'd run into Tom before she did her shopping instead of after. She could just see herself making a third trip to town that day.

On her return to the house, she began making the stew. She knew from experience, it tasted even better warmed up the second time. Having it all prepared ahead of time would be a great time saver.

She browned the onions along with the diced bacon. While these cooked, she peeled and cubed the potatoes. As they were parboiling, she added the cut-up cream cheese to the bacon and onions when those pieces were translucent. Now she added the potatoes (including the water she cooked them in) to the bacon, onion and cream cheese mixture.

"This is a nice gooey mess, ready for the next step," she muttered aloud to herself. She opened the cans of shrimp and minced clam pieces adding juice and all to the pot cooking on the stove. Last of all, she added the can of corn and some of the milk. She let all of this simmer on a low heat, turning her attention to the breakfast and lunch dishes. When she had washed the dishes, she turned off the heat under the pot of stew. About ten minutes later, she placed the stew in the refrigerator.

"There, that's all set. All I need to do now is add some butter and more milk when I heat it up." She didn't hear Addie come into the kitchen behind her.

"You talking to yourself, Ann?" Addie waited until Ann had safely placed the pot on the shelf of the refrigerator before she spoke.

"Addie! I didn't see you there!"

"I thought not. I didn't want to scare you, so I didn't speak up. I figured one of us would be wearing your soup. It smells good, Ann. Can't wait to try it. Looks like you made enough to feed an army."

"Would you like a taste? It's still plenty warm," Ann offered.

"Thought you'd never ask," chided Addie.

Ann retrieved the pot from the 'fridge. She got three cups down and ladled the stew into them. Going to the door, she called out to Frank.

"Frank! Addie and I are testing the stew. Do you want some?" she turned to Addie, "I really wanted to try some myself. I did make a lot. I saw Tom in town and asked him to join us for supper. That's okay?" She had known it would be or she wouldn't have invited Tom in the first place. "You'll want a dab of butter in that and more milk, probably. I'll add them when I reheat it later."

Addie did as Ann said. Frank came in to wash up at the kitchen sink. Ann placed a plate of bread and bowl of saltine crackers on the table and served glasses of water all around.

"Do you want anything else to drink, Addie? Frank?" Addie shook her head 'no' while Frank asked for coffee. There was enough in the thermos from breakfast to serve him while Ann followed Addie's lead and had the water.

Addie tasted the shrimp stew and declared it delicious.

"Can you imagine serving guests leftovers?" laughed Ann, since in essence, that was what they would be doing. "Actually, it's even better warmed up, isn't it, Frank?" He nodded in agreement.

"I'll take your word for it," was Addie's response. "You haven't steered me wrong yet."

After their taste-test snack, Addie insisted it was her turn to do up the dishes. Ann hadn't drained the hot water from the dishes she had done earlier, and in a very short time, Addie was done.

"Frank, you look like it's time for you to take a nap." Ann didn't have to twist his arm. He said he would lie down for 15-20 minutes.

Addie and Ann sat at the kitchen table mulling over the lists Ann had made while they had looked over the items of clothing Addie had stored upstairs. They decided to go ahead with the idea of furnishing the upstairs rooms as they had discussed at that earlier time.

The sound of a car heralded Missy's arrival and the two women went out to greet her.

"Missy, I hardly recognize you out of uniform and without your hair in its net," said Ann.

"Well, this is my leisure uniform, jeans and a tee," Missy replied. "Ya'll ready to get to work?"

"That's right, you think you only have to dress mannequins." The sparkle in Missy's eye told Ann that she caught the careful way Ann had avoided saying 'dressing dummies', not wanting a repeat of the play on words they had started earlier that day. But Missy wouldn't let her off that easy.

"No, I reckoned we'd dress, dummies." The punctuation was Missy's.

"We have a whole lot more for you to do, now we've got you captive, Missy," Addie broke in. "Before we start, have you eaten yet?"

"I grabbed a bite at the diner so I'm all set."

They started to lead Missy into the kitchen when Addie suggested Ann show her the buggy Frank had set up. Addie went into the house while the other women went around front where the buggy sat under the trees.

Missy exclaimed over the grouping Frank had arranged. "What good condition the buggy's in. I remember when Tom suggested it. Has he seen it yet?"

"No, but he will later. He's coming out for supper. Missy, are you blushing?" Missy denied it but there was a rosy tinge to her cheeks that wasn't there moments before.

"Ann, are y'all matchmaking again? You were successful getting Glen Adams and Miz Addie together."

"Me? Matchmaking? No, Ma'am! Besides I doubt very much a pretty lady like you needs help in that department."

The last remark apparently pacified Missy as she turned the conversation back to the display.

"Those clothes are perfect on the dummies! I can't believe they gave them to you for nothing. Why couldn't mean old Ned Foster have done that?"

They heard a call from the house and turned to see Addie at the front door beckoning them to enter that way.

"It's far more impressive to come in this way, Missy. Since you're our guest, we'll give you a proper welcome."

"But once we get you inside, we put you to work. Come into our parlor, said the spider to the fly." Ann threatened.

Missy hesitated, pretending fear of the unknown, but Ann playfully nudged her as if to shove her into the house. As Missy entered, the feigned play stopped so she could appreciate the full impact of the stately foyer and rooms beyond.

"Oh, my! Oh, my! It's lovely, Addie. Thank you for showing me."

"You're welcome to my house anytime, Missy," invited Addie.

"I appreciate your invitation, Miz Addie."

They continued the tour of the large room as Addie referred to the living room, then to the library alcove. From there they entered the kitchen, then returned to the foyer and ascended to the upper level where they looked through the four bedrooms there.

"I mentioned to Addie, she has the makings of a bed and breakfast here," ventured Ann.

"I agree. If you do open one, I can steer tourists here if you like," Missy offered.

"I'm considering it, Missy. If I could be assured they'd be like Ann and Frank, I'd do it in a minute."

Returning to the east front bedroom, they looked through the piles of clothing previously sorted, discussing what they would use. Since they had three ladies, they decided to clothe one in nightclothes and place her on a chaise lounge in that room. In another room that contained a dressing table as well as bedroom furniture, a fully dressed lady would be seated there. A third figure, also fully clothed, could be placed in an alcove seat near the bookshelves upstairs or they might put the remaining lady downstairs, somewhere near the foyer. There had been three stands that accompanied the mannequins. Frank had used two for the children in the back of the buggy. He had said he would relinquish them if the ladies required their use. They really needed just the one for the figure downstairs, according to their decided arrangement.

While Addie and Missy made the final decisions on the clothing, Ann began bringing items from the hidden attic. She heard Frank call up the stairs that he was up so he was pressed into service to bring the mannequins from their storage. When he had done that, he helped Ann finish bringing the antique articles from the attic. Ann directed Frank in putting the items in their designated room and he helped place them around. Each room had their own basin and water pitcher set and even a 'thunder jug' strategically placed under each bed. Hand-crocheted bedspreads and down quilts were arranged to their best advantage. The front bedroom was the forum of attention as it contained a featherbed.

No attempt had been made to conceal the attic from Missy but she was so engrossed in her assigned task, she didn't even notice where Ann was obtaining the treasures.

"Do you need me anymore?" asked Frank. "I thought I heard a car pull up so I'm going down to check it out."

"No, you're done. Thanks for your help, Honey." Ann replied.

Missy nudged Addie when she heard the term of endearment Ann had used.

"You hear all this sweet talking going on out there?"

Addie just smiled and handed Missy the next item of clothing.

"What did they call this pretty thing?" Missy inquired of Addie.

"My mother use to call it a chemise. I figured as longs I had them, we might just as well dress them decent."

Ann came in to see how they were doing. "Looking good, ladies," she commented.

The figures were finally clad in their finery with the first one settled in the front bedroom on the chaise. Ann and Missy then each took one of the remaining 'ladies' and all three headed towards the hall. At the door, they turned to admire their combined handiwork. Satisfied that it was to their liking, they proceeded to the west front bedroom. This room contained the dressing table and the next figure was seated there.

"You've done well arranging my old things, Ann," praised Addie. "They look real nice there."

Missy enthusiastically agreed. The trio continued on to the back west bedroom, admired the arrangement but went ahead with the plan to post the figure near the entrance downstairs. This decided, they peered into the back east bedroom. Ann pulled Missy back and they let Addie enter first. As they followed behind her, they heard her gasp.

"Ann! How wonderful! What a surprise! How could you have known?" She stepped aside, Missy following closely behind her. Ann

125

and Frank had set this room up as a combination nursery/playroom. In one corner there was a crib all made up with an embroidered quilt. A teddy bear sat in one corner of the crib. The other corner of the room had a small iron cot covered with a quilt made up of multi-colored squares in a colorful array that would be especially pleasing to a child. Along the side of one wall was situated a toy chest. The lid was ajar and various dolls and stuffed animals peeked from inside the chest. The lid, when closed, formed a seat with a padded cushion tacked or glued in place for the comfort of one who chose to sit thereon. There was a built-in seat along the full length of the window wall. There were cabinet doors that opened into the room, allowing access to the space beneath the seat.

"It didn't take much imagination to tell us this was a child's room after I found the toys in the cupboards. Frank and I brought the toy chest and crib in from the …, their storage."

"Sister Bessie was taken sick when Edward was little. We fixed this room up for Edward who stayed with us until Bessie was well again. He spent about three months here. I believe it was originally a child's room. We kept the toys in here thinking we might be blessed with a child ourselves someday."

"Is..is it all right to set it up this way, Addie? I don't want to cause you to have any unhappy memories?" Ann stammered.

"It's okay, Ann. It wasn't meant to be." Addie stated matter-of-factly.

"Looks real nice, Ann," said Missy. "It all does."

"Thanks, Missy."

They went back to the first bedroom where Ann handed Missy the stand and went to pick up the last figure that had been placed on the bed after they had attired her. Missy protested and exchanged loads with Ann.

"I'll carry the dummy down the stairs, Ann. Are you sure you can manage going down the stairs with the stand okay?" She asked solicitously.

"Yes, thanks, Missy. Guess it would have been foolish for me to attempt it with our lady friend here."

Missy carried the figure down to the first floor. Then she returned to the stairs where Ann and Addie were slowly making their descent. Missy took the stand from Ann and retreated in front of them but not too far ahead so she could be of assistance if necessary.

"You're a tough bird, Ann. To see you climb on that motorcycle you wouldn't know your legs bother you. My Daddy had arthritis real bad. Is that what you got?" Missy inquired with concern in her voice.

"You've got a keen eye for the obvious, Missy. But you didn't see me get off that bike, did you?"

"No, I guess I didn't. How did you manage it?"

"I put a choke hold on Frank and he stands up, taking me on up with him. Then I swing off," Ann explained.

"Motorcycle. What's that about a motorcycle?" asked Addie.

"It's Tom's, Addie. He was kind enough to let Frank and I use it last night. Guess we forgot to mention it."

"Probably afraid I'd ground you two," fumed Addie. "You're both too old to spank."

Ann and Missy looked at each other and laughed at the thought of Addie taking the two Flanders to her knee and spanking them.

"Yes, Ma'am," Ann said submissively, feigning seriousness for the moment.

"Let's set this gal up here in the hall," suggested Missy.

"You're full of great ideas, Missy. Glad we recruited you for these endeavors."

"Yes, she looks like the lady of the house greeting her guests," commented Addie. "I think we done well."

The ladies became aware of voices outside.

"Who's out there with Frank?" asked Addie.

"Too early for Tom." replied Missy.

"I forgot Frank said he heard a car quite a while ago and came down to check. Well there's only one way to see who it is." Ann opened the door and went out. Seeing who the visitor was, she called out. "Hello, Glen. What are you up to?" She expected the others to follow her. Missy did, but Addie was scurrying back into the house.

"Oh My. Can't let company see me like this," she muttered.

"You look fine, Addie," Ann spoke in a loud stage whisper, but Addie paid no heed. The younger women left her to her own devices and continued out to where the men were.

"Hello, Mister Adams, remember me? Missy, from the diner?"

"Well, yes Ma'am, Missy. Took a minute though, since you don't have your waitress dress on."

"Come and see what Glen's contributed to the cause." Frank said eagerly.

He led the others partway towards the buggy display. When he stopped, they stopped. He pointed towards the buggy. There under the trees, they could make out the outline of a dark horse standing in front of the buggy.

"Oh, a horse! How long can we keep him?" Ann questioned.

"He's yours, take a closer look." Glen stepped aside so Ann and Missy had a better view. They moved nearer.

"Glen! That is great! I've seen something like this before in the shape of bears, dogs and even people, but never a horse. Frank, remember the outline of Don leaning against a tree back home? This must have been quite a lot of work for you, Glen."

"Twarn't nothing, Ann. I do some woodworking now and again. I had a pattern for reindeer I made at Christmastime. I just altered it and there's your horse. Frank painted it black. Made it look real. Now, where's Addie?"

"She's primping," volunteered Missy. "But don't say I told you so." As if on cue, Addie emerged from the house.

"Glen, this is a pleasant surprise. What brings you this way?" Addie looked past the group to see what had drawn their attention. "What's that? A horse? Where did it come from? Did you bring it, Glen?"

Glen took her arm and led her a bit closer until she realized it was a plywood cutout figure.

"Why that's perfect! Looks good there," she exclaimed.

"Doesn't it, Addie? It adds just the right touch to complete the picture," said Ann, appreciatively.

"Glen, I'd say you've earned your supper. We have plenty. Will you stay and join us?" queried Addie.

Frank broke in, "Now, there's an offer you can't refuse, Glen."

"I reckon I couldn't even if I wanted to, Frank. I graciously accept, Addie."

Ann excused herself from the group and entered the house to begin reheating her stew. Addie suggested Missy and Frank give Glen the tour of the house and she went along after Ann. Once in the kitchen, Addie bustled about getting pans and baking ingredients out.

"I thought I'd make us some cornbread to go with your stew, Ann."

"That's just what we need! I was racking my brain because it seemed like something was missing," Ann told her.

"It won't take long. Nothin' like hot cornbread." Addie spoke confidently.

Soon delicious aromas filled the kitchen. Amid their clatter in the kitchen, no one heard Tom Cates drive up. A tap on the back door announced his arrival and Addie sent him to join Missy's guided tour. Together Addie and Ann set the dining room table. Addie used her best china and silverware.

"Looks real fancy, Addie. Wait till they find out there's only one course," Ann said with mock enthusiasm.

"Two. Don't forget we have dessert as well. 'sides, you keep telling me to use my things. Well, I'm using 'em," she added.

"Touché." Ann quipped just as the group entered the living room.

"Y'all come eat, now." Addie summoned them into the dining room. She indicated Tom and Missy should sit on one side of the table with Frank and Ann seated across from them. Glen held Addie's chair for her while she sat down, then took the remaining seat at the opposite end of the table.

Ann stood up and dished up the food from the mirrored sideboard and passed the dishes to those seated at the table. She handed Addie and Glen each a plate of cornbread to pass. She then served herself a bowl of the shrimp stew and returned to her seat. After Ann sat down, Addie bowed her head. The others followed suit.

"Glen, would you do the blessing?" Addie asked.

"I'd be honored. Heavenly Father, we thank you for this food we are about to eat. We ask your blessing on those who prepared it and we who partake. Bless those within and those without. In Jesus' name, Amen." The others echoed "Amen!"

"Let's dig in," urged Glen. "Smells good, Addie."

"It's Ann's dish, Glen. We tested it and I think you'll like it."

"Addie baked the cornbread." Ann willingly shared the limelight.

After a long, leisurely meal, followed by dessert, the friends lingered over their coffee.

"Don't want to break up this pleasant gathering," began Tom, "but I promised Missy a ride on my Harley. Could she borrow your helmet, Ann?"

"Sure, Tom. I'll get it." Ann arose and got the helmet from their bedroom. When she returned, she asked Missy what jacket she had to wear.

"You can take my leather one, but you'll swim in it," Ann offered.

"I have my nylon windbreaker and a sweater. It's mild out so that should do." Missy replied.

Frank and Tom went to bring the Harley around to the door, while out on the back porch, Ann showed Missy how to adjust the helmet strap to fit. Glen and Addie still sat at the dining room table.

"Addie, you 'bout ready for another evening on the town?" Glen asked.

"Not just yet, Glen. I did enjoy myself, though. I'm ashamed to say, I overslept this morning and still had to take a rest later on."

"I ain't been no spring chicken myself today," Glen confessed.

"Glen, did you know Frank and Ann was out riding on that motorcycle of Tom's last night? I overheard Missy ask Ann about it."

"No, can't say as I did. Don't surprise me none. I've heard Frank speak about 'em so I knew he wasn't a stranger to 'em." Then added, "Shall we go see them off?"

"Reckon so, but they give me the shudders." She arose from the table and accompanied Glen outside.

Missy was excited about having her first motorcycle ride. Ann gave her several tips on buddy-riding including the proper way to lean into the curves. Frank told her about 'posting' on the pegs (like horseback riders do in the stirrups) for a more comfortable ride.

"Let your leg muscles do the work," Frank instructed.

"I hope I don't forget any of your lessons," Missy exclaimed.

With a wink, Ann gave a final tip. "Don't worry about remembering how to lean. Just put your arms around Tom's waist and follow his movements. That's the easiest way. More fun, too!"

The others hooted as Missy blushed. Tom turned the key, hit the electric start and soon they were on their way.

"I hope she'll be okay," fretted Addie.

"It's not as bad as it seems," Frank reassured her. "You have to watch out for the other guy. Tom seems to be a careful operator, so I wouldn't worry."

"I hear you two had yourselves a ride last night," said Glen.

"Yeah, a real nice one. I think Tom's taking Missy on the same route. Across the Piney Woods road east of here, " replied Frank.

"This would be a nice night to sit out in a porch swing, if I had one," mused Addie.

"That would be a nice touch, Addie," agreed Ann. "Where would you put one? There are several pleasant spots."

"Well, one would be pretty over there." She pointed to a location on the opposite side of the lawn from the buggy. "'course, it would be more private on the back lawn."

"What you need is a bird bath," commented Frank.

"There used to be one here on the front lawn. I hadn't thought of that in a long time. Must be around here someplace."

"I'll keep an eye out for it, Addie. Haven't seen it yet. If I find it and it's intact, I'll set it up," Frank promised.

Glen followed their conversation with interest while Ann had wandered off and was inspecting Glen's 'horse' closely.

"What are you gonna name the horse, Addie?" She called out.

"Why, Shadow, of course. Don't y'all think that's a proper name for it?" responded Addie.

"I think it's a perfect name, Addie," declared Glen. "Shadow, it is."

"I think everything has shaped up fine for the historical society meeting on Thursday," Ann verbalized what the rest were thinking.

Frank left the others and went to his car. He rummaged around in the trunk until he found Ann's camera, which he then used to snap some pictures of the horse and buggy.

Ann was pleased that he had thought of the camera and asked that he take some snapshots of the interior of the house.

"Yeah, I planned to do that," he replied flatly. "No sense in doing a job halfway. But I'll need the flash attachment for inside." Ann helped him find it and put it in the camera.

"She's the technician in the family," Frank explained to Glen and Addie.

On the pretense of checking the camera, Ann took a casual shot of the older couple.

"Wish I had taken one of Tom and Missy before they left," she commented to Frank. "Remind me and I'll do it when they get back."

Frank agreed to do so as he proceeded to go inside and take the pictures Ann had requested. She tagged along with him to assist in advancing the film. She said it was so stated in her technician's job description. They took the pictures of the interior and as they returned to the first floor, Addie and Glen were just entering the house.

"I was telling Glen about my farm directories. We're just going to look at them." They seated themselves at the table in the library where Frank and Ann joined them.

"I have an old county map at home," Glen mentioned. "If you like, I could bring it over here for your library."

"Or better yet, get it copied, Glen," suggested Ann. "I'm sure the map is valuable. It would be beneficial to have a copy here, but you should retain the original in safekeeping."

"I agree with Ann, Glen," Addie nodded in agreement as she spoke. "I'd be glad to pay the printers to make the copy."

"Well, that's a thought, Ladies. Next time I'm over, I'll bring the map."

"Addie, what was this road out here called before it was named Rainer Road?" asked Frank.

Addie and Glen replied almost simultaneously. "It's always been 'Rainer' as long as I remember."

"Why do you ask?" ventured Addie.

"I thought you said this place wasn't always in your husband's family."

"That's true, but there's an old homestead down that road. We call it Hundred Acres. My husband was born there. Haven't been down there in years. Tell you the truth, I don't even know if the place is still standing. I just pay the taxes on it. They're not very high."

"Could we see it sometime? Wouldn't you like to check it out, Frank?" begged Ann.

"Why certainly, you're welcome to look it over anytime you wish. In fact, I think I'd like to go see it with y'all."

"How 'bout now?" suggested Glen. "We can all go down in my truck. Addie?"

"I'm game. Let me just put on my garden pants."

As soon as Addie had changed, the four piled into Glen's truck and drove down Rainer Road till they came to the end. The old Rainer farm faced the end of the road.

It was overgrown with weeds and second growth. The house was unpainted and the old boards were black with age. The house was built in such a manner as to give the appearance of two separate buildings joined by a roofed corridor that ran through the center of the full length of the house.

"That's a strange design. I've seen quite a few with a deep hall like that in the front but only one other that goes straight through to the back." Ann pondered this unusual architecture.

"That's called a dog trot or dog run. Or a cat run. Whatever critter you prefer," explained Glen.

"I remember Bert used to tell 'bout the chickens roosting there to escape the heat or the rain." Addie laughed.

"Roof line's still pretty straight and sturdy looking," Frank noted. "Wouldn't take a lot of work to restore it, would you say, Glen?"

"Probably not, Frank. This climate here plays an important part in preserving our buildings. That barn out there don't look bad, Addie.

My son may be interested in renting this barn as well. You say there's a hundred acres here?"

"More or less. Can't believe I didn't think of this property when you asked before, Glen. 'Course I thought it'd all fallen down 'fore this."

While Ann and Addie began to poke around the outside of the house looking at the different plants, the men checked out the barn and a shed.

"Addie!" called Frank. "I found your bird bath! It's huge!" The men wrestled the two portions of it over near the truck and hoisted in into the truck bed.

There were several old pieces of farm equipment in the barn and two grist wheels in the shed but little else of value.

They decided against entering the house as it was beginning to get dark out so they left further exploring until another day.

As they passed the Bisbo place, they spotted Teddy outside and waved as they drove by. He recognized them and waved back.

Tom and Missy were just entering the drive ahead of them. Ann insisted on taking a flash picture of the two riders. Missy was thrilled with her 'maiden voyage' as she referred to her first motorcycle ride.

Tom expressed admiration for Missy's bravery. It was obvious to one and all that he was smitten.

"What's that you got there?" asked Tom as he spotted what Frank and Glen were preparing to unload from Glen's truck. Tom lent a hand and he and Frank lifted the massive fountain from the truck.

"Good thing there's two pieces to this. I'd sure hate to try to lift the whole thing. Addie, Frank said it's a bird bath. I call it a bird's hot tub, a giant hot tub!" observed Tom.

They accepted Addie's invitation for a cool drink and then everyone went their separate ways.

CHAPTER SEVENTEEN

Addie's Options

Saturday morning, Ann thought to place a call to Meg Parsons to inform her of the date and time of the Historical Society Meeting. She wished she had made an extra copy of the flyer to mail to the Afton Department store but with the meeting less than a week away, she decided it would be better to call. Fortunately, Meg was at work and free to take Ann's call.

"I will surely try to make your meeting, Ann. The mannequins worked out okay, did they? I was sorry there was only three stands."

"I think you'll be impressed with our setup," Ann answered. "We'll be happy to see you. You know you have an open invitation to come out. It was your generous gift that has made this start to come together."

"I'm glad it's worked out well. I made points with my boss for coming up with the write-off."

"I won't keep you from your work. If I get my hands on a copy of the meeting notice, I'll send it along. Okay to send it to the store?"

"Don't matter, but let me give you my home address and phone number. Got a paper and pencil handy?"

"Right here. Shoot!" Ann copied down the information Meg gave her. Noting that it was a rural address and named a road between

Afton and Route 3, Ann made the comment: "Gee, you're not as far away from us as I thought."

"Not too far. I'll probably bring my aunt for company. She's real interested in local history."

"The more the merrier, see you Thursday! Bye." Ann had no sooner hung up the phone, than it began ringing. She answered it to hear the librarian on the line.

"Miz Rainer," the voice inquired.

"No, it's Ann Flanders. Wait, I'll get her for you."

"No. No. That's okay, Miz Flanders. I can tell you what I called for. I just wanted to tell you that we've got great response for our meeting. This is the shot in the arm we've needed. We've got former members renewing that we haven't heard from in years. I think the library phone has been ringing off the hook with most calls about the meeting. What I'm doing is limiting the meeting to members only and bonafide guests. If we don't do that, it will get all out of hand. Any other people I'm telling that I expect there will be an open house soon. I wanted to tell Miz Rainer about that. Do you think we might arrange an open house? I hate to mislead folks. Tell her we'll help her handle it. We could charge a tiny admission and split it with her. Would she mind?"

"I'll talk it over with her. I think it's an excellent idea. I believe she'll like it. Gee, you haven't even seen the house yet."

"Not inside, but I did drive by there last night on my way over to Afton. I hadn't seen it since it was spruced up. It looks great!"

"Well, let me speak to Addie about your open house proposal. I'll let you know what she says."

"If you don't get a chance to call, you can tell me Thursday at the meeting."

"Fine, we'll see you Thursday." Hanging up the phone, Ann went to find Addie to share Lillian Perkins' idea with her. She found Addie on the front lawn with Frank, overseeing the placement of the birdbath. Addie was in her glory. She seemed to blossom out as the old house's treasures were uncovered.

Addie turned enthusiastically as Ann joined them. "Ann, I should have been here a hundred years before I was. I would have loved to be around when this place was in its heyday."

"When you hear what I have to tell you, you'll realize this place still has a heyday. Lillian Perkins from the library just called." Ann then repeated the gist of the conversation. Addie's excitement over the prospect of an open house was hard to contain.

"But do you think anyone would pay to visit my house?" she asked as she began to have second thoughts about how such an idea would go over with the public.

"They most certainly will. Lillian said 'tiny' admission so she's probably in the range of fifty cents to a dollar."

"Well, we'll see. I'm willing to do this, so give her my say-so."

"I hoped you would. Did I mention she said the society would help?"

"That's even better. And, Ann, I have another idea. What do you think if we dress up like the dummies for the meeting?"

"Now you're cooking with gas, Addie," quipped Ann. "Except I haven't seen any outfits up there in any generous sizes such as I would need. You and Missy, could, though. That's a clever idea."

"Addie," Frank broke in. "You have an ace up your sleeve, you know."

"Whatever do you mean, Frank?"

"The house at the Hundred Acres. That could easily be a museum piece. Wouldn't need any painting, the weather-beaten exterior is 100% authentic."

"What a great idea, Frank!" Ann said with enthusiasm. "See, Addie, you have so many options."

"I never had any idea what I had. All I saw was an old run-down house that I felt I couldn't afford to keep up anymore."

"Glen said he'll stop by one day next week and we'll inspect the old house. I want to check out the condition of the floor and sills. There are not too many examples of that style home around. Ann and I saw one over in the hills above Sparta or McMinnville on one of our drives around before we came here."

"Yes! That's where we saw it! It was in the valley below Beersheba Springs. It was the first time I'd ever seen a house like that. I called that a breezeway running through the center of the house. I thought it might have been an old style two-family house."

"I think y'all know more about Tennessee than I do. You sure get around," Addie remarked wistfully.

Ann and Addie decided to run into town for groceries before lunch. Ann wanted to get to the Post Office before it closed at noon.

"Too bad there's no shrimp stew left. We'd have lunch all sewed up. They..WE all sure enjoyed that, Ann."

"We like it too, Addie. It's pretty rich, so I don't make it too often."

The ladies scurried around and were soon on the way to town where their first stop was the Post Office. Ann removed the Historical Society flyer from the bulletin board and made three copies. She paid the clerk for the copies and bought several books of stamps plus a single stamped legal size envelope. She pulled a slip of paper from her purse, addressed the envelope, placed one copy of the flyer inside, sealed and mailed it.

"I told Meg Parsons I'd send her a flyer," she explained to Addie.

They went to the grocery store next and purchased the items on Addie's list. Ann stopped by the deli counter and ordered Provolone cheese and salami. She asked that they not be sliced, but just an inch thick chunk of each be cut off and weighed. The clerk did as she instructed. Ann also ordered a quarter pound each of ham, turkey and roast beef.

"Making sandwiches for lunch, Ann?" Addie inquired.

"We can, but our main dish will be an antipasto salad. It's an Italian version of a chef salad," she added when she saw the perplexed look on Addie's face.

"Like a Julienne salad?"

"Exactly. It's a delicious source of protein and a quick lunch too! Some stores sell it in the delicatessen section all mixed. Probably not much call for it here."

"We'll need some lettuce, too," reminded Addie.

"You're right, also black olives and tomatoes. Some people put hot peppers in and boiled eggs."

Addie made a face and commented dryly: "No hot peppers for me! I don't mind the eggs. Let me get some bacon. We can have BLT sandwiches for Monday lunch."

"Sounds good. Speaking of bacon, let's get Frank to take us out for breakfast tomorrow morning."

Ann grabbed a head of lettuce, quickly steered to the canned olives while Addie obtained the rasher of bacon from the cooler.

"I really know better than to shop when I'm hungry," Ann said.

"I've heard that before, probably from you. Well, I've got all I had on my list so I'm ready to cash out."

It took longer than usual to check out at the register, since the Saturday shoppers were out in full force. Several people greeted Addie warmly. They seemed genuinely happy to see her out and about. She later commented to Ann that it seemed like she had been sick for a long time or away on a long trip.

"Where were all these friends since Bert passed on? I thought they'd all died as well. I bet some of them thought I was dead, too."

"It's a common complaint, Addie. It's like when people get divorced, their friends don't want to give the impression they are taking sides so they distance themselves from both parties. When people die, I guess they're afraid it might be contagious. Some married women also consider a single lady, whether widowed or divorced, a threat, especially when they're as pretty as you."

"Now, Ann, stop your malarkey!" Addie blushed as she spoke.

"Well, Glen thinks you're pretty nice!"

"Hush! You stop that! Hear?" She was adamant.

"Yes, Ma'am," Ann said meekly. She was pushing the grocery cart to the car, with Addie following. They heard someone yell.

"Hello, Addie. Hello, Ann. Fancy running into ya'll here."

"Hello, Glen." Addie was the first to spot him sitting in his truck.

"I brought my son's wife in to shop," Glen explained. "Here's Brenda now. Brenda, these are my friends, Addie Rainer and Ann Flanders."

A nice-looking young woman approached them. Her friendly face was peppered with freckles. She was pushing a cart more loaded than Ann and Addie's. She smiled at the ladies and expressed her delight in meeting them.

"I've looked forward to getting to know you both. Father Adams has said so much about y'all. I must have your recipe for that dish you served up last night. He can't stop raving about it."

"How do you do, Brenda? It's real nice to meet you, too. And yes, I'd be happy to give you the recipe."

"How do. Glad we ran into you today," said Addie. "Ann, tell Glen about what the librarian had to say this morning."

"About the open house? I guess they've had such a response to the meeting notice that they want to have a public open house with a small admission. They'll keep the meeting closed but for the genuine society members."

"That's good," said Glen. "I was afraid you'd get overrun with curiosity seekers. The admission price will cut it down somewhat and maintain the integrity of their meeting."

"You probably have frozen food you need to get home and put away, Brenda, so we shouldn't detain you," stated Ann.

"Yes, that's true," answered Brenda gratefully. "I hope y'all come by and see us, now we've met. I know Billy wants y'all to stop over, too."

They promised to do so after the meeting and open house were behind them. Ann went to stow their groceries in the car while Glen was doing the same for Brenda, allowing Addie and Brenda a few more moments to chat. When they heard Glen shut the back of the truck cap, the ladies took it as a cue to curtail their conversation. With brief waves, they headed for home.

"That was pleasant. Glen's daughter-in-law seems very nice. She told me Glen's much better to have around since he's been coming over." Addie continued, "His son's decided he shouldn't lift a hand with any of the farming, just lets him putter with his woodshop."

"Well, he must get bored since he's used to being busy. It's not easy to come to a sudden halt. Especially when you're in good health as Glen seems to be."

"Yes, he enjoys good health. He's said so, but Brenda assured me it's true. Mild blood pressure elevation, she said."

"You two really hit it off, I'd say," observed Ann.

"Well, I felt as though I knew her. Glen's spoke about his family and showed me a whole passel of pictures."

Ann wisely did not comment or ask questions at this point. She had become fond of Addie and was happy she had found a friend and protector in Glen. Teasing her, no matter how innocent, might put her on the defensive and mar this budding relationship.

They put the groceries away as soon as they arrived home. Addie set the table while Ann prepared the antipasto salad. She cubed the cheese and salami, cut up several tomatoes and drained the black olives. Addie rinsed the lettuce and put it in her lettuce drier to spin the water off, then patted it with paper towels to remove any residue of water. She broke the lettuce up into bite-size pieces, took the ingredients Ann had prepared and began tossing those while Ann shredded some of the lunch meat (turkey, ham and beef) and threw those in.

Frank appeared at the door, asking, "How soon is lunch?"

"How about now?" was Ann's retort. "We're having an antipasto. What kind of dressing do you want? Do you want a sandwich, too?"

"I'll have French if you have it, but better wait to see if I have room for a sandwich before you make it." Frank's reply surprised Ann. He was one of those people who usually add salt to food before they taste it (which Ann felt was an insult to the cook) and whose eyes were bigger than their stomachs.

Ann placed three salad dressings, on the table: French, Russian and Italian. She and Addie had the Italian.

"More authentic," commented Ann. She noted that Frank reached for the Russian and applied it to his salad. Addie had been about to hand him the French. Confused, she glanced at Frank, then at Ann, who gave a brief nod of her head.

"He always gets them mixed up," she explained to Addie after lunch.

"Then, why not just put out the Russian and Italian?" asked Addie.

"Because he may have his glasses on and read the name and ask me why I didn't put the French on the table."

"Even though he don't really want it?"

"You got it, Addie. I hate to say this, but it's just like a man. He's not too much different than any other."

"I enjoyed your antipasto salad. It was truly nutritious and delicious."

"Addie, you sound like a poet," laughed Ann. "But I've run out of ideas. I haven't the slightest hint as to what's for supper."

"I'll treat to supper out." Addie said generously.

CHAPTER EIGHTEEN

Historical Society Meeting

*S*unday through Thursday passed routinely for the Rainer household. There was a thread of excitement that permeated the atmosphere as everyone was eagerly looking forward to the Historical Society meeting. Frank, mainly to have it over with, but he gamely did whatever the women asked of him to prepare for it. When they were engrossed in something that didn't require his presence, he'd get out of their sight.

He and Glen had gotten their heads together and had a few projects going which they did not mention to Ann and Addie. The Adams' had finalized their rental agreement with Addie and the women grew accustomed to seeing Glen's truck head down Rainer Road. They didn't notice that he frequently picked up a hitchhiker headed the same way. When he was able to get away, Frank would head down to the hundred acres on foot, timing it so he would be past the drive when Glen came along. Glen tried to be sure to come by regularly every day so Frank could plan on him being along at the same time. Glen would pick him up and they'd be gone an hour or so. The ladies were busy with their activities and were unaware of what was going on.

The tools Frank needed were kept in the back of Glen's pickup truck and the men enjoyed their conspiracy. Ann's camera frequently accompanied them and the progress they were making at the old homestead was thus recorded for later sharing.

When Thursday arrived, everyone was so busy and excited, they almost forgot to eat. Frank's tactful comment, "When are we going to eat?" reminded the ladies and a quick repast was prepared. Frank grumbled that he'd be glad when they got back to their normal routine, but the women didn't take him seriously.

Missy had traded her shift with another waitress, Rosie, so she could attend the meeting. She had eagerly agreed when Ann told her of Addie's suggestion to dress in turn-of-the-century clothing. Missy was delighted with the outfit Addie had selected for her to wear. It was a long, black skirt with a white Gibson girl blouse. Addie looked her over very critically, frowning slightly.

"What's wrong, Miz Addie?"

"Something's missing, Missy. I think I know what it is." She disappeared into her bedroom. Ann and Missy could hear her rummaging around in her closet. She emerged carrying an object resembling a molded wire frame.

"It's a bustle, Missy! Just what you need!" exclaimed Ann.

"How perfect! But how do I wear it?"

"Don't look at me, Missy, I never wore one." Addie said, shaking her head.

"We'll improvise," Ann commented. "We need some string or belt or even long shoe laces will do." They managed to secure it in place and when Missy's skirt was settled over it, the extra material gathered in the back laid over the framework properly to everyone's satisfaction.

Addie had decided on a plain dark brown dress for herself. She located a crinoline underskirt to add to its authenticity. To Ann's surprise, Addie handed her a gingham dress in a generous size. It had a low cut neck and a long flowing skirt

"See, Ann, there were some healthy ladies back then. But I think you should add some lace to the bodice and try this little apron. Makes you look like a hostess."

"With the mostest," Ann replied dryly.

Missy had taken her hairbrush from her purse and bending from the waist, was brushing her hair down over her head. She placed a rubber band at the crown of her head and made it into an upsweep style, asking for bobby pins to pin it in place. Addie again arose to the occasion and supplied the necessary items. After completing her hairdo, Missy insisted that Addie and Ann have their hair similarly 'coifed'. After mild protests, this was accomplished.

"I almost forgot, Addie. I have something for you." Ann presented Addie with a cardboard box, about 6" x 8" in size. Addie opened it to find a Guest Register Book. Ann had put the day's date and 'Peckville Historical Society meeting' at the top of the first page.

"I thought it would be nice to keep account of the people who visit Rainer Manor. After tonight, we'll label the next page, 'Open House – (date).'"

"I wouldn't have thought of it myself, but I like the idea. Thank you, Ann."

"Ladies, we all look so elegant and gracious," burst Missy.

Frank gave a shout from the kitchen, "Looks like your first person's here early."

"Probably Lillian Perkins," Ann guessed, correctly it turned out.

They went to the front door to greet her.

"Welcome to Rainer Manor, Ms. Perkins," Addie spoke first and ushered the librarian into the foyer.

"Please call me Lil. My, don't y'all look so precious!"

"I believe you know Missy and you remember Ann." Addie gestured towards the other women.

"Yes, I do." Replied Lil, adding, "I just love your horse and buggy out front."

"We hoped it could be seen easily," commented Ann.

They moved into the front room then across to the library, where Addie called Lil's attention to the farm directories. Lil was impressed with the number and content of those books.

"Actually, I'm impressed with all you have here, Miz Addie."

"Wait till you see the upstairs, Lil!" gushed Missy. "Shall I show her?"

"Good idea, Missy. Ann and I will stay here if anyone comes along."

"Yes, the ladies on the refreshment committee should be along shortly," said Lil. "I didn't tell you how many we expect to come, did I?"

"How many?" asked Ann.

"Twenty-five, which is a goodly number. We're lucky lately if we get 10-12 members to attend."

"We are honored that so many are interested in coming out here." Addie stated.

"Especially on such short notice," expressed Ann.

"I told you, this was the shot in the arm we needed!" Lil called from the stairs where she and Missy had already begun the climb to the second floor. Addie and Ann could hear her exclamations of pleasure as Missy led her from one room to the other.

The arrival of a car distracted them and they went to the front entrance to assist the two ladies who comprised the refreshment committee. They helped carry plates of cookies and jars of punch while one of the ladies carried a large punch bowl and the other a grocery bag containing clear plastic punch glasses, paper napkins and small paper plates. They went through the formalities of introducing themselves to one another. The taller of the two women was Michelle Frazier, while a shorter, rounder lady was Barbara Clarke. They busily set about arranging the paper and plastic goods around the table and placing the cookie platter and punch bowl in easily accessible positions.

"We'll wait to pour the punch out just before we break up the meeting," explained Barbara, who seemed to be in charge of the refreshments.

"Where is Lil?" asked Michelle, "Or isn't that her car out there?"

"She's here, she's upstairs with Missy. They should be right down," responded Ann.

"I love your outfits," commented Barbara. "What a lovely idea!"

"We wanted you to feel like you have really stepped back in time for this evening, anyway. It was Addie's idea."

"And a very good one," replied Michelle. "I think we'll really enjoy tonight's meeting."

Their conversation broke off when they heard Missy and Lil laughing at the head of the stairs. The four ladies walked to the foot of the stairs to see TWO Gibson girls descending.

"I let Missy talk me into changing my attire." Lil said as she carefully negotiated the stairs in the long skirt. Seeing Barbara and Michelle, she added, "Sorry ladies, this is the last authentic outfit!"

"Actually, we rearranged things," Missy began apologetically. "The chaise lady is at the dressing table and the bookcase lady has a flannel nightie on and has become the bed lady. Hope that's okay?" Missy looked aghast at her own boldness to make such a change.

"Certainly, it's fine, Missy." Addie assured her, continuing, "Ladies, on the library table, we've a guest book we'd like y'all to sign."

Before long, the other members began arriving. Within fifteen minutes after the appointed hour, there were thirty people in attendance. One man had thought to obtain twenty folding chairs and so there were sufficient seats for all.

They were pleased to see Meg Parsons and her aunt were able to come as special guests. Glen Adams had come by and picked up Frank. Before they left, they helped set up the folding chairs and asked if they were needed any longer. No further help on their part was necessary, so they left.

The business meeting progressed through the usual agenda. Minutes of the previous meeting and treasurer's report were read and old business discussed. When the floor was opened for new business, the prospect of assisting Addie with an open house was introduced. It met with approval on all sides. They decided to hold it the following month to allow time for advertising. It was suggested that several ads be placed in both the weekly Peckville paper and the Afton Daily Herald. The society secretary, Amanda Bates, wrote a monthly report which appeared in the Peckville Weekly. She agreed to include a write-up of the planned open house in her report.

Admission fee was brought up. Lil made the motion that it be set at $1.50 for the initial open house. Addie would receive $1 of this and the Historical Society would get fifty cents. It would generate money this first time to revive the club's floundering treasury and furnish money for Addie to use to maintain the property. Lil went on to explain that if Addie decided to open her home later for visitors, she could set the price as she desired.

"We want to take advantage of the public's initial curiosity. You may want to have open house two days on a weekend." Lil summarized.

Addie agreed to this proposal. Lil then reworded her motion to formalize dates and price. Further action was taken to name the necessary committees to handle the arrangements.

A vote of appreciation was made and carried, thanking Addie for her hospitality in allowing them to hold their meeting at Rainer Manor. It was established that they would have the next meeting in two weeks at Addie's to see how the open house plans were shaping up with the committees meeting each of the two weeks after that before the open house.

"After that, if Addie's not sick of us, maybe we could hold our monthly meetings here," proposed Michelle.

"Yes and I wonder if this might not be named a historic site," suggested Barbara.

"Okay, Barbara, you head a committee to look into that aspect." Lil said. "There are many options to be explored which would benefit both Addie and our Historical Society."

"Oh!" Ann suddenly broke in. "I almost forgot. These mannequins have been donated by the Department Store in Afton through this lady, Meg Parsons, to the Peckville Historical Society for use at Rainer Manor."

A vote of thanks was enthusiastically supported by all members. Contributions of all who had a part in preparing Rainer Manor for the meeting were formally acknowledged. Addie ventured that Frank and Ann had done the most but made sure that Missy, Glen, Tom and Teddy Bisbo were not overlooked.

The meeting was adjourned and they progressed to the refreshment table. Thoughts were traded back and forth more freely in the informal atmosphere that pervaded the social part of the evening. The members toured the upstairs guided by Lil and Missy. Addie and Ann presided over the refreshment table to allow Barbara and Michelle to join the tour. Several members had brought their cameras along to record the meeting.

Michelle verbalized what most were thinking. "I don't know when we have had such an interesting and fun meeting. We have never had a two hour business meeting since I joined."

"I told y'all it would be great!" was Lil's response.

"Could we dress up for the open house?" pleaded Amanda Bates. "We should be able to scour up more dresses." Several others nodded in agreement with this suggestion.

Since it was beginning to get dark outside, several members went outside to take photos of the horse and buggy. Frank and Glen returned and were invited to join the group at refreshments. They were the center of attention of the group at the buggy who were plying Glen with questions about the cost of a plywood figure such as the horse. Missy told Glen that his contribution was officially on the record.

The membership chairman, Wayne Coates, took advantage of the renewed interest and collected some delinquent dues. These were good-naturedly paid since all those in attendance had come prepared to pay them. Lil had warned them that due to the expected high turnout, only members in good standing would be allowed to attend. Wayne had convinced her to extend it to any member who would update his status at the meeting. He also recruited five new members: Addie, Missy, Glen, Meg and Dottie Parsons. Frank and Ann were accepted as associate members.

"I meant to collect these dues during the business meeting," Wayne apologized.

"Naw, Wayne, you're better off to have waited 'til the cookies and punch softened us up," laughed one of the other men.

"I wish I'd thought to make name tags for us to wear," remarked Ann.

"It's a good idea for the open house for the guides and members. I thought the guest register was appropriate, also." Lil said approvingly.

It was with reluctance that Meg and her aunt Dottie were the first to leave. They were delighted to be a part of this and promised to attend the monthly meetings. Meg commenting that "Afton being such a large town, it's difficult to get to know your neighbors. That's why I moved back out to live with Aunt Dottie."

"We are pleased you could join us and we truly appreciate the role you played in the success of our endeavors," exclaimed Lil.

"Please come again and don't stand on formality. Stop by anytime you want." Addie said to Meg and Dottie.

"We will. Thank you, Miz Addie."

While the Historical Society ladies made fast work of cleaning up so it wouldn't be left for Addie and Ann, Frank assisted Wayne in loading the folding chairs. It was long past eleven o'clock before the last guests were ushered to their cars. Addie and Ann couldn't believe their eyes that all of the clean-up work was done. After they bid Missy goodnight, they buttoned up the house and raced to bed.

Ann's sleep that night was fitful. In her dreams, the halls at Rainer Manor were full of mannequins who became flesh and blood people dressed in period clothing. Plywood horses pulling buggies went flying by so quickly she could just catch a glimpse of their passengers. They were her grandchildren! She reached out to embrace them but the buggy went by too fast and all she could see were the children waving and blowing kisses to her. Then all faded into a maze of gray and sepia tones until it became nothing and she slept deeply until the next morning.

CHAPTER NINETEEN

Something's Up

*A*fter breakfast the next day, Ann noticed Frank was acting a bit mysterious, which was unusual since he was always open and shared whatever was on his mind. Ann wondered if he had been this way for a while, but because she had been so preoccupied with the Historical Society, she had missed the signs. She determined she would devote her entire attention to him to reassure him.

He pulled her aside and asked for Glen's phone number. She looked it up and gave it to him on a slip of paper but he didn't make any move to make his call.

She and Addie went upstairs to take care of the outfits that had been worn the previous evening. They decided since none was soiled and the same people would no doubt wear them at the open house, they would just hang them in the closet. Slips with the wearer's name were pinned to the garments to eliminate any confusion the next time.

"I'm afraid, because of their age, they might become damaged when laundered," Addie declared.

"My thought, exactly," said Ann, adding, "Before we put these away, I want to get my camera and take pictures of them. I realize there were pictures taken last night but I'm not sure we'll get copies.

Wish I had thought to get my camera out then." She went back downstairs to get it.

As she came back to the stairs with the camera, she overheard Frank on the phone. His tone of voice sounded conspiratorial to her and her curiosity overcame her good manners so she brazenly eavesdropped.

"Well, today's the day. It's time to tell Addie and Ann. (pause) Well, I thought I'd take them to lunch first. Then all hell can break loose. (pause) No, I don't think Ann is even suspicious of what I've been up to. Missy seems to know. She made a remark to me about it last night. (pause) Well, Tom must have told her. There's nothing goes on in this county he's not aware of." He stopped speaking, partly to let Glen speak and partly to catch his breath.

"Yes. Well, Glen, I couldn't have pulled it off without your help. I hope Addie doesn't chew you out for not telling her about your part in this. If they hadn't been so wrapped up in their own stuff, they wouldn't have to be the last ones to find out."

Ann sensing the conversation was closing, scurried up the stairs as quietly and quickly as anyone with her arthritis could manage.

"Ann, why are you so flushed? What's wrong?" queried Addie.

"Nothing, I just came up the stairs a little too fast." To herself, she wondered, "What was that all about? Well, I guess I'll find out at lunch today."

When the ladies finished their task upstairs and retreated to the first floor, Ann went looking for Frank. "Wonder if it's too late to mend fences," she mused. "Guess I have had him on 'hold' for quite a while now."

He wasn't in the house so she went outdoors to search for him. He wasn't in the front yard or the back. Their car was there so he couldn't have gone anywhere. She continued to look for him in the barn and the back barn. Tom's motorcycle was in its usual place, even Teddy's bike was leaning where he always left it when he caught the school bus.

"I find it hard to believe he went out for a walk, alone," she said aloud, thinking to herself, "I must be crazy, talking to myself all the time."

Normally, Ann would be frantic by this time, believing Frank was lying somewhere, injured. Her search had been so thorough, even looking up and down both the main road and the side road as well as looking under the old Ford and their car, she felt he was not on the property. It had to be somehow connected to his clandestine phone call earlier. How unlike Frank.

She returned to the house and found Addie in the kitchen looking through the refrigerator and freezer.

"What should we have for lunch?" she asked Ann.

"Oh, let's have a late lunch, give us more time to think about it," suggested Ann.

Addie agreed to that, then asked, "What's Frank up to out there?"

"Oh, he wasn't in sight. I just strolled around a bit. It's really nice out today. He's probably out in the back barn, working away on something." Ann didn't want to tell Addie she couldn't find Frank.

They heard a horn honk and looked out to see Glen's pickup pull out of the lane. He was alone. A short time later, Tom Cates pulled up out front in his patrol car and Frank alit from the front passenger seat.

"Look what I found! A lost runaway boy. Didn't even know his phone number. Best keep an eye on him, Ann." Tom laughed.

"I'll try, Tom," she responded. "It isn't easy since he learned how to walk," she continued dryly.

Tom waved goodbye and went on his way. Ann didn't question Frank on his whereabouts. It sounded like Tom had seen him walking and picked him up, but the possibility existed that Frank had been puttering in the yard and Tom stopped and took Frank with him. Still it wasn't like Frank to just take off without telling her where he was going and approximately when he would return. Ann wouldn't give him the satisfaction of asking now. She had thought Frank was with Glen until she saw Glen alone in his truck.

"You about ready for lunch, Frank?" Ann inquired sweetly. "Addie wanted to start it but I suggested we have a late one."

"What if I take the two of you out for lunch? You've been so busy, it'll give you a break," Frank suggested.

"Sounds good to me. Addie?"

"Okay, I'm game. Just give me a minute to freshen up."

Ann caught Frank smiling to himself. He's smug about something, that's for sure, she decided.

Ten minutes later, they headed out to the car for the trip to town. Ann, as she usually did, suggested Addie sit up front with Frank. Addie, as usual, turned down the offer and sat in back.

"It's kind of you, Ann, but I don't mind as long as your car has four doors. If it had only two, I'd take you up on your offer to sit up front."

Ann laughed, "If it only had two doors, Addie, Frank would be sitting in back as I'd insist on driving, and you and I would both be up front!"

Their expected destination was the Main Street Diner even though this had not been verbalized. The food was good, the prices were right and the company cordial. There was no need to go anywhere else for lunch. Missy was on the afternoon shift so wasn't there yet. Rosie brought water and menus to their booth.

"Coffee for everyone? How was your meeting last night? Missy was all excited about going." She had subtly absorbed their nods in answer to her question regarding coffee.

"It turned out great, Rosie. Missy looked lovely. We really appreciated all she's done to help us," praised Addie.

"And thank **you** for changing shifts with her. Addie and I don't do stairs well so we really counted on her help," Ann was quick to tell Rosie.

Another patron entered the diner as they spoke. As Rosie left to return behind the counter, a clear view opened to reveal Glen sitting there on a stool.

"Why, there's Glen!" said Addie. "Glen, hello. Why don't you join us?"

"If y'all don't mind. Hello Ann, Frank. How y'all today?" he asked innocently.

"Resting up from last night. Taking it easy," was Ann's response. The others readily agreed.

"Well, you're not alone. I overslept this morning. Brenda made me get my own breakfast for being so lazy. Now I couldn't wait till I got home for lunch so I cut in here."

They all ordered the special, Fish Fries, deciding to eat a light supper. Various customers came in and out while they were there. Several of these were in attendance at the meeting the night before and warmly greeted Addie and her friends.

As they paid their bill and prepared to leave, Frank asked if anyone had any errands to run in town before they left to go home. Neither Addie nor Ann could think of anything they needed to do.

"Addie, why don't you ride back with me?" suggested Glen. "The company will sure make the drive seem shorter."

Addie agreed and Ann noted she did not get flustered, a good indication she was becoming comfortable in her relationship with Glen.

"You go on ahead," Frank told Glen. "I need to buy some gas before I leave town." He and Ann went to their car and drove over to the station where Frank regularly purchased gas. He always had his car tuned up and felt it was best to be consistent with the brand of gas for best mileage and engine performance.

They were only about ten minutes behind Glen and Addie in Glen's pickup truck, but when Frank turned down Rainer Road, there was no truck in the drive. This puzzled Ann. Even more confusing, Frank did not pull into the drive but continued on down the lane.

The plot thickens, thought Ann. Frank drove the full length of the lane to the '100 acres' farm. There sat Glen's truck in the drive. Ann realized that was a feat in itself as they had been unable to park there on their first trip down because of the heavy second growth of bushes which had overgrown the drive and lawns. Not only was the drive cleared, but the lawns as well.

Addie sat there with a look of amazement on her face. When Frank and Ann approached the truck, Glen alit from the driver's side and went around to assist Addie down from the passenger's seat.

"Whoever did this? Whenever did they do it? Glen, you did this! You're the only vehicle I've seen come down here. I thought you were doing something at the barn!" Addie exclaimed.

"Frank did more than I did. Guess y'all didn't notice he was kidnapped every day this week."

"Is this where you were this morning? But we saw you coming from the other direction with Tom. And Glen came out of the lane alone," sputtered Ann.

The two men were enjoying putting one over on the gals. They looked at each other to see who was going to answer all their questions. Frank went first.

"I was in the back of Glen's truck. I got out a ways up Rt. 3. Tom happened along and gave me a ride. Worked out great!"

"Frank would wait at the corner and when I came by, I slowed down and he climbed in." Glen explained. "Boy, you're sure agile for such an old fellow," he teased Frank.

"You two were so busy, I don't think you ever realized I was gone. I was on 'ignore,' instead of 'hold'," Frank complained.

"Don't feel bad, we thought we were on 'neglect'," was Ann's retort.

"Can we go inside? Is it safe?" asked Addie.

"Oh, yes. Glen and I checked it out. Only had to replace a board or two. Come on in." They followed Frank into the old farmhouse. The ladies were delighted to be able to gain entrance without having to wade through all the weeds and shrubs they remembered from their first excursion here.

There is a special thrill in exploring an old home. You wonder who lived there and imagine what stories the walls could tell if granted the power of speech. Because Frank and Glen had inspected the premises and made repairs, the scary part, the dangerous aspect had been removed. Being as old as it was, the house did not contain any type of wall-board. It lacked the musty, chalky smell Ann remembered from visits to abandoned houses as a child. Her father had been a carpenter and was interested in old houses and the methods by which they had been constructed. This love of architecture had been inherited by her older brother who had studied to be an architect and worked to restore older houses. Ann mused over the thought that one seldom saw an abandoned house anymore. If a house was vacant, it either had a for sale or for rent sign, a posted sign or was burned to the ground. She commented on this in an aside to Frank.

"Probably most places are condemned if not fit for occupancy. Fire departments use them as a controlled burn for training purposes. It's a whole lot safer than leaving them open for trespassers to explore. The owners are scared of lawsuits." Frank explained.

"Like an attractive nuisance, they could be held responsible." Ann said in comprehension of his explanation.

"Exactly," Frank replied.

"You two take the cake," Ann expressed admiration of their workmanship.

"I agree," Addie chimed in.

They continued exploring the old place. As is common in really old homes, it was hard to determine what the function of each room was. There is usually nothing to distinguish one room from another.

Sinks were dry sinks with no plumbing traces or holes in walls to furnish clues as to their purpose. Cupboards were seldom built-in, but were movable pieces of furniture and usually were long since hauled off and sold to antique collectors. If there were built-in cupboards in a house, you would frequently find one in almost every room. (If you had a carpenter in the family, you could always think of something for him to build.) Room sizes are not always a clue. Most rooms were small. All of this made it quite a puzzle to solve. It was fun to guess at, anyway.

Addie said Bert had been born in this house, but his family had left when he was an infant and moved to Chattanooga where he grew up. Addie had met him there and they had lived there for quite a few years. He was too young when his family had moved away from 100 Acres to remember the layout of the rooms in the old house.

By the time the young couple moved to the area, the old homestead was vacant. Over the years, occupants had used the rooms however they needed to with no set pattern. This particular structure had all rooms opening onto the center walkway. During the depression, two families had called it home. The worn threshold attested to the numerous feet that had trod in and out since the house was built.

Ann sat on the steps and had sunk into a reverie thinking of all the stories this place would hold. It was one of the oldest houses she could remember being in. At least it looked like it. She slowly became aware that Addie was speaking to her.

"What do YOU think, Ann?"

"Oh, Addie, I'm so sorry. I was daydreaming and didn't realize you were speaking to me."

"I should have realized you were deep in thought.. I was just wondering if I shouldn't give this place to the Historical Society. I don't have any use for it and I'd hate to see it rot and fall down. Would I be crazy to do that, Ann?"

"That sounds like a wonderful idea, Addie."

"It's not that the taxes are high, but would save me that little bit."

"If you didn't plan to leave the manor to your nephew or have anyone in mind, you might consider donating that to the Society as well. You could have life occupancy rights. They would then be responsible for all taxes, maintenance, maybe utilities or at least a share of them. When you get to where you didn't feel you could stay there alone, have them furnish a caretaker or couple. You wouldn't be alone then. If they open the Manor to visitors, you could exclude the back part of the house (kitchen, dining room, bath and the two bedrooms.) and have those your private quarters."

"Was that what Lil Perkins meant when she said I had options?" wondered Addie.

"Maybe, she hasn't said yet what she meant. You might want to consider it. If you decide to go ahead and do it, be sure you have a reputable lawyer set up the terms and leave a loophole. Something that if some manipulative person got in charge of the Historical Society and treats you badly or fraudulently, that the pact is invalid and all rights revert to you. A guardian would be named on your behalf to look out for your interests."

"Ann, you should have been a lawyer yourself. Wish I knew all that stuff," marveled Addie.

Ann laughed, "Wish I knew what I know. Sometimes my memory banks don't always retrieve data from my central files."

"Memory banks, central files, I don't understand." Addie did indeed look confused.

"Computer terms, Addie," explained Addie.

"Oh, like that machine in the library," remembered Addie.

"Exactly, Addie, you've got it!"

The men joined them. They had gone over every inch of the house, admiring its condition and proud of the work they had done to make it last longer.

"What's up, Ladies?" asked Glen.

"Well, Glen, if you must ask, we're discussing how poorly our memory banks are operating these days, retrieving data from our central files," volunteered Addie. She looked from one man to the other relishing the looks of amazement on their faces.

"Addie, you sound like a computer expert," said Frank.

"I'm taking lessons from the best here," she replied, placing her arm across Ann's shoulders. She continued on, "'sides that, we're discussing my options for the future. Why don't we head back to the house? I'd like to talk this over some more and see what Glen and Frank have to say about this, Ann." Addie turned and looked at the 100 acres property. "Y'all have worked so hard for me. I do appreciate all you've done. You're good friends, all of you."

They returned to the respective vehicles they had driven up in and headed back down the lane to the Rainer 'big house' as Frank called it.

Ann made coffee and they sat and had a coffee klatch confab while Addie told the men the details of what she and Ann had discussed back at the old house.

"I wouldn't gain much by giving them the old place, but it would be saved for posterity." Addie summarized.

"There must be an historical landmark designation which could be applied to both," Frank suggested.

"That's right. Lil Perkins assigned Barbara Clark the task of looking into historic sites for the next meeting," remembered Ann. "That was before you and Glen rejoined us."

Glen interjected, "I like Ann's suggestion that you donate this place to them with the life occupancy clause. If you give them both maybe they'd be willing to assume all costs and let you live here free."

"Could this little association afford to assume all costs?" asked Ann.

"Probably, with the increased membership and the income they'd generate by opening them up to the public for an admission," Glen answered Ann.

"Perhaps they could get a state grant to assist with the maintenance and taxes," Ann threw in.

"We'll give Lil a call Monday and get her feelings on the matter," decided Addie.

"Yes, we should take care of it soon since Ann and I should head north in 3 to 4 weeks." Frank revealed.

'Can't believe time has flown so quickly," said Ann. She couldn't bear to look at Addie. If she had looked, she would have seen a somber look cover her face like a cloud passing overhead.

The discussion ended there. Glen arose to leave and Addie walked outside with him.

"I think I'll kick back for a little while," Frank told Ann. This meant he was going to lie down for a while, something Ann hated to do in the daytime, regardless of how tired she was.

"Put a spread over you, it feels like it's gotten a bit chilly," she suggested. While he went in to nap, she got the morning paper and brought it to the kitchen table to read. After she perused the headlines and read a few articles that interested her, she skipped to the crossword puzzle. She had been secretly pleased when she had discovered that Addie wasn't interested in either the puzzle or the 'word jumble'. She did the jumbled words mentally or on a scrap paper, just in case Addie did become intrigued by it.

Finishing the puzzle, she realized she hadn't heard Glen's truck leave. About the same time she thought about this, she heard Addie call her. She went outdoors and heard a second call. Rounding the corner of the house, she came upon Glen and Addie relaxing in a lawn swing.

"Did you build this, Glen? When did you bring it?"

"Well, you're full of questions, Ann, aren't you?" Glen laughed.

"Ain't this just the grandest thing for Glen to do?" exclaimed Addie.

"I was going to put it at the old place but knew you'd get more use of it here," he explained.

"I guess all my dreams have come true." Addie declared. "Somewhere we have an old, old picture of this place and there's a swing like this sitting out front."

"I saw it in your album you were showing me one night," mentioned Glen. "I could set it out there. I just put it around back here to surprise you."

"Oh, I like it fine right here, Glen. I don't want to set out there where all going by can see me. It'll be more private here. I intend to use it and enjoy it. I thank you again, Glen."

"A special gift for a special lady, Addie," Glen said gallantly. Turning to Ann, he added, "My son and I brought it right after y'all left for lunch today."

CHAPTER TWENTY

Trouble Abrewin'

*F*rank and Addie had driven to town for Adelaide's doctor's appointment. Ann was finishing up the dishes from their lunch and relishing a few quiet moments alone when she heard the crunch of tires as a vehicle entered the front driveway, that was seldom used.

She glanced out and saw two scruffy-looking men emerging from an older model pickup truck with mismatched fenders. Ann thought about the articles she had often read up north about itinerant people preying on older homeowners with construction or repair schemes. She wondered why such a thought would occur to her, though it did put her on her guard as she answered the knock on the front door.

"Oh? Miz Rainer here? We thought she might want us to do some chores for her." The younger of the two men spoke first.

"Yeah! We do this all the time, to help out. Thought she lived all alone. You kin to her?" The older man really looked shifty-eyed, Ann thought. Instinctively she felt her initial reaction when the two drove up may not be too far wrong. Her eye for detail had taken in the Kentucky license plate on the pickup.

"No, Aunt Addie's not here. She's shopping with my husband at the moment. My son's down cellar, he could probably use some help, if you don't charge much." Ann appreciated the unexpected help from the clunky old furnace as the open front door caused a draft to hit the thermostat. As usual, when the old furnace started up, it sounded like someone WAS down cellar banging on the pipes. This was the first time Ann didn't mind the noise.

"Oh, no," the older man spoke as the two edged out the door. "Sounds like your son has things under control. We ain't much on plumbing. Sorry to bother you." They almost fell over each other trying to get to their truck. The driver started the truck up and spun the tires, throwing gravel as they left.

Adelaide won't appreciate the hole in the drive they made in their hurried departure, Ann decided.

She had made up her mind that she would call Tom Cates at the Sheriff's office and tell him about these fellows, just in case they were the bad apples she presumed. Just as she approached the phone, Frank and Addie were pulling in the back drive. She hurried outside to meet them and tell them of her recent encounter. Addie got quite nervous when Ann described the truck.

"Frank! That truck was pulling into Frances Edwards' drive as we drove by. Remember you commented it could use a paint job?"

Frank burst out, "And you said it was one you'd never seen before. I'll run down there and check it out. If they're as skittish as Ann says, just the sight of a man driving up should scare them off." He quickly got into his car and headed back towards the Edwards' house on the way to town.

"Oh, Ann. We'd better call Tom," Addie cried, clutching her purse to her chest. "I'm so afraid Frank will get hurt."

"Well, I'd honestly worry more about those fellows than Frank, if I were you. Frank is one guy who can really take care of himself," was Ann's response. Nonetheless, she ran into the house and dialed the Sheriff's number, glad that Addie had the foresight to post it near the phone for ready access. She asked the deputy who answered her call if Tom Cates was on duty. When informed that he was not, she quickly explained their suspicions. She then gave him details of the last sighting of the truck, adding that Frank had gone there and described him and their car, adding "Tom Cates knows Frank."

"Can you stop him from going there?" the deputy asked. "The descriptions match two bad dudes who have already harmed at least six elderly folks. Especially with the Kentucky plate and type of vehicle."

"No, I have no way, other than to call the Edwards' residence. The elapsed time causes us to believe they had already gained entry. Frank can take care of himself, I firmly believe." Ann wished she had called the law enforcement office sooner, before Frank and Addie had returned.

"We're on our way, Ma'am. Meanwhile I suggest y'all lock all your doors and don't open them to anyone you don't know." The haste in which the deputy disconnected the call led Ann to believe help was indeed on the way.

Several miles down the road, Frank was just knocking at Frances Edwards' door. He willed himself to look as meek and mild as he could and to fake a limp and slow steps as he approached the door making himself appear as a man in his eighties. His white hair and shaggy white eyebrows added to the deception, if one didn't peer into his face and spot his smooth skin. He had the presence of mind to carry one of the small bags of groceries Adelaide had bought while in town. With this new chain of events, they had been left in the car.

His ears still smarted with the recollection of a remark aimed at him which he had overheard while shopping with Addie in town.

"Carpetbagger," a local had snorted. "Living down here on Easy Street."

Frank hadn't heard another's reply. "I don't think it's too easy. Haven't you seen all the improvements he's made out at the Rainer place? You ought to drive by and have a peek. You'd change your tune, if you knew."

Frank's taste for justice and excitement overrode his anger at the recollection of the overheard remark and he concentrated on the task at hand. The older 'scruffy' as Ann had described him, answered the door.

"What do you want?" the man snapped, peering around Frank to see if he was alone.

Frank saw a reflected image from the next room in a mirror on the wall as he pushed his way into the room. Instinctively, he sized up the situation as he took in the picture of the younger man holding his hand over Mrs. Edwards' mouth, while pinning her to a chair with his other arm. Frank sensed, more than saw, the terror in the woman's eyes as she weakly sat in her captor's clasp. Frank realized that she couldn't know that he was not part of this gang.

The older of the two intruders seemed to become aware that Frank knew things were not as they should be so Frank sprang into action. Unaware of the true danger involved, his body responded as if he had trained his whole life for this moment. He shoved the bag of groceries into the face of the nearest intruder. The fellow called to his companion for help to overpower this old guy, as he got the idea that this was not going to be as easy as he had first thought.

With a hasty threat to his elderly prisoner, the younger man ran to grasp one of Frank's arms as his companion grabbed the other.

This is too easy, Frank thought, slacking off slightly on his resistance, making his two attackers believe the same thing. Frank finally decided the ruckus was probably too upsetting to the old lady cowering in the next room and decided to put an end to the fight. He moved both arms together as if to clap his hands. The two would-be captors, both with unbelieving wide-eyed expressions on their faces, smashed heads and dropped limply to the floor. Frank snatched up the telephone cord lying where the intruders had ripped it from the wall, rendering the phone useless. He used the cord to tie the two back to back, only binding their arms. He sort of hoped they'd regain consciousness and just TRY to make a dash for it, adding to the pleasure of the game. He felt more vital, more alive than he had felt in a long time.

Now his thoughts turned to concern for Mrs. Edwards. She had crawled to the door where she sat leaning against the door casement with a disbelieving look in her eyes.

As she slowly assessed what had happened, she too felt more life arising in her veins as she viewed the satisfactory ending to what could have had tragic results.

A team of deputies arrived, relieved to see the hard work already accomplished, yet doubting that this old guy had captured the two men single-handedly.

Just as they were escorting the two fugitives into separate patrol cars, Tom Cates drove up in his personal automobile.

"Frank," he called. "You okay? I was having a coffee break at the Diner when I saw these cars head out this-a-way. I figured they'd need my help even though it was my day off."

"Yeah, I'm all right, Tom. Better give these boys a few aspirins, though."

"You know this feller, Tom?" asked one of his fellow officers.

"Uh-huh. This is Frank Flanders from Addie Rainer's place. Fellow who tuned my bike."

Today's escapade would be the topic of conversation for quite a while, especially when they repeated Frank's calm response when Tom informed him of the duo's past crimes and dangerous reputation.

"I just taught them that it don't pay to tug on Superman's cape." Frank commented dryly.

CHAPTER TWENTY·ONE

A Tour for Teddy

*F*rank took his leave to return to Rainer Manor to assure Ann and Addie that everything turned out well. Addie had been beside herself fretting about Frank's welfare and Ann had found it hard to reassure her although she felt sure Frank could take care of himself. They had worried too, about Frances Edwards, Addie's neighbor.

It was with great relief that they heard the car horn as Frank pulled into the drive. Tom Cates wasn't too far behind him.

The ladies were abuzz with questions, which the men answered, reassuring them Mrs. Edwards was fine in spite of being roughed up. Tom told them one of the deputies was to remain with her at the emergency room until her daughter's arrival.

"Emergency room?" questioned Addie.

"Just a precaution, Addie. They want to be sure everything's okay. Figured it'd calm her to be out of the house while they get it straightened up and get the phone reconnected." Tom explained.

"They ripped it out," Frank answered the questioning look Ann gave him.

"And Frank used the cord to bind them old boys up!" was Tom's gleeful comment. "After those boys put their heads together and agreed to give up."

"I bet they put their heads together." Ann said dryly, then added, "With a little help from our friend here."

"Just a little," Frank modestly agreed.

"Hey! Why don't we all run up to the Steakhouse for supper tonight? We'll pick you up. Addie, you and Glen will join us. Hate to leave you home alone after such a day. I'll call Glen."

Addie just stood there confused. Ann led her into the house and sat her down at the kitchen table.

"Addie, are you all right? It's been such a scare for you, I know."

"I'll be all right. I was just afraid for Frank, and myself. Ann, suppose y'all had never come to stay here? I would have been here alone.. I might not have been so lucky as Frances was today."

"But we ARE here, Addie. Why don't I make us a cup of tea to settle us down." She filled the teakettle and put it on the burner, then went to see if Tom and Frank wanted to join them for tea or coffee. They opted for the latter so she returned to the kitchen and made coffee.

When the men came in, Tom went to the phone prepared to call Glen when Frank told him that Glen was just driving in. Addie went to the door to greet him. They could read the concern on his face as he embraced Addie.

"I...I heard there was t...trouble over this-a-way," he stammered. "Addie, I was so worried about you."

"I was never in any danger, Glen. But I shudder to think what could have been if Frank and Ann had not come to be here with me. What will I do when they go?" she cried.

"We'll work out something, Addie. Don't you fret." Glen comforted her. He turned to Tom. "What happened here? I just heard there was trouble, but no details."

Tom filled him in on the recent events, while Ann poured their hot beverages. By the time their cups were ready to be refilled, their jangled nerves were soothed. Tom and Frank were embellishing their story in a manner to amuse rather than scare. A few smiles were seen on the ladies' faces and Glen grinned broadly several times.

"I'm glad you gave 'em one for us good old boys, Frank," remarked Glen appreciatively.

"I was just about to call you, Glen, to see if y'all wanted to join us in dinner at the steakhouse tonight. I figured Frank's earned a steak after all he's been through today."

"I guess I'd like that," replied Glen. "Addie, do you feel up to it?"

"I might, after I take a little rest. Frank, will that make me as strong as you are?" Addie quipped.

The others laughed in relief to see Addie beginning to relax after all the excitement.

"If my gal's willing to go, then we will." Glen left no doubt as to who his gal was as he rested an arm across Addie's shoulder.

"Missy and I will pick y'all up here 'bout six," stated Tom. "See y'all then," he called as he went out the door. Glen left for home shortly after.

"Daylight or not, I'm taking a rest, too!" declared Ann when the visitors had departed.

While the residents of Rainer Manor were napping, Tom and Missy were not. They placed several phone calls; one to Lillian Perkins who then set her informal telecommunications network in motion and a plot was hatched.

To her credit, Addie was the first to rouse from her nap. Her resiliency was to be admired.

Ann arose next and the two set about making soup and sandwiches for lunch. Frank was up before it became necessary to call him to lunch.

It was quieter than usual at the table. Addie was deep in thought. Frank was prone to talk about the morning's episode, but did not because of the upset it might cause Addie.

Ann did make the remark, "This will teach those crooks not to mess around these parts. There may be snow on the roof, but...."

Frank interrupted her. "I doubt that saying fits this situation, Ann."

"Oh, I guess you're right." She was a bit dismayed at her near slip of the tongue.

"I can't believe that you'll soon be leaving," worried Addie.

"Not until the 5th of next month," said Ann. "If the weather is still bad up there, we'll stay longer."

"It's still 3 – 4 weeks away," comforted Frank.

"Wh..what are your plans for next winter? Do you reckon you might come back here? I was thinking, maybe I won't give all the acreage to the Society. Then if y'all didn't want to stay at the big house, you might like a little one built down there? I'd sure like for y'all to come back here."

"Addie, that's sweet of you to suggest that. I expect we will be back. The climate and people suit us just fine. Isn't that right, Frank?"

"Don't worry, Addie. I think we'll most likely be back here in November. We'll be in the area and will see you often. As to where we'll stay, we'll cross that bridge then. I COULD build a small two-bedroom cottage down there," pondered Frank. "It might be a good idea to be able to overlook the farm sites. Addie, would you prefer to live here in the big house or would you like a smaller one, if you had your choice?"

"I hadn't really thought about it, Frank. I guess I never believed I had any other course than here or an old folk's home."

"Things have been really moving fast around here, haven't they, Addie? You'll have to rest up over the summer for another whirlwind winter. I guess we've stirred up a lot of activity that will carry through the summer to make it pass faster." Ann said, soothingly.

"I will endure it better if I know my two good friends were coming back."

A light tap was heard at the kitchen door. Ann opened it, disclosing a white-faced Teddy Bisbo.

"Why come in, Teddy. Would you like a soda? Have you had your lunch?"

Teddy entered looking quickly around the room. "Oh, there you are, Mr. Flanders! I was down to the gas station and they said you was in a fight with two guys. Are you okay?"

"I'm fine, Teddy." Frank was touched by Teddy's concern.

"You oughta see the other guys," laughed Ann.

"Well, you do look okay," said Teddy with relief. "Wisht I was there to help," he said bravely, but tears welled up in his eyes. Ann went over to him and gave him a big bear hug.

"I know you would have been a great help. When I see all you two accomplished together around here, I guess your teamwork would have made an even quicker end to it."

"I was sure wishing I had time to get an extra hand," remarked Frank. "Everything happened pretty fast."

Teddy was full of questions which Frank answered willingly. The two strolled outside to give Teddy a close look at the silhouette horse Glen had made. Frank was making an attempt to reassure Teddy that things were normal at the Rainer house. Teddy hung closely to Frank, shadowing his every move. Ann peered out the window and then motioned for Addie to look at the man and boy.

"Teddy's going to miss Frank, too, Addie."

"No doubt about that." Addie agreed. "Me and him will have to console one another."

Outside, Frank decided he'd better give Teddy an advance warning and not wait until the last minute to let him know of the Flanders' impending departure.

"Next winter when we get back from up North, I may have a real big project I'll be looking for your help on."

"Wh..when you heading north?" Teddy's voice quavered.

"Not for three or four weeks yet. What's that long face?"

"I didn't know it'd be so soon."

"That's still a long ways off, Teddy. Now! I don't believe you saw the display the ladies did inside. How about if I give you the grand tour?" offered Frank.

"Will Miz Addie mind?"

"I'm sure she won't, but I'll ask her to be polite."

Teddy waited out by the buggy while Frank went to check with Addie. He returned quickly.

"Teddy, I'd like to show you Tom's Harley." Frank directed him to where the motorcycle was kept.

"She didn't want me traipsing through the house, did she?" Teddy asked hesitantly. Frank thought 'sharp kid' to recognize his delay tactic, even though for the wrong reason.

"No, she said it was fine. It's just that I was afraid I'd forget to show you this and I knew you were dying to get a close look at it."

"Wow! Them things look a whole lot bigger, close up! Hope I can get one when I get a job!"

Frank pointed out all the features of the machine and took the opportunity to give Teddy some riding tips, as well as care and maintenance pointers. His confident manner gave Teddy assurance that Frank had no doubt but that someday Teddy would become the proud owner of such a fine vehicle.

After they looked it all over, they headed towards the house. Ann greeted them. Addie was not in sight. It bothered Teddy that she wasn't around. He liked Miz Addie and wondered if he had done something to offend her.

Ann showed Teddy the library and helped him research the house he lived in to see who lived there years ago.

"Who owns it now, Teddy?" Ann asked and as soon as she did, regretted it for fear of sounding too nosy.

"My Mama does," Teddy answered. This surprised Frank and Ann as they had just assumed the Bisbo's rented.

Next the three ascended the wide staircase. Teddy seemed awed by the massive surroundings, and made frequent comments.

"Why, I didn't know this place was so big!"

They went to the room where the chaise lounge was. Teddy was taken by how real the mannequin looked, until he stepped closer. As they viewed the room, Ann pointed out the various items of interest. They proceeded to the next bedroom where a figure reclined in bed. Teddy drew back.

"Someone's sleeping in there," he whispered.

"It's just a dummy," Frank assured him. "Go see."

Teddy approached the bed tentatively. He looked like he was afraid of the figure.

"It's okay, you can touch it," offered Ann, whereupon Teddy did so.

"Kinda scary, is it, Teddy?" Frank asked kindly.

"Yeah, I guess it *is* spooky-like." Teddy ventured.

As they headed to the third bedroom, Teddy spotted the figure seated in the alcove seat.

"THAT lady looks real, too, don't she?" he looked quizzically at Frank. Frank gave him a wink in reply. Teddy looked again, then said to Ann, "This was nice, thank you for showing me your display."

"Oh, we're not done yet, Teddy," said Ann, continuing on to the third bedroom.

They entered the room where a costume-clad figure sat at a dressing table. Ann was telling him about the old time featherbeds and four poster beds as they walked towards the desk.

The figure at the desk slowly turned.

"Welcome to Rainer Manor, Teddy Bisbo."

Teddy burst out laughing. "Miz Addie, you sure fooled me."

"Not for long, Teddy. Be honest, did Frank warn you what we were up to?" Ann questioned.

"Oh no. I didn't let on," sputtered Frank.

"To tell the truth, I was suspicious of the lady at the bookcase seat, she looked so real. I remembered you said you only had six figures. There were three in the buggy, one in bed, one on the lounge chair and one in the seat. I wasn't sure if you got some more someplace or not, but I decided I was gonna be on my guard."

"Well, you're a sharp young-un." Addie said admiringly, adding, "Just for being so alert, you get a prize." She led the way to the last bedroom.

"When Addie opened the door, Teddy's eyes widened at the sight of the toys. He circled the room, looking at each in turn.

Addie said generously, "Teddy, you may have your pick of any toy in here."

Ann swallowed a gasp, but did not interfere.

Teddy immediately selected a baby doll, one of the more modest objects in the room.

"Teddy," Ann asked gently, "How did you decide so fast which one to take?"

"My little sister will love it. She has an old rag doll but she'll just love this baby," he explained.

"How old is your sister?" asked Ann.

"She's four. She's a good little gal," he answered.

Addie rummaged in one of the cupboards under the seat. "Here," she said, handing a box to Teddy. "You may take the doll to your sister, but I want you to have this for you. You deserve it." Ann detected the glint of tears in Addie's eyes as she spoke, though Addie quickly turned to hide them.

"Anyway, Teddy, I'm glad we didn't scare you," commented Ann. "We may have stunted your growth."

"This would make a good haunted house for Halloween," suggested Teddy.

"Now there's a good idea!" Frank exclaimed. "A lot could be done with that theme."

"A mixture of mannequins and live people dressed in period clothes! Buggy rides and hay rides! Old time games like dunking for apples, with cider and donuts for refreshments," cried Ann enthusiastically.

"We'll keep it in mind, Teddy," assured Addie.

"Let's see what you have there, Teddy," asked Frank

Teddy held out the box so they could see the game Addie had given him. It was one they recognized as a long popular game, editions of which could still be purchased. The prime condition it was in made it a valuable article.

"That's a fine gift, Teddy." Frank told the boy as they all headed back down-stairs. "It's quite valuable. You could probably sell it to a dealer and have enough money to buy a new game AND a new bike."

"I wouldn't sell this game Miz Addie gave me for anything," responded Teddy.

"Teddy, I gave it to you for you to do what you want with it. If you can sell it and make some money, I wouldn't begrudge you that. I would be happy you could benefit from it." Addie told Teddy, "Now let's have that soda."

They sat at the kitchen table to enjoy their beverages. Frank and Ann were delighted that Addie and Teddy were becoming fast friends. This would help to fill the void when they headed north.

"Teddy," began Addie. "Can I count on you to work for me, mowing lawns and raking leaves for me this summer? I'll need a good hand around here."

"Yes, Ma'am, I'd like that fine," replied Teddy respectfully.

"Good, that's settled. All I need now is to find me a good woman to do my heavy housework and I'm all set."

When Teddy finished his soda and set his glass on the table, he asked Addie, "Miz Addie, could y'all write me a note to give my Mama telling her about y'all giving me them toys? I don't want her to worry none."

"No, we don't want her to worry. I've a better idea. You run along home and we'll bring them down to you. I'll tell your momma in person that I give them to you. Just tell her we'll be along."

Teddy exited hurriedly with this news. "See y'all!" he called back.

"Frank, you don't mind running us down there, do you?" asked Addie.

"No problem," replied Frank. The ladies went to get their coats while Frank went out to start the car.

As they drove down the lane, Addie remarked, "I'm ashamed to say I've never been neighborly to the Bisboes. I remember when they moved down there. Tom Cates told me who it was. I believe he said she was a widow."

"I wondered if she was. I've only seen her once. When we went down to ask about Teddy working with Frank. She seemed like a nice person. Looked like she sure worked hard. They keep a few chickens and a goat, if I remember correctly," said Ann.

"I wonder how she makes ends meet," marveled Addie. "You think you have it tough until you hear 'bout someone worse off.'"

"Here we are!" announced Frank, as he turned into the grassed-over drive. "And here's Teddy."

Teddy was eagerly awaiting their arrival. He had told his mother they were coming. She was anxious as to why, but Teddy's anticipation assured her there was a pleasant reason for the visit.

He led the visitors into the little house where he resided with his mother and sister. It was sparsely furnished but neat and clean. The living quarters were L-shaped. A small kitchen in the back, dining area in the front corner with the living room across the front of the house to the opposite corner. There were three doors off the L. The first, off the kitchen, led to a pantry. The other two, from the living room end, apparently led to two bedrooms.

Mrs. Bisbo was just wiping her hands at the sink. They noted the water source was a hand pump. Frank hadn't missed the small structure behind the house next to a little barn. From his childhood days, he recognized an outhouse when he saw one and remembered the days when he had endured the cold to make the mad dash down that path. For the first four years of his marriage to Ann, there had been such a structure behind their home, too. It made them appreciate the wondrous luxury of indoor plumbing even more.

"Hello, Miz Rainer, Miz Flanders, Mr. Flanders. Welcome to our house. May I offer y'all some tea?"

"That would be pleasant," replied Addie.

"Yes, please," responded Ann.

"None for me, thanks. Teddy's offered to introduce me to Nanny goat." Frank and Teddy left the ladies to their woman-talk.

"Did Teddy tell you about Frank's adventure today?" Ann began the conversation.

"Yes, he did. He was all excited about it." Mrs. Bisbo peered from Ann to Addie, quizzically.

"Teddy stopped this morning to ask about Frank and we give him the grand tour of the house." Addie began by way of explanation.

"We had it all set up with mannequins dressed in old-fashioned clothing. We did it for the Historical Society meeting last week." Ann interjected.

"Yes, he told me about that." Mrs. Bisbo waited for the rest.

"Well, I've grown fond of Teddy," Addie spoke softly. "I've never had any of my own. You've done a fine job of raising him." She paused, then continued, "One room is a playroom and I give Teddy the choice of any toy in the place." Addie turned and motioned for Ann to finish for her.

"He selected a toy for his sister, instead of himself, so Addie selected a game for him. We decided to bring them over so he wouldn't have to try to carry them on his bike. We wanted you to know that the game is his to do as he wants. It's a very early edition and in fine shape so if he wanted to sell it to a collector, he could buy a new game for himself and have money left over. Of course, years from now, it will be worth even more."

Mrs. Bisbo was speechless.

"Well spoken, Ann. Couldn't have said it better myself." Addie praised her.

"Thank you, Miz Rainer." Mrs. Bisbo found words to express her appreciation.

"Call me Addie."

"My name is Thelma," Mrs. Bisbo said shyly.

"Thelma, that's a pretty name. I'm Ann and of course, my husband's name is Frank." Ann said as they were joined by Frank and Teddy who were just coming in the house by the back door. Teddy carried a paper bag containing the toys.

"Ma-Ma, I'm awake," came a voice from one of the other rooms.

"Get up, then, Mary," the mother spoke kindly. "Teddy, will you bring her out, please?" Teddy did as his mother requested. He returned leading his sister to the table where the visitors sat.

"I told Mary we had company," he said as they approached. "Mary, these are my friends, Mr. and Miz Flanders and Miz Rainer."

"Hello," the child responded, wide-eyed.

"Hello, Mary," the visitors chorused.

"Teddy, why don't you give her what you selected for her?" Addie's suggestion pleased Teddy. He reached into the bag and brought out the baby doll. The delight in the child's eyes rewarded the visitors for the time they had taken to bring the toys in person.

"Is THAT for ME?" Mary asked unbelievingly.

"Yes, it's from Teddy," Addie said generously.

"Thank you, Teddy." Mary turned to her mother and asked "Is it my birthday?"

"No, dear, not just yet." Thelma answered. "Soon though," then turning to Addie, "I can't thank you enough for your kindness to Teddy. And y'all, too," she addressed the Flanders.

"Teddy's a fine boy." Frank tried to sound gruff.

"Teddy says you hired him for lawn work, this summer?" It was more a question to Addie than a statement.

"Yes. Ann and Frank are heading north soon. I'll sorely miss them but Teddy will be a great help to me. All I need now is to find me a lady to help me with my housework and I'll be set."

"I'll be glad to give you a hand, anytime." Thelma said tentatively.

"Could you? Pay's not great, but I'll try to make up for it in other ways. Mary can come with you."

"I didn't mean for wages. I mean to get a job when Mary gets in school."

"I insist to pay you. It would be a blessing to me to have someone I trust in my house."

"I thank you kindly, Miz Addie. It sure would help out. Not to burden you with my tale of woe, but it's been a tight squeak since we bought this place. I didn't want to raise my young'uns in the city, so I gambled on this."

"However do you manage?" asked Addie.

"You do what you have to do," replied Thelma.

"Is there anything you need?" asked Ann. "What can we do to help?" She felt inadequate. Obviously, there was a lot one could do to help, but it was just as obvious Thelma wasn't one to take a hand-out.

"We are self-sufficient." Thelma explained proudly.

"Ann's quite expert at saving money," Addie said. "She's taught me a thing or two, believe me."

"Just the usual stuff, cents-off coupons, rebates, buying generic." Ann stated.

"Don't be modest, Ann. This lovely coat I have is one she got for me over in Afton at the Salvation Army Shop." Addie fingered the lapel of her coat.

Thelma displayed interest in the garment. She turned to Ann and asked about the other types of items one could buy there. "I know about those shops, didn't realize they had any around here. That coat looks like brand new."

They made small talk for a while longer, then the visitors made their departure amid mutual invitations to visit. Mary held her baby doll closely, waving goodbye.

After they left, Mrs. Bisbo hugged her children to her side, telling Teddy, "Your friends are real nice, Teddy. I'm proud they speak so highly of you." Teddy's beam of joy told his mother all he felt at that moment.

CHAPTER TWENTY-TWO

A Hero's Reward

*O*n the ride home, Addie expressed what they were all thinking. "She's a proud lady, very independent. I'm glad we went down there."

"Teddy was really happy that we did," Ann responded.

As soon as they arrived home, Frank announced that since they were going out for dinner that evening, he was going to kick back for the second time that day. Addie expressed concern to Ann.

"Do you s'pose he's hurt himself?"

"No, I'm used to this. If he doesn't have a project going, he frequently will lie down for a while. He catches a few winks and he's raring to go. He conserves his energy and so when he really needs it, his energy level is high. I wouldn't fret about him, Addie. That was child's play for him this morning."

"I guess he's got the right idea. I believe I will rest a bit too, Ann."

"Should I be concerned, Addie? Are YOU feeling all right?" Ann chided her, then relenting, admitted, "It sounds like a wise thing to do. I think I'll sit and write some letters, myself."

Ann got her notepaper and busied herself at her correspondence. She enjoyed writing letters although she had seldom written to anyone other than immediate family since she had been in

Tennessee. It did not bother her that the people she wrote to did not answer each and every letter. She realized writing letters did not come so easily to some others as it did to her. Her mother had this gift and Ann had naturally followed suit. If you were a friend of Ann's, you could be assured that if she thought of something she wanted to share with you, you'd hear from her. There was so much to share. Living at Rainer Manor, the visit to Bessie, the trip to get the mannequins, the lovely motorcycle ride, the preparations for, and the Historical Society meeting, the house at 100 Acres, and now, Frank's adventure at Frances Edwards' house this morning. She almost wished she had a computer or word processor at her disposal so she could type it once and print as many copies as she desired, adding a handwritten, personal note to the report she would prepare. It would certainly save quite a bit of repetitious writing, she knew.

The time passed quickly for her, as she became engrossed in writing the letters. She was surprised to see how late it was getting. She stopped writing and went to shower. When she finished she woke up Frank so he could do the same.

Addie had taken a short nap and decided to write her sister. She covered many of the same topics Ann had. She called out to Ann when she heard her in the hall.

"Ann, I can't spell manakin."

"M-A-N-N-E-Q-U-I-N," Ann came to the door of Addie's room where Addie sat in a chair at the window, writing. "I had to look it up myself, just now."

Ann was intrigued by the lap-desk Addie was using. The solid flat top was held in a practical writing position by a weighted cushion, which was contoured to rest comfortably on one's lap. Ann had never seen one up close before but had admired a similar lap-desk in a gift catalog she had received in the mail quite a while ago.

"I'm taking your lead," Addie commented.

"If I knew you were awake, I wouldn't have called Frank yet." Ann apologized.

"That's all right, don't fret about it. When he's done, I'll have plenty of time." That is what she did. By the time six o'clock rolled around, the three residents of Rainer Manor were dressed and waiting for Tom and Missy to pick them up. Glen's daughter-in-law, Brenda, dropped him off a few minutes before six.

A car was heard to pull in the front drive. Its arrival was heralded by a melodious horn blast. The waiting group moved towards the front entrance. Frank arrived at the door ahead of the others and opened it.

"What on earth? Are we expecting the President or the Governor?" He asked. Ann was quickly at his side with Glen and Addie close behind. They peered out the door and were astounded at the sight they beheld.

Sitting in the drive was a black stretch limousine. A uniformed chauffeur got out of the driver's seat and came around to open the back door, where Missy and Tom sat in luxurious comfort with broad smiles.

"Hop in, celebrity!" Tom welcomed Frank and motioned for the others to get in also. Ann scurried inside the house to get Addie and her own evening bags and to lock up the house. She was glad they had decided to dress up for dinner.

"Well, this is a thrill for us!" cried Ann as she returned to the limo and climbed in. Addie and Glen chimed in their agreement.

Tom broke open a chilled bottle of raspberry ginger ale and poured them each a cool, bubbly, long-stemmed glass of the soda.

"I remembered y'all didn't drink, so I substituted this," explained Tom.

"Excellent year, Tom," Frank quipped. "I'm really honored that you went all out on my behalf."

"Frank, it's just a token of the esteem the people in Peckville and surrounding area hold you in. Have you seen the news reports?"

"No, we never turned the TV or radio on," replied Frank.

"I taped it on my VEE-CEE-ARE. I'm surprised they didn't come looking for you." Tom winked at Glen. Frank apparently didn't see this, but Ann did. She decided to just sit back and enjoy herself.

As the limo continued the drive to the Steakhouse, the group of friends chattered away and polished off their liquid refreshments, drinking toasts to Frank and each other, friendship, Tennessee, New York State, the South and the North. They thoroughly enjoyed this mode of transportation which allowed everyone to visit including the men, at least one of whom usually would be driving. The rear seats faced each other to facilitate conversation between the occupants. Six was the optimum number of occupants and all had plenty of room.

"Tom, I didn't know Peckville had a limo rental agency," commented Ann.

"It don't," Missy broke in. "Tom's friend helped him arrange it."

"See the deer," Tom interrupted. "Oops, there they go!" Everyone craned their neck to look towards the spot Tom pointed at. Missy shoved him as if he was fooling them.

"Oh you!" she exclaimed, but then changed the subject to the planned Historical Society open house.

"Everyone I've talked to is real interested in it. Word's got out what a nice meeting they had there and Lil Perkins said considerable interest has been generated for the Society, too!"

The limo arrived at their destination and pulled up to the door.

"Good thing you made reservations, Tom," commented Missy. "This place is packed!"

"I'm glad we don't have to find a parking place, either." Glen said. "Don't believe I've ever seen it so full."

"Probably Chamber of Commerce night," suggested Tom, adding, "They won't bother us none. They meet in their own room."

He led the way into the foyer. The restaurant was a huge log cabin and all the interior beams were smooth, highly polished wood. The décor was Western traditional with wagon wheel chandeliers and huge steer heads in every room. Everything looked massive and well cared for.

Tom gave his name to the hostess, who met their group, explaining that they had reservations.

"I'm sorry, Sir. The party at your table hasn't left yet. If y'all step into the lounge over yonder, we'll be happy to serve y'all free or'deuvres and drinks. It won't be long?"

The group moved in the direction she indicated with Tom first, Frank next, the rest following. As they entered the next room, Tom stepped aside allowing Frank to enter where he was greeted by thunderous applause. The room held about fifty people whose attention was riveted on Frank. He hesitated, started to turn as if to escape but the others formed a wall behind him forcing him to enter the dining hall and receive the accolades presented to him. Some of those present were people who were members of the Historical Society, while Ann also recognized Peckville business owners. Everyone had nametags adhered to their jackets or dresses. Lil Perkins came over with nametags for the new arrivals. Frank's simply read "HERO", while Ann's said "ANN, WIFE OF HERO."

"Lil, however did you get this together on such short notice?" Ann exclaimed.

In answer to Ann's question, Lil said, "Oh we have our ways. Pretty good grape-vine we got us, don't y'all think?"

"Well, I guess so!" Ann replied.

A flurry of activity at the dining room entrance heralded the arrival of a television crew from Nashville. Frank dutifully stood where directed and agreeably answered their questions.

"He must be in shock," Ann whispered to Missy and Addie. "He never expected such publicity or to be honored like this."

After the news interview was completed, Tom ushered Frank to the head table and motioned for Ann to follow. Frank was seated next to the town's mayor, Dan Nolan. Tom's boss, Sheriff John Wilson sat at one end of the head table next to the Mayor's wife, June, with Ann seated on the opposite end. At a round table immediately in front of where Frank and Ann sat, were Tom, Missy, Addie, Glen, Lil and her escort. The remaining people were seated at other round tables placed around the room. Some other people entered until there were about 60 in attendance.

"Frank, I promised you a steak dinner," laughed Tom. "Here it is!" The meal was served family style with platters of steak and chicken, serving dishes of mashed potatoes, gravy, steak fries, corn and green bean casserole. There were plenty of rolls and relishes. Everyone dug in and enjoyed the generous spread.

Even the TV crew were seated and fed. Dessert was served to all with refills of coffee. At this time, Mayor Nolan, Master of Ceremony, stood and addressed the assemblage.

"Y'all know what brings us together this evening. We're here to honor Frank Flanders who this morning single-handedly captured two criminals who have been terrorizing elderly people in their homes across two states before coming to this area. Thanks to Mr. Flanders, that's where they made their mistake. So we got us together tonight to expediently show our appreciation." Turning to Frank, he went on to say, "Mr. Flanders, we thank you for your heroic efforts and want to tell you we are honored to call you 'neighbor'. That's a fine job you did at the Rainer house, too." Frank stood up and the mayor shook his hand. The audience broke into applause. Frank started to sit back down, but the M.C. asked him to remain standing a while longer.

"Mr. Wilkinson, I believe y'all had a few words to say." As a portly gentleman worked his way to the podium, Mr. Nolan introduced him, "B. C. Wilkinson, our county legislator." Polite applause accompanied his arrival at the speaker's stand.

"Mister Flanders and other honored guests, Ladies and Gentlemen, it is with great pleasure that I present to Frank Flanders, this $5000 reward that was established for the person causing the apprehension and arrest of these desperados which met their match in our fair county today." He handed Frank a check as he shook Frank's hand.

"I…I don't know what to say. This is certainly a big surprise to me. I'm just glad that I got there in time to prevent serious injury to Mrs. Edwards. Ann and I want to thank you all for your kindness to us and now, for this, too!" He waved the check and quickly sat down.

Tom Cates said with a grin, "You spoke well, Frank, for someone who had nothing to say."

Mayor Nolan spoke up and said, "There'll be music for your listening and dancing so don't hurry off, folks." Everyone laughed because no one was rushing off. They just were enjoying visiting with one another. People got up and table-hopped with everyone stopping at the head table and speaking to those seated there.

When the band began playing, among those who danced were Tom and Missy. Before the evening drew to a close, even Glen and Addie, as well as Frank and Ann, took a spin or two around the dance floor.

It was just a few moments before midnight when the limousine was summoned for the return trip to Rainer Manor. They proceeded to the Adams' residence first to deposit Glen at his door, then retraced their way to Rainer Road.

"Tom, thank you for all you've done. I feel like 'King for a Day'." stated Frank as the limo drove up to Addie's door.

"Frank, it was my pleasure. Not all my idea either. They wanted a forum to present you with the reward money. You're a celebrity and you deserve it."

"Thanks again. Goodnight Tom, Missy." He called as the limo pulled away from the house. Ann and Addie's voices blended with his as Tom and Missy returned their goodnights.

"What an evening," said Ann as she slipped her shoes off. She absentmindedly turned on the TV just as the late report was being given.

"Frank, Addie, look!" Frank and Addie both came to where they could see the TV. There was Frank, being interviewed and the reward check presentation, following a brief news item telling what had happened at Mrs. Edwards' home earlier that day.

"I wonder if this is nation-wide," commented Ann.

"Oh, I doubt that. Probably just a local newscast item," was Frank's response.

"I declare, I've never been in the limelight like this before. See, Ann! There we are!" Addie pointed to the screen.

"I see, Addie and there – big as life – is Glen Adams, with his arm around some lady." Ann pointed to the same image, while Addie blushed, sputtered and good-naturedly stomped off to bed.

"I SURE HOPE it ain't nationwide," she was heard to mutter as the door to her bedroom was closed.

CHAPTER TWENTY-THREE

Adventuresome Addie

*F*rank arose before Ann or Addie so he decided he'd do the breakfast honors. He was a good cook and didn't mind making a meal now and then. Ann would tell you that she appreciated this talent, especially during her pregnancies. Eating didn't really bother her then, just the smell of food cooking, so it helped tremendously to arrive home from her work to find the table set and the food all prepared. It was handy that Frank's shift began about an hour earlier than hers, so he got home that much earlier.

The smell of coffee brewing roused the ladies with Frank's invitation following shortly after the aroma reached their rooms. Ann tumbled out of bed, ran a comb through her hair and donned a robe.

"Don't stand on ceremony, Addie, just throw on your robe. I did," she called to Addie as she passed her door.

"Or if you like, I can serve it to you on a tray," Frank good-naturedly suggested.

"Yeah. Hey Addie, would you rather have breakfast in bed?" asked Ann. A robe-clad Addie quickly emerged from her room in answer to their clowning around.

"Y'all are frisky today. Frank, you made breakfast? Looks good."

"Smells good, too, Frank," added his wife.

They settled down to their meal. As usual, Ann was done first and she arose to place her dirty dishes in the sink.

"More coffee, anyone?" Ann asked as she poured herself a second cup. The other two indicated they would have more as well.

"I'll probably miss y'all most at mealtime," Addie remarked wistfully.

"Probably because we eat almost all the time," Ann said dryly.

"Ann," Frank interrupted. "I left my hammer down at the old place. I'm gonna shoot down there on Tom's bike to get it. Addie, how about it, are you game to ride down there with me? I won't go too fast."

Addie looked at Frank as if he'd gone completely out of his mind. "You can't be serious, Frank? Why would an old lady like me want to do such a dangerous thing?"

"Because there's a first time for everything," said Ann. "Addie, you'd love it! Put on a pair of slacks and you're all set."

"I can't believe I'm saying this, but yes, I will!" Her response took both Frank and Ann by surprise. They looked at each other in amazement.

"Atta girl, Addie. I'll be real careful," promised Frank.

"I know you will, Frank. I trust you and I've seen how confident Ann is about it. I may never get such a chance again." She retreated to her room to get dressed. Once she had made up her mind to take the ride, she was really eager to do so.

Frank brought the motorcycle to the back entrance and parked it parallel to the steps. When Addie came out, Ann followed her with her helmet in hand. She adjusted the strap for Addie and fastened it on. She assisted Addie while she climbed onto the motorcycle behind Frank. Frank indicated the pegs she should rest her feet on. Addie placed her arms around his waist as Ann instructed.

"Ready, Addie?" asked Frank. When she shook her head 'yes', he twisted the throttle gently. Slowly adding power, he drove it to the end of the drive, checked to be sure nothing was coming, then took off down Rainer Lane towards the 100 Acres. Ann had her camera and was snapping pictures as they drove away.

As Frank and Addie neared the old place, they passed Teddy on his bicycle. When they pulled into the drive, Frank turned the motorcycle around and stopped in the drive between the house and barn. He removed his helmet and called to Teddy who rode up to where they were.

"Teddy, I left my hammer on the sill in the barn. Will you please get it for me so I don't have to make Addie dismount?"

After a moment of gaping at Addie, Teddy eagerly retrieved the hammer from where Frank had left it.

"Thanks, Teddy.. It's a good thing you happened along. We hadn't thought that far ahead."

"I never give it a thought, either! I owe you one, Teddy," Addie lapsed into some of Frank's slang.

"Do you suppose I could have a ride with you sometime?" Teddy asked hopefully.

"If you get your Mom's say-so, sure." Frank answered without hesitation. "Thanks again, partner."

"You're welcome!" replied Teddy, waving as the two headed back out the drive, then roared up the lane, Addie hanging on for all she was worth. She was in no danger of falling off, but to a novice, this is not readily apparent.

Frank slowed at the Bisbo's house and pulled up in front. Thelma appeared on the porch just as Frank removed his helmet.

"Hello, Mrs. Bisbo, remember us?" he called to her.

"Yes, of course, Mister Flanders," she replied.

"I wanted to ask if I could give Teddy a ride on Tom's motorcycle. I'll be real careful," he promised.

"He is a very careful operator," Addie endorsed his claim.

"Why Miz Rainer, is that you?" Thelma asked in disbelief.

Addie laughingly shook her head, clunking her helmet against Frank's head. He shook his head in mock confusion and put his helmet back on his head.

"Sorry, Frank. I ain't got the hang to this hat yet," Addie apologized.

"I guess if it's safe enough for Miz Rainer, I give my consent for Teddy to have a ride," said Thelma.

"Great, see you later," called Frank as they took off again, somewhat slower than they had departed from 100 Acres, much to Addie's relief.

They returned to the house. Ann heard the bike coming and went out to greet them. Frank circled around and came in close to the back steps for Addie to dismount. Ann steadied her as she swung her left leg off the motorcycle.

"However did you manage down there?" Ann asked.

"Teddy was nearby so he got the hammer for Frank, thank goodness!" Addie answered.

Frank stayed on the machine but shut it off and removed his helmet.

"You did real good Addie. I'm proud of you," he said admiringly.

"Well, thank YOU, Frank! I hate to admit it, but I enjoyed myself."

"I told Teddy I'd give him a ride." Frank explained to Ann.

"You checked with his mother" Ann asked him.

"Yes, Addie and I stopped. She said it was okay. Seeing Addie on here really helped to sell the idea to her."

Addie offered Frank the helmet. "Y'all need this. Where do I put it?"

"Ann, fasten it on the seat rail for me, will you?" He handed the helmet to Ann who did as he asked while he donned his own helmet again.

"See you when we get back," he said as he restarted the Harley and headed towards the Bisbo's.

Teddy was awaiting him as he rode up. "I haven't dared ask her yet," he confided in Frank as his mother appeared on the porch.

"Mr. Flanders, will you please give my boy a ride on your machine?" asked Thelma as she smiled at Teddy's confusion.

"Well, if you insist. Can we get anything for you? Bread, milk?" He offered.

"Why that would be fine, thank you." She went into the house and returned with an envelope which she handed to Teddy. "How can you carry things on that?"

"We'll manage." Frank assured her.

Teddy's excitement over his first motorcycle ride was hard to contain. While it pleased Thelma that her son and Frank had forged a bond over the past few months, she knew that Teddy would be inconsolable when the time came for the Flanders to return to their home in the North.

The man and boy headed off on their shopping trip. Teddy expected they would drive the few miles to the little combination gas station/grocery he usually rode to on his bicycle. When Frank signaled a right hand turn instead of a left at the Route 3 intersection, Teddy realized to his pleasant surprise, that the trip would extend to Peckville instead. Frank had decided he could save Thelma some money if they purchased the items in town. This would also afford Teddy a longer ride.

Frank pulled up in front of the grocery market and shut off the engine whereupon Teddy agilely dismounted and removed his helmet, handing it to Frank.

"You did that like a pro," Frank told him admiringly. "You go ahead, I'll just sit here with the bike." Teddy did as instructed. Once inside the store, he recognized the bag boy as an upperclassman who rode the same bus to school that Teddy did.

"Hello, Todd." Teddy grinned to see the reaction of his acquaintance who had seen the mode of transportation which delivered Teddy to the store.

"Hello, Teddy. That's a fine machine you're on. Good day for riding, huh?" was Todd's response to Teddy's greeting.

Teddy couldn't resist swaggering a bit as he walked past Todd, answering, "Sure is. That's the only way to travel on a day like today."

"Ain't that Mr. Flanders you're with?" Todd asked. "I saw him on TV last night."

Teddy's joy was complete when he heard the respect in Todd's voice. "Yes, that's my friend, Frank Flanders. That Harley is Tom Cates', the deputy. I 'spose you know him." Without waiting for a reply, he quickly obtained the items his mother had asked for and took his place in the express line. He soon rejoined Frank at the Harley and holding the plastic bag of groceries in one hand, he steadied himself with the other as he swung deftly onto the buddy seat behind Frank. He glanced sideways towards the store and saw that Todd's attention was riveted on the two cyclists as they prepared to ride off.

Frank, of course, was aware of Todd's interest and perhaps he gunned the motor just a bit extra as they roared off down the street. Remembering that his passenger was a novice, and heeding the promise to be careful he had made to Teddy's mother, he eased it back down to road speed. Actually, he wasn't going that fast, but taking off in the lower gear as is necessary, it gave the impression they were really 'smoking.'

The return trip seemed much too short to Teddy, but he wisely knew that his mother would be anxious about him and he was eager to share the details of this new adventure with her. He thoroughly enjoyed the attention Todd had given to him. He wouldn't have to say a word to anyone about his weekend activities since he knew Todd would take care of spreading the news about that. He simply relaxed and enjoyed the ride home. The scents of the budding flowering trees hung in the air and the sun warmed them as they motored along. Since Teddy usually was on his bicycle traveling around, he was familiar with these smells. He didn't realize that for people who traveled in enclosed vehicles most of the time, the aroma of the surrounding vegetation was one of the pleasures of motorcycling. Frank and Ann would be quick to point out to the uninitiated that there were drawbacks to this. They referred to the occasional encounter while in the vicinity of a freshly manured field, as enjoying the 'fresh country air.'

Their arrival at the Bisbo residence was greeted by Thelma and Mary's appearance on the porch. They were full of questions for Teddy and amazed that they had ventured as far as Peckville in such a short period of time. Thelma and Teddy both expressed their appreciation to Frank for his thoughtfulness, waving enthusiastic good-byes as he rode back down the lane to Addie's.

CHAPTER TWENTY-FOUR

Smoky Mountain Trip

*F*t was a lovely golden morning. One of those days when the sun beckons you to arise even though your body desires to remain in bed longer. Addie had declared she would make some sour milk pancakes for breakfast. The quantity she prepared was more than the three of them could eat at a sitting, but they made a good attempt to clean them up. While enjoying their breakfast they began to rehash some of their activities over the past few months. Addie spoke of the satisfaction she found in the visit with her sister.

"I can't get over it! I should have taken a bus trip to go see Bessie years ago. It just seemed so far away. Now it was like no time and we were there. These new highways seem like something from the future. When you've been stuck in one place as long as I have and haven't seen the building of new roads, they make you think they've appeared out of nowhere." Addie almost gushed out this statement, adding, "In your words, Ann, you two have really broadened my horizons."

"Let me know when you get ready to travel again, Addie," said Frank. "I have another trip planned for the three of us. It won't be overnight, probably." Seeing he had piqued their interest, he continued, "It would retrace one of our drives, Ann, but it's worth seeing again."

Ann nodded agreement, as the hints he had dropped were all she felt she needed to know to figure out the destination of the planned trip.

Addie seemed quite eager to start out whenever Frank and Ann wanted to. Their car was comfortable. If Frank stopped as often as Ann did so she could stretch her legs, she could see no reason they could not take that trip. Certainly, Frank had been working so hard; it would give him a much-needed rest.

"Do you want to go today?" asked Addie.

"Today?" Ann expressed surprise. "Are you sure you feel up to it?"

"Yes," said Addie, "if y'all like, I'm game."

"That's fine with me," was Ann's reply. "Frank?"

"Hey, if you two are willing, let's go!"

Within the hour, the dishes were done, snacks and a thermos of hot coffee were packed. Ann tucked the goodies carefully in a little brown insulated kit. On the side of the zippered bag was emblazoned 'Survival Kit". Addie recognized it as one Ann had taken on the trip to see Bessie. Inside were individual serving packets of coffee, tea, sugar, powered creamer, sugar substitute, as well as matches, a candle, Band-Aids and aspirins. It also contained a coiled electric gadget that was used to heat water for hot drinks.

At Ann's suggestion, they decided to take an overnight bag for each in the event they strayed further away than planned and didn't get back home that day as expected. Addie called the Adams' residence and left a message to tell Glen about their trip so he wouldn't get concerned if he stopped by or called in their absence.

The three stowed their bags in the trunk of the Flanders' Buick. Frank checked the oil, water, transmission and windshield washer fluid as a matter of routine and they were soon on the road towards Afton. When they arrived at the interstate, they turned north. A half-hour later they again changed routes heading east on I-40.

They proceeded along this route until they came to the exit marked "SEVIERVILLE, GATLINBURG". Here they exited and drove south, through Sevierville and Pigeon Forge. As they drove through Pigeon Forge, Addie marveled at the resort town, wall-to-wall shops, stores and restaurants. Ann pointed out "DOLLYWOOD", country singer Dolly Parton's enterprise. Traffic through this area was heavy and slowed them down quite a bit but eventually they arrived at Gatlinburg. Here they stopped for lunch, taking their third rest break of the day. Although Frank hadn't explicitly told Ann where he was headed, the route confirmed her guess.

The restaurant they ate in was comfortable and the food was good. Addie had gasped when she saw the prices, explaining, "Not like our truck stop at Asheville, is it Ann?'"

"Hardly," laughed Ann in swift agreement, "but better than a place Frank and I stopped at once for pie and coffee. $8.50 was the total. Remember, Frank?"

"Yeah, I do. Up home we usually get a full meal for both of us for that amount of money. Maybe not quite the same atmosphere as here, huh, Ann?"

"Definitely NOT the same ambiance as our usual haunts," Ann agreed, referring to the simple diners and restaurants they often frequented.

Addie sat back and enjoyed their banter. Once again, she marveled at how easily they had fit into her life, aware that their departure would create a tremendous vacuum in it. Frank's comment directed at her, roused her from her thoughts. She apologized and asked him what he had said.

"I said, I bet Glen would have enjoyed this trip if we'd planned ahead a bit and thought to invite him." Frank repeated.

"Yes, I believe he would. But Glen and I have a lot of time to enjoy one another's company. For now, I'm relishing your undivided attention." Addie candidly admitted.

"Good," said Ann. "Enjoy!" she added as their waitress brought their order.

They ate a leisurely meal causing Frank to remark to Ann that he had noticed she was no longer eating as fast as she usually did. "I'm glad to see you've learned to relax and slow down your eating habits, Ann."

"Yes, I've become aware of the same thing, myself, Frank. Years of eating lunch in a short lunch period is probably what caused me to eat so fast. No reason to hurry now, thanks heavens!" she answered

The trio enjoyed lingering over coffee refills, then finally took their leave to continue on their way.

Outside Gatlinburg, they passed Christus Gardens, which Ann pointed out to the others, mentioning that friends from NY State had visited there and were impressed with the religious attraction. Near Cherokee, they turned onto the Smoky Mountain Trail. The road wound over the mountainous terrain, past split rail fences, log cabins and a little white chapel in the woods. They stopped several times at scenic overlooks where Ann snapped pictures of the views with Frank and Addie in some shots. At first Addie's enthusiasm was evident but after a while she grew very quiet.

Ann respected Addie's silence and ceased her usual chatter. She concentrated on the view, periodically pointing out various items of interest to the others. Finally, Ann could no longer contain herself.

"A penny for your thoughts, Addie," Ann gently prodded her.

"They're worth far more than a penny," replied Addie. "Do you know, Ann, I've spent most of my life here and this only the second time I've visited this park."

"I guess we often take places, things, like people, for granted. We think we don't deserve to enjoy them or we don't take the time. We save the good things for a special time. Sometimes we wait so long to enjoy them, it's too late." Ann seemed to be talking to herself more than to Addie. "Sorta like saving the frosting from your cake till last so you can savor it and having someone reach over and snatch it from your plate," she continued.

They left the mountain trail at one of the intervening highways and headed North towards I-40. Frank stopped to gas up the car at a gas station near the interstate access ramp. After he paid for the fuel, they were again on their way. At this point, the highway was three lanes wide in both directions, divided by a median strip of grass.

Near the next interchange, an 18-wheel tractor-trailer truck was entering the highway on the access ramp. Frank moved over to the center lane, yielding the outside lane to the truck. Ann flinched as she realized the larger vehicle was moving into the lane they now occupied, the driver staring straight ahead as if he had no idea they were there. She called a warning to Frank who was already aware of the problem and was moving over to the third (high-speed) lane. To their dismay, the tractor-trailer was still coming into that lane. In a desperate bid to escape a collision, Frank maneuvered his car into the median, speeding up in an effort to keep his car upright and maintain a forward motion.

Other than a few gasps and an "OH! OH!" or two from the ladies, there was silence in the car as Frank skillfully wrestled with the steering wheel, counteracting each slide the car careened into. The tractor-trailer continued speeding down the third lane, the driver apparently oblivious of the problem he had created for Frank and his passengers. As the truck sped on down the highway, Frank saw the lane was clear and brought the car back onto the highway.

Ann swung around in her seat and looked back at the median. The path their car had taken was evident by the trail of skid marks where the grass was torn up by Frank's maneuvers. The piercing sound of a siren split the air as a state patrolman whisked past them with lights flashing, chasing the errant truck driver ahead. They watched as the officer pulled the truck over and, with his partner, approached to ticket the driver. Frank pulled behind the patrol car several car lengths in back of it and shut off his engine.

Ann raised her hands towards Heaven and said, "Thank You, Lord! Praise You Jesus!" Frank and Addie chimed in "Amen!"

Frank added, "Somebody up there likes us."

Addie corrected him, "Oh, it's not just SOMEbody!"

After the officers completed their official duty, one walked back to the Flander's vehicle. He asked if everyone was okay and they assured him they were. Frank asked if they needed to make a statement about the incident.

"No Sir, both my partner and I saw what occurred. As long as you all are okay, and if there's no damage to your vehicle, that won't be necessary."

"Yes, I better check it out," Frank said as he got out of the car. He checked the undercarriage and all the tires, satisfying himself that there were no problems with the car. He reported this to the trooper.

"That was a fine display of driving expertise, Sir," the officer said admiringly. "Would you be a retired member of the force?"

"No, Officer, just survival training from the school of hard knocks," replied Frank.

Inside the car, Addie wondered why he had waited to check the car, thinking he could have been doing so while the officers were ticketing the other driver. Ann explained that he probably hadn't done so for the same reason he had stayed so far behind the patrol car when he pulled to the side of the road. "If he had pulled in too tightly behind the patrol car or had got out of the car during the time they were occupied with the other guy, it would have been distracting to the officers. One would have had to keep an eye on us in the event we were some kind of threat to them. By staying back, shutting the car off and remaining in the car, Frank was indicating to them that he was not a threat and was simply waiting until they could direct their attention to us. If he had been some kind of hot head and jumped out of the car, yelling and so forth, he might have been ticketed too or at least aggravated the situation."

When at last they were able to continue their journey, they all began to speak at once. Ann worried about Addie. Her face was still as white as a ghost.

"Sorry about the rough ride, Addie," Frank began. "Are you okay?"

"I'm fine, Frank. You are a skillful driver as the policeman said. I just wasn't prepared for such a wild ride."

"I was," Ann commented dryly. "I HAD clean underwear on."

Addie's reaction to this comment was totally unexpected. She started laughing so hard, she couldn't stop. Finally, with tears in her eyes, she managed to compose herself enough to sputter, "Your mother told you that too, did she?"

"You never know when you might have an accident," added Frank.

"I never had so much fun in my whole life," declared Addie.

"Well, if you like that so much, we'll have to detour through more medians." Ann quipped.

"I'll pass," was Frank's comment.

"Me, too!" Addie quickly responded.

The rest of the drive home was uneventful, punctuated only by several rest stops and their supper stop at a Shoney's. They ordered their meals from the Seniors' menu and were pleased to each obtain a full meal with meat, potatoes, vegetable, salad, roll and beverage. The total of all three meals was less than $20. Once outside, Ann and Addie broke into their 'peanut butter shuffle' as they now referred to their 'bargain' dance step.

When Frank drove the car into Addie's back drive well after dark, Ann breathed a prayer of thanks. "Thank You, Lord, for Your journey mercies, and Your tender care, Amen!"

Again even Frank echoed, "Amen!"

CHAPTER TWENTY-FIVE

Open House at Rainer Manor

*T*he day for the long planned open house at Rainer Manor finally arrived. Addie had asked the Historical Society to move it up a month so that Frank and Ann would still be there. Addie said she felt better having a 'whole passel' of strangers in her house if Frank was around.

As predicted, the turnout was heavy. Both Tom and Missy arranged their work schedules so they could attend. Tom made the comment that Frank's notoriety probably increased the attendance, with many people coming to meet their local hero. Frank modestly pooh-poohed that idea though Ann secretly believed Tom had made a valid observation. Certainly Frank was quite the center of attention.

Brenda Adams came over with Glen. He had talked her into wearing a long gingham dress and bonnet his grandmother had worn. Although self-conscious at first, she soon felt at ease due to the Society ladies wearing similar attire. Addie enlisted Brenda's help in manning the guest register for a while assuring her that she fit right in.

Thelma Bisbo attended with her children. She had first told Teddy to go alone but he begged so and Mary pleaded as well, breaking down Thelma's resistance till she finally agreed. It was evident she was going to lose this battle so she gave in graciously. Addie had sent a personal invitation to the family to come as guests. Thelma baked some miniature cupcakes to take to Addie that caused Teddy to swell with pride. Cars were lined up and down both sides of the lane and if it had been up to Thelma, she would have retreated to her home. Her sacred promise to her children prevented her from wavering, much to the delight of Teddy and Mary.

The refreshment tables were wisely set up on the front porch where punch and cookies, as well as other miniature goodies, were served. Missy and Lil prepared signs for the front and back entrances that read: "PLEASE – NO FOOD OR DRINK ALLOWED INSIDE. THANK YOU".

After touring the manor, Thelma volunteered to help out in the kitchen where Ann and Addie were baking more tea cookies for fear they would run out. Mary soon made friends with a little girl about a year younger than she and they played quietly in a corner of the kitchen. Addie dug out a set of small tin dishes from a cupboard and slipped the girls several cookies so they might have their own tea party. Their play was the sweet play of innocent children.

"Would you like more tea, Mary?" the younger child inquired.

"Yes'm please, Lacey. Thank you," Mary replied.

Ann took a tray of cookies out to the front porch to refresh the supply at the tables. She overheard a young man's worried question directed at a woman his age, apparently his wife.

"What do you mean, you can't find our daughter? Nancy, in a crowd like this, you can't take your eyes off her for one second!"

"I thought she was out here with you, Peter. Where could Lacey have gone?"

Ann quickly interrupted, "I know where your daughter is. She's playing in the kitchen with Mary Bisbo. They're having a tea party. Follow me." She led the way to the kitchen, holding her finger to her lips as they entered that room.

"I'll have more tea, Mary," Lacey was heard to say.

"Say the magic word," chided Mary.

"Please, Mary, and thank you," Lacey quickly responded.

The young parents looked at one another. Thelma sensed something was in the air and stepped over to where Lacey's parents stood with Ann.

"Is anything wrong? Ann?" she asked, a worried look creasing her forehead. The two children looked up from their play. Mary timidly went to her mother and clung to her skirt, as Peter and Nancy explained their concern when they couldn't locate their daughter.

"Momma, Daddy!" Lacey called excitedly. "I been playing with my new friend, Mary."

"Mary," Thelma asked gently. "Where did you find Lacey?"

"She finded me, Momma. She said her Momma and Daddy got losted so I said she could play with me till they found themselves. Big people can do that better'n us, I guess."

The grownups had to laugh at such wisdom. Their shared laughter broke the tension and they introduced themselves to one another. The young parents were Peter and Nancy Jamieson. They decided the girls should be allowed to play together a while longer. Thelma and Ann accepted Nancy's offer to help them in the kitchen while Peter went back outside to continue to poke around.

Thelma and Nancy hit it off right away. Nancy related that Lacey had no play-mates. They had recently moved to the area from Illinois as the company which employed Peter had relocated. The move had been a financial drain on them forcing Nancy to get a job to help make ends meet.

"My landlady is caring for Lacey now. She's competent but patience is not her long suit. She's never had children of her own and she's really not enthusiastic about this arrangement. Does anyone know where I could find a sitter?" Nancy's voice quavered as she asked the question. She was glad now that she had let Peter talk her into attending this open house. Having to go to work immediately after moving to the area had not allowed her the luxury of meeting anyone and making friends. She wished they hadn't had to make the move. Back home, her sister had cared for Lacey. This family support system was lacking here and she direly missed it.

"I wish I could help you out, Nancy, but I just recently told Miz Addie I'd work for her, cleaning and such. I 'spose I could work out an arrangement as to days and I could watch Lacey at my house some days so to give your landlady a break a couple times a week."

"I've a better idea, Thelma," proposed Addie who had overheard their conversation. "You could bring both gals with you the days you're working here. They play together nicely and it would help entertain Mary. Don't you agree?" Another plan was hatching in Addie's mind but she wanted to discuss it with Frank and Ann before she mentioned it to anyone else. She decided to get to know the Jamiesons better. Maybe there was a possibility she could entice the young couple to move into Rainer Manor for the summer. Time would tell, she thought.

Nancy's relief at the possibility of locating a reliable, congenial babysitter with a ready-made playmate for Lacey was evident. She and Thelma retired to a corner of the room to discuss the logistics of this new arrangement. Thelma had no idea of the wages a sitter would earn and when Nancy said she would furnish Lacey's meals, Thelma wouldn't hear of it. They tried to arrive at a figure Thelma would accept.

With tears in her eyes, Nancy told Thelma, "If you knew how wonderfully confident I am about this, but I feel so guilty you won't accept more. Thelma, I'm paying my landlady three times this amount. Won't you please take more?"

Peter entered the room and became concerned to see his wife near tears. "Why Nancy, what's wrong? Lacey?" A glance at the girls playing assured him his daughter was fine.

"Peter, Thelma's consented to babysit for us but we can't agree on the price."

Peter drew himself up to his full height. "Well, we can go as high as $80 a week and not one penny more!" He practically sputtered this statement.

Everyone in hearing broke out in smiles, even Nancy had to laugh. "No, No, dear. The problem is Thelma won't take enough. I must confess I've never found myself in such a situation before. It's unheard of! Begging a babysitter to accept a better wage!"

"Well, as Addie pointed out, the girls do play nicely together and Mary gets so lonesome when Teddy's in school. I believe I will benefit from this arrangement as much as you so I can't take advantage of you."

Ann took Peter aside and suggested, "Why don't you accept Thelma's terms? There are ways you can repay her other than monetary. Perhaps if your wife took her shopping once a month. You might have a chore or two Teddy can help you with once in a while. He's a well behaved boy and has helped Frank with the painting and tasks around here."

Peter considered these ideas and convinced Nancy that they could talk more about it later but that Ann may have solved the issue. One of the thoughts Peter came up with on his own, was to help Thelma figure the income and social security taxes on the wages they paid her. The Jamiesons could pay these taxes as part of Thelma's wages. Thelma would become eligible for the household credit on her federal taxes as well as make her currently insured under social security. She could still be at home with Mary, yet be gainfully employed. He wisely decided not to broach this topic to Thelma until he and Nancy worked out the details and determine the legality of such a move.

Once they were in agreement, Nancy immediately telephoned her landlady to tell her of this new day care plan. The relief in the older lady's voice reinforced Nancy's belief that the woman did not relish the career which had been thrust on her in her effort to help her tenants out of a bind.

Missy came looking for more punch just as Nancy was making her call so was in earshot when Thelma approached Addie and said, "You must be a good fairy, Miz Addie. Seems like you have a way of solving problems every time you're around."

Addie gave her a quick hug and confessed, "Tain't me, child, but thank you for thinking so."

"Things do have a way of falling into place easily here at Rainer Manor," commented Missy.

CHAPTER TWENTY-SIX

Eve of Departure

*A*s the time finally wound down on the Flanders departure, Frank spent the afternoon stowing boxes and bags in the trunk of the Buick. Early the next morning, he and Ann would be on the road headed north for the summer. The few months since they'd been in Tennessee had passed quickly and he looked forward to the two day trip to their New York State home. If they drove through, they would be there in 15 hours but they preferred to drive eight or ten hours, spend the night in a motel and drive the last five to seven hours in the daylight.

Both Frank and Ann enjoyed traveling and had trekked to California. They had visited forty of the lower 48 states. The remaining eight were in the Northwest (Washington, Oregon, Colorado among those eight). Later in the summer, they would probably journey the distance to take in these final eight. Their plans did not include Alaska and Hawaii, but you never could tell with these two what would happen next. They would be content just to cover the Continental United States.

The arrangement with Addie for their quarters for February, March and April had been an economical blessing for them in that their budgeted savings for their stay in Tennessee had not been depleted. Addie had also been able to save a considerable amount due to Frank and Ann buying all the groceries, running errands and taking Addie to her appointments. Ann had insisted on paying the telephone bill since she felt she used it most for calls to their relatives and friends back in New York State. This eased financial burden did much to calm Addie's fears about her future security. The great improvement to her property was invaluable and had done much to lift her spirits.

It saddened Addie to think of the loss of her companions, but she was determined their last day with her would not be dampened with her long face. She invited Glen, Tom and Missy to join them for their final evening meal at Rainer Manor. Tom and Missy were both working the evening shift at their respective places of employment so regretfully had to decline Addie's invitation. Glen readily accepted and Addie pulled out all the stops to set out a bountiful spread. The main dish was roast pork since Addie knew it was a favorite of both Frank and Ann. Sweet potatoes, candied carrots, turnip greens and fried apples accompanied the roast. Hot biscuits and corn bread were in plentiful supply as well as homemade bread.

The dessert was Addie's 'cahn pie. Ann later declared she would never again order pecan pie for dessert since it was bound to be a disappointment next to Addie's.

In all of the preparations, Addie insisted she alone would be in the kitchen. Ann was not to lift a finger to help. Ann did not go against Addie's wishes but rather busied herself getting things packed so Frank could stow them in their car.

As much as she knew she would miss Addie and the other new friends they had made, still Ann was eager to get back home to see the family and friends there. She wanted to hug her grandchildren and see how much they had grown, especially the youngest who would be a year old next month. She had kept in contact with letters and occasional phone calls but there was nothing like seeing them first hand. She was anxious to see how her parents had weathered the winter.

At dinner that evening, Glen inquired if they had finalized their plans for next winter.

"I don't want to pin you down none, Frank," began Glen, "but have you given thought to coming back?"

"I hope so!" Addie burst in.

"Yes, I believe we definitely will be back," Frank answered quickly. "The climate and certainly, the people, agreed with us."

Ann readily added her affirmation. "There's no sense in looking any further. We like it just fine here!"

"Good! I'm relieved to know I can look forward to seeing you in the fall!" Addie said excitedly. "We're going to have us a grand Christmas this year. I'll get it all planned this summer. Will you help me, Glen?"

"I sure will, Addie. We'll roast chestnuts and the whole works!"

They spent the next fifteen to twenty minutes tossing Christmas ideas back and forth. Frank and Ann mostly sat there listening.

Ann commented, "It sounds like a Christmas out of a story book, Addie."

"It will be, Ann. I've decided to let the Society give tours here through the summer but stop them just afore Thanksgiving. Maybe I'll relent and have one again near Christmas. I can call it 'Storybook Christmas at Rainer Manor'."

Glen added, "I like the sound of that, Addie. Some folks hereabouts make crafts. You might consider letting them sell some here then."

"I'll think about it, Glen, but it sounds good to me."

They lingered over their coffee cups for a long time this last evening. Glen finally roused himself from his chair.

"Why don't you folks go to bed so's I can go home," he laughed. "Unless, Addie, can I help you with those dishes?"

"No, I'm gonna let them stay in the sink tonight. After these two leave tomorrow, I'll need some diversion to keep me from feeling blue."

"I'm sorry Tom and Missy had to work tonight. I thought we'd get to see them one last time before we left," spoke Ann wistfully.

"I know they regret not being able to join us." Addie comforted Ann. Tom and Missy had become good friends to Addie as well as to the Flanders.

They said goodnight and farewell to Glen. Frank and Ann felt secure in the thought that Glen would be keeping an eye on the place and Addie. As Ann said, it eased the pain of parting to know that Addie was not being left as alone as she had been when they met her not so long ago.

Frank was off to bed immediately after Glen's departure. He did all the driving on their trips so it was imperative he get his rest. Ann, on the other hand, could always catch a few extra winks along the way, though she usually didn't. She enjoyed watching the scenery and would point out interesting sights to her husband.

Ann and Addie sat quietly visiting at the table for quite a while. Ann offered to help with the dishes but Addie stood firm on her position that she really wanted to have that chore to concentrate on after Frank and Ann left.

One of the topics of conversation at dinner regarded Addie's thoughts about the Jamiesons and the possibility of their staying with Addie over the summer months. Their apartment in town was small, the day care arrangement with Thelma was working out well but required quite a bit of travel on their part to bring Lacey out and pick her up. By sharing quarters with Addie, they could not only cut down their travel time and expense but could also save some money towards getting a place of their own.

"Be sure to consider what it will be like to have a small child around constantly," cautioned Ann. "It will surely change your life style if you do."

"I've given that a lot of thought. I think I could get used to it. It would only be evenings and weekends except for the days Thelma would have the little gals here whilst she cleans."

"It might work out, Addie. I'm sure they would jump at the opportunity." Ann stifled a yawn but not before Addie noticed.

"You best be getting to bed, Ann. You've got quite a trip ahead of you tomorrow."

"I know you're right, Addie. I hate for this evening to end, though. I'll really miss you. We've enjoyed our stay here so much. Frank's become quite fond of you, as well!"

"I'll sorely miss you both," replied Addie, blinking back tears.

"I'll write to you this summer, Addie," promised Ann.

"I hope you will!" Addie exclaimed, as she went about the room turning off lights. Ann flipped off the switch near her and checked the door. Before they went to their respective bedrooms, she gave Addie a quick hug and bade her goodnight.

CHAPTER TWENTY-SEVEN

Headed North

*T*he Flanders were awakened early by kitchen sounds as Addie prepared a generous breakfast. Delicious smells of frying bacon and brewing coffee greeted them, hastening their arising. Donning bathrobes, they scurried down the back hall to the kitchen where the table was laid awaiting their arrival at breakfast.

"Addie, I should have helped you with all this!" cried Ann upon entering the kitchen.

"I wanted to make it myself, but longs you're up, you can put the toast down to cook. By the time it's done, these eggs should be ready and we can set down."

Ann did as directed while Frank stepped back down the hall to throw on his shirt and trousers and splash some water in his face.

Ann was admonishing him not to take too long as breakfast was practically on the table. She did know he would enjoy his breakfast more if he felt comfortable. He reappeared just as the ladies had finished placing the last plate of bacon and eggs on the table. Addie had already poured glasses of orange juice that she set at each place setting.

As they pulled up their chairs, Addie announced that she wanted to say 'Grace.'

"Father, we thank You for this food we're about to eat and these friends that share it. Bless this food and those who receive it. I thank You for the many blessings You have bestowed on me, and Father, I especially thank You for bringing Frank and Ann into my life. Let us not lose touch with one another. Grant them your journey mercies on their trip north and keep them safe on their trip back to Tennessee. Thank You, Amen!" Addie and Ann were both sniffling by the time Addie finished.

"Beautiful, Addie, just beautiful. Thank you for that," Ann stated when she was able to speak.

"Yes, that was very nice, Addie," Frank joined in. "Now, let's eat!"

"Just like a man," was Addie's dry response.

Their meal was eaten in comparative silence. They had grown so comfortable with one another there was no need for idle chatter and each felt the moment too emotional for banal conversation. After the plates were cleared away and their coffee warmed up, all seemed to speak at once.

"Remember the time we…"

"Wasn't that funny when Glen…"

"I'll never forget the look…."

Their statements ran all over each other's comments, like water tumbling over rocks, splashing randomly, rolling on its way with the pull of gravity. Then followed their laughter as they realized no one was listening to anyone else. Both ladies wound up with tears streaming down their faces.

Embarrassed, Frank arose saying he'd better check out the car. Ann quickly jumped up to get washed up and dressed so she could put the rest of their toiletries in their travel bags. By the time Frank had checked the car's fluid levels and the tires, she had their remaining luggage lined up by their bedroom door so he could finish packing the car. They had decided to leave their small TV with Addie instead of hauling it back up north. It wasn't needed there and they felt that Addie might enjoy watching it now and then. Of course Addie fussed that it wasn't necessary to leave it, but Ann convinced her she would do them a favor to store it so they had more room in the car.

"Be sure to turn it on now and again, Addie. It doesn't do them any good if they're not operated periodically," Frank winked at Ann as he made this statement to Addie.

By seven o'clock, everything was neatly stowed away in the trunk of the Buick. Addie took several items out to the car and handed them to Ann.

"Here's a care package and your thermos. I filled it with hot coffee for you."

"Thank you, Addie! That was thoughtful of you. What's in here? Biscuits! Oh Boy!" She couldn't resist snooping in the bag, though Addie chided her and playfully slapped her wrist.

"Now, at least wait till you're over the mountain afore you eat 'em all up." She pointed north, indicating a mountain range looming in the distance at least ten miles away.

"After such a bountiful breakfast, I would hope we can get more than ten miles down the road before we get hungry!" Ann laughed.

With all the last minute things done, it was finally time to say 'Goodbye' to Addie. It was no easier than any of them expected. Ann was disheartened that they hadn't arranged to have someone be there with Addie as a distraction but Addie held her head high, determined not to get foolish over this. Still she knew that she had let Frank and Ann get closer than she had ever let anyone outside her family.

The final words of departure said, the last embrace given, quick waves and they were off. Ann turned in her seat gazing at Addie until they had left the back drive and turned onto Rainer Road for the short distance to Route 3. Addie stood waving as long as they were in her sight, then she shrugged her shoulders as if to rid herself of these unwelcome emotions, spun on her heel and entered the house. Here she began to wash the dishes she had declined help with, clattering pots and pans to her heart's content. Every once in a while, she'd sniff; now and again drying her hands so she could use a tissue to blow her nose. She'd mutter to herself, until finally her dishes were washed, then still muttering, she picked up her dish towel and dried them all, stacking them on the countertop until she was finished with the drying. She then put them away in the cup-boards and turning, surveyed her kitchen, satisfied her efforts were complete. A glance at the clock revealed that her work did not use up anywhere near the time she hoped. She decided to go lay on her bed awhile, hoping for some sleep to pass some time away. She hadn't slept well the night before so the rest would be welcome.

Miles away on Route 3, the Flanders were riding in silence mostly, while occasionally one or the other would make a comment about the scenery or Addie or one of the events of the past few months.

"Are we over the mountain, yet?" Frank queried.

Ann understood that he was hinting she should break out one of the biscuits, which she did, also pouring a cup of coffee from the thermos for him to wash the food down.

When he finished the snack, she handed him a napkin to wipe his hands on, leaning over to steer the car as he did so. Within seconds, he took the wheel again. He had not slackened the car's speed while this change of control had occurred, confident in her ability to steer the car from the passenger seat.

Shortly after this had taken place, Ann noticed Frank was peering intently into the rear view mirror.

"Is something wrong?" she inquired.

"Yeah, we got a tail, looks like. Probably saw the NYS plate and is waiting for us to pull a boner," Frank replied.

"I've checked your speedometer once in a while, and you haven't been speeding. When did he show up?" Ann asked, wrinkling her brow.

"A mile or so back. There goes his lights." Frank eased the car onto the edge of the road, half expecting the law enforcement vehicle behind him to pull around and continue on down the highway to some emergency call. Instead the officer pulled his patrol car to a stop behind Frank. He got out of the patrol car and approached the driver's door of the Buick.

"Is there a problem, Officer?" asked Frank.

"Could I see your driver's license and registration, Sir?" the officer inquired.

Frank retrieved the items from his wallet and as he handed them over, repeated his question. "Is there a problem?"

"My orders are to detain you, Sir." These words were no sooner spoken than a second patrol car loomed into sight, parking behind the first police car.

Frank started to laugh as two occupants of this second car got out and began to approach the Flanders's vehicle. Ann looked at her husband as if he had lost his mind.

"Look, Ann. See who's here." Ann peered around him to see Tom Cates peeking in through Frank's window. A laugh on her side of the car caused Ann to spin around to see a smiling Missy at her window.

"If you think you're getting outta here without saying goodbye to us, you're wrong!" exclaimed Missy, extending her left hand towards Ann, practically waving it under her nose.

"Oh, Missy, what's this? Look at Missy's diamond, Frank. Does this mean…? Of course it does." Ann answered her own question, continuing, "I take it that congratulations are in order, Tom. Missy, when's the big day?"

"When will y'all be back? We want you to stand up with us!" Missy bubbled. Tom nodded in agreement.

"Well, can you hold off till November?" Frank answered her.

"Guess we're going to have to," Tom responded. He turned to wave as his fellow officer climbed back into his car and drove off. The others nodded at the departing patrolman.

"Your co-conspirator, hey Tom?" Ann asked sweetly as she climbed out of the Buick to hug Missy while Frank got out and shook Tom's hand.

"I was so disappointed that we didn't get to tell you guys goodbye," said Ann. "What a surprise!"

"Yes, sorry we couldn't make it last night. Bet Addie put on quite a spread." Tom commented.

"She did, indeed," agreed Ann. "I think she'll be lost for a while without us underfoot. I'll worry about her."

"We're planning on looking in on her. And Glen says he's gonna get Bessie and bring her over for a visit in a day or two." Missy told them.

"That's great!" was Ann's enthusiastic response. "Just what she needs to perk her up. Hearing your news will do the job, too!"

"Yes, we'll stop by and tell her on our way back to town." Tom beckoned to Missy, "Now, we best let these folks be getting along."

The ladies embraced, Ann hugged Tom and the men shook hands again. Ann promised to write to Missy as the Flanders got back into their car to continue on their way.

"Well, that's perfect!" Ann said to Frank. "I'm so glad they caught up to us. They are the first people we met in Peckville and the last to see us off."

"Can't wait to get back this fall to see what we can get into next," Frank dryly commented.

"Everything in good time, Frank. Right now, Ah can't wait to see all mah babies."

"You not only got Tennessee in your blood, but also in your talk," kidded Frank. "Y'all sound just like Addie."

"Why, what did Ah say?"

"Ah, Mah!" Frank began.

"Well, you're no different, you said y'all." Ann scolded.

"How'd you like one up side your pumpkin head?" Frank threatened her in a familiar mocking manner.

"You and who else?" Ann retorted. "Besides, I've just spent three months trying not to lose my New York accent 'cause I didn't want anyone to think I was imitating them, so now Ahm just gonna relax."

"Are we over the mountain yet?" Frank asked plaintively, in an effort to change the subject.

"Yep, we're over the mountain, old man, but not yet over the hill!" Ann smiled because she had the last word.